Praise for Momma's Baby, Daddy's Maybe

"Sensual and intriguing! Dames weaves a tale full of swing and passion. A sassy new voice in contemporary fiction."

—Tracy Price-Thompson, author of *Black Coffee*

"Jamise L. Dames has crafted a superb novel that will keep your eyes locked on the page with intrigue. With surprises, plot twists, and fascinating turns, *Momma's Baby, Daddy's Maybe* is a tale that will touch your heart and stay with you long after you've put the book down."

—Earl Sewell, author of *Taken for Granted*

"*Momma's Baby, Daddy's Maybe* absolutely sizzles . . . Eavesdropping never felt better. I loved it!"

—V. Anthony Rivers, author of *Daughter by Spirit*

"Jamise L. Dames is a sassy new novelist on the scene. Make room for her on your bookshelf."

—Linda Dominique Grosvenor,
author of *Like Boogie on Tuesday*

"Dames's debut novel, *Momma's Baby, Daddy's Maybe,* starts off fast and sexy and keeps that hot pace throughout. Interesting characters, with plenty of attitude and drama, make this story fresh and readable. Dames is a new AA writer on the scene with the talents to back up her stay in the literary arena."

—Shon Bacon, Chief Editor, *The Nubian Chronicles*

"Great novel! Suspense, drama, and tragedy—a great combination. It made me laugh and cry . . . I didn't want to put it down, not even at the end. Dames is to be commended."

—Michael Porter, MPTN

"*Momma's Baby, Daddy's Maybe* is a literary treat and then some. From its succulent love scenes, to the finger licking good drama, you will find it difficult to resist coming back for seconds and thirds."

—Nakea Murray, founder, As The Page Turns Book Club

Momma's Baby,
Daddy's Maybe

A NOVEL

Jamise L. Dames

ATRIA BOOKS

New York   London   Toronto   Sydney   Singapore

ATRIA BOOKS
1230 Avenue of the Americas
New York, NY 10020

ISBN: 0-7434-9199-8

First Atria Books trade paperback edition November 2003

10 9 8 7 6 5 4 3 2 1

ATRIA BOOKS is a trademark of Simon & Schuster, Inc.

Manufactured in the United States of America

For information regarding special discounts for bulk purchases,
please contact Simon & Schuster Special Sales at 1-800-456-6798
or business@simonandschuster.com

Poem "Joy" printed courtesy of Carl Dean, Jr. and Eye Rise Press

For my love, my life, my everything—my three reasons for laughter, smiling, hope, prayer, patience, and consistency: TreDayne, Cinque II, and Kyran, upon your graduations.

IN LOVING MEMORY

Vera Howard, my most cherished aunt and true friend. May your soul ascend high enough to tickle the angels. I miss you . . . I love you . . . and I feel your presence. Take care of your buddy.

Acknowledgments

As I sit here compiling names of the people who have positively touched my life I realize that I've been extremely blessed. So in advance I'd like to thank you all. Thank you for being you and for the role that you've played in my life. Please forgive me if I have a memory lapse and forget to include your name . . . my memory lapses—not my heart.

First and foremost I thank the Creator for giving me a gift so wonderful and special that I am compelled to share it with the world. I'll do my best not to let you down.

For my mother, Barbara Gill, I love you more than I can say and you can imagine. Your unconditional love defines unconditional love; my grandmother, Viola Box, another beautiful soul. Thank you for being a positive, steady force in my life; my figure skating aunt, Judy Box, your beautiful words of encouragement means more than you know; my great-grandmother, Pearlie Box, you're the backbone of five generations and loved by all.

My appreciation and gratitude goes out to all of those who I've mentioned in the previous editions. Life would be monotonous and unentertaining without you. Special thanks to those who have supported me endlessly and realize that I'm in the business of writing novels, not giving them away. Selfless acts do not go unnoticed or unrewarded. Therefore I have to especially thank Michelle Green, Lashon Fryer, Nickie Blakely, Nakea Murray, Sharone Box, Robin Box, Shelly Box, Riccardo Box, Chuckey and Lynne Charles, Bill Murray and Raven Cannon, Stan Penix and family, Howie and Stormy Rickerson, Tommy and Crystal Whipple (The bouquet was wonderful as is your constant demand for more chapters! Thanks x2), Trevor Randolph and family, Divine Saddiq Dubar, Jerry and Gary Dorton, Ms. Carolyn (Cal) Groom, Danny and Joann Smith, Paradise Payne, Doug McCory, Marc Buckner and family, Robbie Farwell Rivers, Velma Wade, and LaRoy Berry.

Many heartfelt thanks to the amazing people who've made this literary journey a pleasant one: My literary manager, Ken Atchity—serendipity it is—let's make the best of it. Here's to us . . . Cheers; the ever reachable and always upbeat Margaret O'Connor; my extraordinary and amazing editor, Brenda Copeland; Chandra Sparks-Taylor, who never misses a beat; Ron Martel, Mr. divine design; the irreplaceable Kim Rose, what would I do without you? Thank you for being more than a publicist; Nicole Childress, producer, publicist, researcher—renaissance woman . . . Simon says red; Wade Blackman, the excellent attorney; Susan Mary Malone, Michael Porter, and Michael Slaughter.

To my fellow authors who've positively influenced either my life or career—thank you: Tracy Price-Thompson, Travis Hunter, V. Anthony Rivers, Toni Staton Harris, Shawna Grundy, Carla Rowser Canty, Brenda Thomas, Earl Sewell, Gerald K. Malcom, Cherryl Floyd Miller, David Charles, Shonell Bacon, Carl Dean, Jr., Alex Hairston, and Steve Perry.

A great big thank you to two wonderful professors at my alma mater, UCONN. Dr. Willena Kimpson Price, a wonderful altruistic woman. The guidance and care that you so easily give are untouchable; Michael Bradford, a dazzling playwright and Mr. dialog himself. I may not have followed all of Aristotle's rules in the *Poetics* but I paid attention.

Cinque, if love were visible it would be you. You've supported me in everything, caught me when I thought I'd fall, and held my hand every step of the way. You believed in me when I was too tired to, and reminded me never to let go of my dreams because they're mine for the taking. If I could live up to just one-tenth of the faith you have in me I'd be supernal. I can never thank you enough.

Thank you, thank you, thank you to my children, TreDayne, Cinque II, and Kyran, by order of birth, not importance. I love you all equally. Thank you for all the patience that your young hearts muster up while I write. I do this for you. So, please do as Mommy does, not just as I say . . . don't just follow your dreams—make them happen. All of me . . . to all of you—in all ways for always.

Rukiya La'Shay Murray, Eligio (Zap) Bailey, and Christopher Ferraras—God-Mommy loves you all very much.

A special thanks to the wonderful people who've played a major part in the success of this novel: Learie and Kevon at Culture Plus Books, Eric and Karen at A & B Books, Reflections Bookstore, Staten Island Book Club, Jonestry Book Club, As the Page Turns Book Club, Sisters in Sprit Book Club, R.A.W. Sistaz Book Club, Odysseys Book Club (Janice Aaron and friends), Girlfriends Reading Circle, Circle of Friends X, Psst Book Club, Jackson Mississippi Readers Club, and the great people at Nile River Coffee House. Also many thanks to the Alpha Kappa Alpha, and Delta Sigma Theta sororities for their warm support.

For my terrific readers who've made my career a fulfilling one—I couldn't ask for better, more honest, encouraging, and truly fantastic people. Your letters, emails, and comments are appreciated equally as much as your showing up to book signings in the rain, sleet, snow, and sun. I aspire to make your support worth it. And for those who've asked, pushed, and reiterated for *Pushing Up Daisies*—it's on the way. I promise.

Love, laugh, and enjoy life as carefree as children.

Enjoy,
Jamise

Momma's Baby,
Daddy's Maybe

JOY

A million dreams swimming
To a beautiful beginning
So precious indeed
Just one in a million received
The strongest union conceived
And from the moment they first breathe
So hard to believe
The joy a baby brings
A joy . . .
     Wondrous like Niagara Falls
     Magnificent like China's Great Wall
     Everlasting like the Pyramids
     Precious like all children
Count the fingers, count the toes
Count the greatest blessings this side of Heaven knows

All the joys a child brings to one's soul
Must be placed back within the child as they grow
So they too will know
They are precious indeed
Truly unique

Thus within their soul . . . a wonderful feeling
They are truly, ONE IN A MILLION

                 —Carl Dean, Jr.

~ 1 ~

Kennedy Jacobs eased off her lover, Michael Montgomery, enjoying the delicious ache lingering between her thighs. *If Simone could only see me now,* Kennedy thought with a tad bit of guilt. Her sister would kill her. Kennedy knew Michael was off-limits and of course she understood why, but when it came to Michael, she was powerless to control herself.

Michael had taken Kennedy to heaven and back with just his mouth. He was everything any woman in her right mind would need or desire. *Simone must be crazy if she thinks that she can keep me away from this man,* Kennedy thought and smiled to herself.

She gathered her clothes from the floor, wondering how the hell she'd fallen asleep on top of him. Michael hadn't even penetrated her, and still, she'd be sore all day. Every step she took would force her to think of Michael and how he'd orally pleased her to ultimate climatic heights. Carefully she tiptoed into the bathroom, determined not to wake him, although it was doubtful he would hear anything over his satisfied snores. Checkout time was at one o'clock. She decided to let him sleep until noon, and let his alarm clock be the sound of the hotel room door as it closed behind her.

She really hated sneaking around, especially to hotels. In a way she wanted to be found out. So tired of lying and making up excuses, she wanted everyone to know that she and Michael were together. Hell, her best friend Miranda didn't even know *who* Michael was, only that he existed and that Kennedy was *not* telling.

She noticed Michael's burgundy silk boxers lying on the cream-colored marble-tiled floor and picked them up. Crushing the suede-like slick fabric between her fingers, she pressed the boxers to her nose and inhaled his scent. His masculine essence overpowered her, washing over her in succulent waves. Damn. Even the man's underwear smelled good. She was hooked. Who had ever heard of such a thing? A woman smelling a man's underwear? *Her* smelling a man's underwear? She heard the sheets ruffle and then the bed creak, and immediately threw his boxers back on the floor. Pulling back the shower curtain, she turned the chrome spigot and allowed the rush of water to cascade over her freshly manicured hand. She adjusted the dial until the temperature was on hell, as Michael would say, referring to how scalding hot she preferred her water. A swishing sound made her pause and listen. Michael was dragging his feet on the carpet. When the swish grew louder by the second, indicating his closeness to the bathroom, she jumped into the shower as if she'd been there all along.

Above the sound of the water, Kennedy heard the distinct beeping of Michael's pager. Hers was in her purse, on vibrate. Seconds later, she heard his voice, low and smooth, apparently talking into the telephone. Concentrating on the soothing baritone whispers coming from his mouth, she gradually decreased the water pressure to almost a trickle, hoping Michael wouldn't notice, and listened intently to his private conversation. Who had the gall to page him and interrupt their lunchtime rendezvous? Like anyone would know that lunchtime was *Kennedy's* time. She heard him say Simone's name and cringed. Damn, didn't the heifer know when to stop? She was always calling or paging or something. Anything.

Kennedy knew her sister had every right to contact Michael, but whenever she did, somehow Kennedy still felt betrayed. The stolen afternoons belonged to her alone. Michael was on her time, not Simone's! The mere thought of Michael made Kennedy's jealousy dissipate into steamy lust, and before she could stop herself, she reached between her legs and began a slow, sensual soaping of her throbbing triangle.

Caught up in her rapture of self-pleasure, Kennedy spread her legs, then leaned weakly against the marble shower wall. She never heard the end of Michael's call. Never heard him enter the mist-filled bathroom and close the door softly behind him. As he pulled back the shower curtain, a gust of chilly air caressed her, making her nipples harden. Her eyes shot open and her jaw dropped, embarrassed by being caught in the act.

Instead of teasing her, Michael covered her mouth with one hand and fingered her parted lips with the other. Grinding slowly, he pressed his naked body against hers. His hardness moved back and forth between her legs. Shuddering and bending slightly forward to accept him, Kennedy invited Michael into her temple to be baptized by her heat and soft wetness. Declining the invite, Michael turned her around and kissed her passionately. His hand never left her spread; his fingers delved deeper as he touched, rubbed, and explored her until she literally screamed, but her scream was muffled by his full lips and expert tongue. Thank God for Michael's kiss because hotel security would've been banging on the door. Kennedy began sliding down the wall, drained and limp. Reaching out to catch her, Michael washed and rinsed her and himself off and stepped out of the shower, smiling. Apparently satisfied with his work, he never uttered a word. Dazed and dizzy, Kennedy reluctantly turned off the shower, got out, and began to dry off.

"Kennedy, I'm sending my pants down to be starched and pressed. Do you want me to send down your dress?"

"No thanks. It's not really necessary."

Michael laughed as he walked into the bedroom. "Are you sure? Did you *see* it?"

"Yeah, I saw it. But it's okay. It's linen, and linen *always* wrinkles. Besides, no one will ever be able to tell the difference between me walking around in it or rolling around in it. Don't you just love linen." Kennedy playfully batted her eyes. "Oh, before I forget, did someone call here? I told the front desk that we didn't want to be disturbed, but I could've sworn that I heard you on the phone."

"No, no one called, but Simone paged me and I had to get back to her, it was important."

"Damn, Michael, it's like she knows when we're together. I mean I could put money on it and win. She never stops. I hope you haven't given her any indication. Have you, you know, about us? Because I don't know how I would explain. I don't want to have to try to explain. I mean, I know that I should feel guilty—and I do, in a way. She is my sister and I love her, and I know she loves me, but she would never understand or accept it. If I was in her position, I can't say that I would either. But I can't help myself. Even if I could, knowing you the way that I do, I still don't think that I would even try to restrain myself. Maybe I'm wrong, but I just wish the wench would get a grip and stop paging you on my time."

Michael raised his eyebrows, exhaled loudly, and rubbed the stubble growing on the side of his face. "Kennedy, don't call her that. You know that's not right, she's just doing her job. Simone and I work together, not sleep together. Anyway, she was just calling me to give me an important message about a meeting we have tonight, that's all. Okay?" Michael grabbed her chin and kissed her.

"Fine, but remember there are only seven days in a week. And if she can have you the majority of the time, I feel that I'm entitled to at least the weekends, most of them anyway, and when you're on your lunch break. Remember, Michael, I am a client, too, even if I'm not a paying client, I'm still in the books."

Michael's pager went off again. With pleading puppy-dog eyes he looked at Kennedy, then down to his pager, then back at Kennedy, and back down to his pager again. He shrugged. As he was reaching for the phone, Kennedy rolled her eyes in disapproval and turned and walked back into the bathroom, picked up his boxers from the floor, and stuffed them into her overpriced black Chanel purse. She made a beeline to the front door and Michael reached out to stop her, but the phone cord wasn't long enough. Immediately she looked down and stared at his privates, which were no longer private but fully exposed and hanging, and then reached out to grab his penis. She squeezed it, bringing life back to it. She kissed the tip of it and blew it a kiss just to make Michael stutter during his conversation with Simone. She walked toward the front door.

Michael stammered and quickly told Simone that he'd call her right back just as Kennedy opened the door. "Kennedy, wait. Don't leave, not like this."

Kennedy rolled her eyes, turned around, and seductively licked her mahogany-glossed lips. "I bet you wish you hadn't sent your pants down to be pressed," she said as she walked out and slammed the door behind her, hard.

Leaving the hotel, she reached inside of her purse for her

car keys and saw Michael's silk boxers. She laughed out loud. He thought that she was going to do him while he was on the phone. Surprise! The only blowing that he'd get was when he was free and swinging in the wind. Besides, one was never supposed to leave a man the same way that one met him.

In the car she reached into her purse and pulled out his boxers and rubbed the silk. Again she inhaled his scent and shivered. Even the man's dirty drawers smelled good. Her chest heaved as she collected herself, and threw them on the passenger seat. "A token, just a token," she said and started her car. Her cell phone rang.

"Yes, Michael," Kennedy answered.

"Who in the hell is Michael?" Jared Reid, her daughter's father, asked.

"Nobody. And why are you concerned anyway?"

"Don't tell me that you're still mad at me. Or are you mad at Big Mike?"

"Look, Jared. Not that it's any of your business. But if you must know, Michael does my taxes. So don't be starting any shit with me. I am not the person you want to mess with today. Okay? Anyway, what do you want?"

"All right. Calm down. I just want to know when I can come and get Kharri. That's all."

"School's out in June. You can come and get her then." Kennedy lowered her voice and said very calmly and slowly, making sure to emphasize her point, "but don't, and *I mean don't* have her around any of your women. She's not ready for that."

"See you in June."

Although Jared was her daughter's father, Kennedy couldn't stand him. At one time she had loved him with all that she had. But then, he had been her childhood sweetheart and her first in everything. In her heart she knew that she would always love him as her daughter's father. But just because you love someone doesn't necessarily mean that you have to like them.

It had taken Kennedy a long time to get over Jared. When they were together, he was nothing but good to her. He treated her like a queen, and because of him, her standards were high. Her motto after him had been, *Why be one man's trash when you can be another man's treasure.* She didn't know if she was Michael's treasure, but she knew for certain that she wasn't his trash.

She wanted Michael. Hell, she wanted him desperately, but couldn't let him know that. She had to stand her ground because once you lay down, someone would walk over you. And she wasn't about to be anybody's doormat. But as much as she wanted Michael, she often found herself thinking about Jared. She reminisced about what they had, almost had, and didn't have. Who was he having something with now? As much as she tried to convince herself that she didn't care about his seeing someone else, she couldn't lie to herself. She was no different from most women. She still considered Jared as belonging to her even though she didn't want him. *Once mine, always mine,* Kennedy thought, smirking to herself.

Kennedy decided to call Jared back to apologize for being so rude. After all, he was a great father, and she saw no reason that they shouldn't get along. Because of Kharri they would be connected for life, and being friends would be easier on them.

She would call him from home. After her hectic afternoon she needed to relax. Her disagreement with Michael and her petty argument with Jared had caused her temples to throb.

At home she could tell that her sister had just left. The living room reeked of her Happy perfume and the strong garlicky aroma of whatever she had eaten for lunch. Had Simone paged Michael from the office or the house? Kennedy set her purse on the sofa out of habit. Her grandmother had taught her a long time ago the old superstition, if you leave your purse on the floor you'll never have any money.

In the kitchen she picked up the phone. Feeling silly, she hesitated and then thought *what the hell* and pressed the redial button. The digital voice on the other end told her that she had reached Michael Montgomery's service and she could either leave a voice message or a number.

Simone had been home all day. Being the vice president of a successful accounting firm, Simone had been afforded the luxury of working by phone, fax, in the office or out. Simone had it made. Kennedy twisted her face. What pager number did Simone have? When Kennedy called, she heard a different message, one in Michael's voice.

Michael only had one pager. Evidently it was hooked up to two different numbers. He never told her that or even bothered to give her the other number. Why? She thought he had given her all of his numbers, or at least he said that he did.

After searching the refrigerator for something to snack on, she decided to have a glass of wine. So what that it was the middle of the day? She had had a long morning and afternoon and for the call she was about to make, she needed a few. Although the call she made to Michael's pager still invaded her head, Kennedy put thoughts of Michael aside, went to her room and locked her door, and dialed Jared's number. The phone rang twice. A woman answered. Kennedy hung up. She must've dialed the wrong number. Ever since she left Jared, she could never remember his number. "You know that's a shame," Kennedy said to herself and got up to get her phone book from her desk.

When she had found the number she dialed it again, and again some woman answered. Kennedy hung up. Obviously Jared had changed his number again and not told her. Her adrenaline rushed from frustration. She ran her fingers through her short black hair and headed toward Kharri's room to retrieve Jared's number from her daughter's Barbie phone book. Just like him to give it to Kharri and not to her.

The number looked familiar. It was the exact one that she had dialed. She called back anyway. Again, the same woman answered.

"Yes, may I speak with Jared, please?" Kennedy asked, waiting for the woman to tell her that she had the wrong number.

"Who's this?" the woman asked a little too confidently, as if she knew that Kennedy was the one to hang up on her twice in two minutes.

"Oh, I'm sorry, I must have the wrong number."

"No. No, you don't. He's here, but who is this?" the woman snapped.

"Who wants to know?" Kennedy demanded, not liking the interrogation from some strange woman.

"You don't call my house and ask me who I am. You tell me who you are and what you want first, if you want to speak to Jared."

"This is Kennedy. Can you put Jared on the phone now?"

Muffled voices came over the line while someone apparently covered the phone with a hand, as though mute buttons didn't exist. She couldn't believe that Jared allowed someone to answer his phone that way. The woman obviously knew who she was because the "who's this" and "what do you want" game had ended as soon as Kennedy said her name.

"Kennedy, I'm sorry. Let me call you right back. I got something to take care of real quick," Jared apologized in an aggravated voice that Kennedy had never heard before.

"Uh-uh. Talk to me right now, Jared. I'm not waiting for anybody to call me back, not after all that childish bullshit that I just went through. You owe me for that one because you know me, Jared, and that, that right there could've gotten very ugly. I almost had to step out of character. But you know that's not my caliber. I'm not that immature where I forget how to speak to people, and I deserve the same respect as I give. You understand?"

"Yeah, Ken. I understand," Jared said between a clicking sound on the phone. "Answer your other line."

"No. Whoever it is can wait."

"Ken, answer the phone, okay? Just do me that one favor," Jared almost pleaded.

Kennedy clicked over to the other line. "Hel-lo?"

"It's me, Ken. That's why I wanted you to answer. I switched to my cell phone. Now where were we? Oh, I am really sorry that you had to go through that. I'm sorry that I had to go through that."

"Who was that, Jared?" Kennedy asked, afraid to hear the answer. "And why was she answering your phone? Don't lie to me. Because I know that she's somebody to you, otherwise you wouldn't have switched to your cell phone. And I know that you switched so that you could leave the house because I can hear the wind blowing through the phone. Cell phones don't sound the same as house phones, so don't lie."

"Yeah, you're right." Jared laughed nervously. "I left the house. I needed to go for a walk. A brother needs some air, ya know?"

"Who was that, Jared? And what gave her the audacity to speak to me like that? She must be pretty important to you because you left her in your house."

"Ken, I've got something to tell you. I was calling to talk to you earlier but you didn't seem to be in a talking mood," Jared said. Kennedy's heart sank. "That was Tasha." He hesitated. "My fiancée."

"Fiancée, *fiancée?* What do you mean, your fiancée? Fiancée? Since when?"

"Ken, look. I was going to tell you before Kharri came. I promise you that. I thought it would be something that we should discuss. I thought that maybe you would help me explain it to Kharri, or at least tell me how I should try to explain it."

"You don't need to explain anything to Kharri because

Kharri ain't coming. Do you hear me? I don't want my daughter anywhere near Sasha, Tasha, or *whatever* her name is."

"*Our* daughter," Jared corrected. "And yes, Kharri is coming. Tasha won't be anywhere around Kharri because Kharri and I won't be here. I'm taking her back to Virginia Beach and we're going to visit my parents for the summer. So don't worry about that. I wouldn't confuse my daughter by having some woman around her that she doesn't know, Ken. I know better than that."

"All right, but please don't let me find out different," Kennedy almost whispered.

"You all right, Ken? You don't sound like yourself. Why did you call anyway? I don't think you've ever called my house without Kharri being there," Jared asked.

"I'm straight. Actually I was calling to apologize for earlier today. I just figured that since we have a child together, the least we can do is try to be friends. But I can tell from the tact of your fiancée that all we'll ever be is Kharri's parents. I'll be your baby's momma and you'll be my baby's daddy," Kennedy responded coolly, trying to cover her bruised feelings.

"Ken, Ken, we'll always be friends. How couldn't I be your friend when you were the first to know more about me than I know about myself? I wouldn't want to lose that, I'd be a fool. We had something special and from that we created someone special. And people think that only God Himself gives blessings but that's not true because you blessed me. Through Him, you blessed me with Kharri. I can never repay you for that and I can never thank you enough. Because of that I will always have a love for you that no one can take away. We always remember our firsts in life and you gave me my first child, you were my first love, and you will always be my friend despite my new life," Jared explained in the usual warm and caring way that belonged to him and him alone.

"Um-hmm. I gotta go now. Bye, Jared. Bye forever, okay?" Kennedy said very quietly, feeling as lost as she did the day that she left him. The pain was stabbing her soul, wringing all the happiness out of her heart, making her numb. She had lost him twice in one lifetime.

A lump grew in her throat, a burning in her stomach, and tears welled up in her eyes. How easily words fell from his mouth, how easily he told her that he was engaged. How could he tell her he was going to marry some other woman and say that he would always love her in the same breath? Jared had spoken about a lot of firsts, not onlys. First love. First child. First person to know him better than he knew himself. Kennedy broke down and cried. A first meant that eventually a second would follow.

~ 2 ~

"Simone, I know you're home, so pick up the phone, it's me, Kennedy."

"Hey, Kennedy. How did you know that I was at home? I'm supposed to be at work, you know?"

"Because you paged me, remember?"

"Oh yeah, that's right. I was wondering if you could pick me up a couple of bottles of that wine that I like so much on your way home."

"Piesport, right? You ordered it, right, because it has to be ordered, you know."

"Yeah, Ken, that's the one. And yes, I ordered it, a few of them actually."

"I'll pick them up for you. But now I have to go because I'm in the car and you of all people should know that these cellular bills aren't anything to play with after you run out of minutes." If Simone couldn't do anything else, she could run her mouth nonstop.

"Okay, but before you hang up like you always do, I wanted to inform you ahead of time that I'm having company tonight."

"And?"

"And you should find something to do." *Click.*

Simone had really gotten on Kennedy's last nerve, hanging up on her like she ran the world. But she didn't run Kennedy. No one did. Simone ran her mouth, and maybe her job, which Kennedy couldn't figure out because she never took her butt to work. Kennedy didn't know how she made all that money sitting at home on her lazy behind. She didn't want to see Simone anyway. Who Simone thought she was, trying to tell her to find something to do, Kennedy didn't know. Besides, she already had plans, some major plans. Michael. And she was going to do him too. Kennedy decided that it was time for her to move because the house-sharing thing wasn't making it, especially with her having her older sister as a roommate. Hell, she must've been crazy. What was she thinking? "More money and less rent. But as they say, all good things must come to an end," Kennedy said to herself as she accidentally drove past the liquor store.

Kennedy called her best friend, Miranda, for the third time that day. She couldn't wait to tell her about Michael. She had to tell somebody before she burst.

"Miranda, pick up!" Kennedy yelled into Miranda's answering machine. What was up with everybody screening their calls nowadays?

"Hey, Kennedy, what's up, girl?"

"Nothing much. What's going on with you, and where have you been? I've called you about a million times today."

"Oh, I was at the grocery store, and not a damn thing is going on. So did you see your friend?"

"Did I?"

"Kennedy, don't be holding out on me. So tell me what happened and don't leave out anything. I want to know everything. So do tell."

"All right, but you have to wait until I get there, okay? You know."

"Yeah, I know. Your cell bill is not to be played with and so on and so on. Right?"

"And you know it."

"Kennedy, honestly I don't know why you're so cheap. You have money, and besides you haven't paid for anything ever since you got with this new guy."

"Yeah, well, I'm on the BQE, I'll see you when I get there. Bye."

Kennedy pulled up in front of Miranda's house and was captured. The sweet scent of the flowers rushed to meet her and overpowered her thoughts. For a moment time stood still as she gazed at the luscious harmony, a mix of flowers, bushes, and plush velvet-green grass. The entire yard screamed that it had been designed by a landscape architect. Miranda had been smart in choosing her colors for the remodeled Long Island home. The beige-peach stucco was topped with a red-tiled Spanish roof, and adorned with floor-to-ceiling windows. The house was inviting. She had never taken a real good look at it before. Then again most people didn't, and anytime people were newly in love, as she was, they admired everything as though love revealed something in a different light.

Kennedy stepped up on Miranda's porch and rang the bell even though the front door was open. She was forced to laugh at the different ranges of dings and dongs that seemed to ring for a small eternity.

"Come on in, Kennedy, the door's open," Miranda yelled.

"Miranda, did you know that your doorbell sounds like a Mozart concert? Every time I come here I hear a symphony."

"Cute, Kennedy, cute." Miranda playfully sucked her teeth and dramatically rolled her eyes.

Kennedy set her keys on the red crescent-shaped table that sat opposite the front door. She turned in a full circle, taking in the décor. She nodded and bumped Miranda with her hip. "I really like what you did with this place, Miranda. I'm feeling it, and I haven't even seen everything that you've done to it yet. I wish I had a place of my own." She sauntered behind Miranda, following her to the adjoining room.

Miranda patted the sofa. "Girl, sit down and tell me the news. You can look at the house later. I know you got major dirt for me, right? You better have dirt for me, making me sit here and wait for an hour, so it better be damn good." Miranda laughed and lit her cigarette as she always did when preparing herself for the latest news.

"Light me one too. I need it right now, just like after sex, you know." Kennedy fluttered her eyes and crossed her legs.

Miranda shook her head. "Kennedy, no you didn't. Was it *good,* girl?" Miranda scooted to the edge of her seat.

Kennedy held up her hand. "Slow down, Miranda. We didn't go there yet. Well, at least I didn't. But *he* did and did it well, I might add." Kennedy pointed between her legs, stuck out her tongue, and wiggled it.

Miranda and Kennedy fell out laughing.

"When, where?" Miranda jumped up and clapped her hands. "I knew it! I knew it! You can't tell me your hot ass didn't give him some. I know you," she said, pointing, "and your hot ass was on fire. So did you let him extinguish you, or what?" Miranda sat down and slowly crossed her arms and legs at the same time, waiting for her answer.

Kennedy fanned her hand. "No, I told you already. *He* does me and that's it. I believe he has this fetish with my— hell, you know. Either that, or the brother's hungry." Kennedy laughed as Miranda sat up and gave her a high five. "Anyway, let me finish. Check this out. I met him for lunch at this little bistro on the Upper East Side. We talked. We ate. We drank, and I had just a few too many Cosmopolitans."

Miranda nodded. "That'll do it. Works for me every time."

Kennedy sat stone-faced until Miranda got the hint to be quiet. "Can I finish?"

Miranda huffed and sat back.

"Thank you. So I came out and asked him what he wanted from me and he kissed my hand and said he wanted all of me. Girl, I almost creamed my panties right there, on the spot. No, that's not true, because I wasn't wearing any panties."

Miranda choked. "Uh-uh girl. Don't you ever tell me some shit like that while I'm inhaling. You made me choke." Miranda patted her chest.

Kennedy laughed. "That's what you get. I told you to let me finish. Now where was I? Oh, and you know me, Ms. Curious, I asked him why. Why did he want me? He started saying how nice and sophisticated I am and how my eyes are like the color of rain, and how my complexion reminds him of pure honey and that my lips are soft and my tongue tastes good. Oh and let's not forget that I'm an intellectual and one of the smartest people he has ever met." Kennedy stood and curtsied.

Miranda jumped up and hurried to the coat closet. Kennedy could hear hangers scraping loudly against the wooden bar. Miranda giggled, piquing Kennedy's curiosity.

Kennedy walked up behind her, put her hands on her hips and shifted her weight on one foot. "Miranda, what are you looking for?"

Miranda turned around and smiled. "That mess that your friend told you. That old line, your eyes are the color of rain—*please,* that was played out years ago. I just knew I had it in the back of this closet with last season's clothes." Miranda held her stomach and stomped her foot, laughing as tears welled up in her eyes.

"Forget you. It wasn't a line. I know it sounds like one, but trust me, it wasn't. It's true, he was saying all that extra B.S. I've heard before. But this time it was real and I was on a whirlwind. I'm serious. Stop laughing. And you know me, I'm not the one to be B.S.ing around, so I asked for the check and we left. So after we're in his car—I left my car at the bistro—he asks me where to? I came right out and told him we've been playing around for a good three and a half months so now it's time we put some work in, if you know what I mean."

Miranda regained her composure and sat back down. "So you mean to tell me that all this time you and him have been together y'all didn't fuck yet?" Miranda poked out her lips and rolled her eyes. "I'm not buying it. I know you too well."

"That's right." Kennedy put her hands on her hips defensively. "And do you have to be so vulgar? He's always been so patient, such a gentleman. But I must admit, I do want to sex him and see what he's working with. Hmm, but you know a sista doesn't mind being the main course."

"I know that's right. Girl, you better work that shit out. If that's what he likes, hey, then so be it. Who are you to starve that man? You better feed him, child." Miranda doubled over. "Girl if we keep this up, I swear I'm going piss on myself. And before you say it, I can say any vulgar thing I want. It's my house, remember?" Miranda ran to the bathroom.

"Just hurry up," Kennedy yelled. "I got to get this out of my system."

Kennedy sat on the sofa and thought about Michael. She'd only had a taste of what he had to offer. She couldn't help wondering if the rest of him would be as good as his mouth.

Miranda threw a pillow at Kennedy. "Okay, I'm back. You can stop daydreaming now."

Kennedy returned the throw. "I wasn't daydreaming. I was wondering what Michael's like. Is he going to be good, mind altering?" Kennedy licked her lips and paused.

"I would hope so. It would be dirty of him to tease you like that, just to disappoint you. You better hope he isn't using his mouth to make up for a lack of something else."

"Yeah," Kennedy said, nodding, "but you know how they are. The ritzy type. The *I*-make-so-much-money type." Kennedy reached for the cigarettes, lit two and passed one to Miranda. "If they really like you then they wait to push up— most of them anyway. They do it to impress you because they can get some every night from some groupie. So it's not like they're a fiend. And if they really want you to be a permanent part of their lives, you can't just jump in the bed with them because you'll turn them completely off. They'll think less of you and assume you're after something. But *I've* waited long enough and besides, I've got my own money." Kennedy snapped her fingers.

"That's true. And yes, I'm going to be vulgar. We women cry that make-love nonsense, but we cannot deny that we don't love a good fuck as often as possible." Miranda slapped her hand against her leg and laughed.

"Yeah. Yeah. Yeah. What school of etiquette did you attend again? Anyway, back to the drama at hand. We drive to his place and it is fab, as in fabulous. You hear me, his place is tight. This man has a remote control for everything. Lights, blinds, music, you name it, he's got it. And you remember the Huxtable house on *The Cosby Show*—"

The front door closed. That meant Rich was home. He was the last person Kennedy wanted to see. As much as she wanted to bend over and throw up at the mere sight of him, she decided to be nice. There was no way in hell that she was going to let him disrupt her mood. He wasn't worth it.

"Hey, baby. Hey, Kennedy." Rich acknowledged them. Something rare for him.

"Hey Rich, how have you been?" Kennedy asked, forcing politeness.

"Not bad. Not bad at all. You sure are looking nice today." Rich winked behind Miranda's back.

Kennedy cringed and Miranda shot her a be-nice look.

Rich kissed Miranda on the cheek. "Hey, baby. Did you cook something? I'm starving."

"Boy, please. *Cook?* It's too hot to cook."

"All right. I got ya. Anyway I'm heading out. I just forgot something. Damn one of y'all smell good in here," Rich said to Miranda but stared at Kennedy as he bent down to whisper something in Miranda's ear.

Miranda giggled and rubbed the top of his head. Rich bent over her shoulder and kissed her. Miranda's eyes were closed and Rich's eyes were on Kennedy.

"See you later," Miranda said before the front door closed.

They sat in silence for a moment. Miranda glowed and stared into space. Kennedy couldn't believe the effect Rich had on her friend. What did he do to her? What did he whisper in her ear that caused her to tune out the world? Did she look like that when she was around Michael? Because that was the way she felt. Heavenly.

Miranda moaned and breathed deeply. Either she forgot Kennedy was in the room with her or she didn't care. "I'm sorry," she said, coming to. "He just does that to me. Damn!" She shivered. "Now where were we? Oh, the Huxtables. What about the Huxtables again?"

Kennedy was halfway across the room. Miranda jumped up and ran to catch her because she knew Kennedy was going to the kitchen. There was no way that Kennedy was going to get out of finishing the story this time.

"Uh-uh wench," Miranda jumped in front of the refrigerator. She knew Kennedy had to be thirsty after chain smoking. "Finish."

"Oh, come on!" Kennedy stomped her foot. "You know I'm thirsty. How do expect me to finish with a dry mouth?" Kennedy turned around. "What y'all got to snack on?"

"Nothing until you finish." Miranda laughed and grabbed a bag of chips from the pantry and sat down. "Get the soda. You know where the glasses are."

Kennedy poured her soda. "Okay. You remember the Huxtable house, right? Well it looks just like that, only bigger and better. So we're at his town house and he offers me some of that wine I got Simone hooked on, well he knows that it's my signature drink. So of course we're indulging a little bit and he takes me on a tour of the house. Exactly what I was waiting for, and as I said, his place is tight. While we are upstairs he takes me into a sitting room and we're talking. He asks me what I want from a man. I went through the usual routine—"

"Honesty. Integrity. Confidence. Humor. Intellect. Friendship. Personality. Stability. Love," Miranda interjected.

"Exactly. *And* someone to really know and love me for who I am. Someone who is willing to accept me for what I can bring to the table, no more and no less—"

"Let the church say amen." Miranda popped a chip into her mouth.

"So now he's all into it, right, so I decide to catch him off guard. I then tell him that all of those things are of great importance, but they do not ice the cake. Of course he wanted to know what does—"

"What did you tell him, Kennedy?" Miranda asked, waving her hand in the air like she was guiding a plane.

"Be patient, my child. I told him there's only one thing that ices the cake and that's great sex and I grabbed his hand and put it up my dress."

"Damn, girl, you don't mess around, do you?" Miranda said, her mouth falling wide open.

"If you want something, that's the only way you can get it!" Kennedy laughed, knowing that she startled her best friend.

"So what did he do?"

"What do you think he did? He grabbed me and kissed the hell out of me. Then he picked my little ass up as though I was air. And check this out. Remember I told you we were in a sitting room, well that was just the entrance to his bedroom. Miranda, I'm telling you, it was just like a

Harlequin romance novel. He picked me up and laid me on his bed and gently undressed me. If Gianni Versace were still alive I would have kissed him for designing my clothes to glide off."

"Keep it coming." Miranda crossed her long legs and took a deep pull from another cigarette.

"Miranda, if you would be quiet for a minute I would finish. So I'm lying there wearing nothing but heat 'cause you know that a sista was hot. And he's standing at the end of the bed fully dressed, just staring. I felt like a Picasso painting at a major exhibit. So I tell him to kiss me. And he said no, that he just wanted to admire me first. So I came right out and told him he could touch me and admire me at the same time. Damn it's hot in here." Kennedy got up to open the French doors.

"The only thing hot in here is your ass. The AC is on. Now close my doors or start paying some bills around here," Miranda teased.

"For real. It's him, I'm telling you." Kennedy fanned herself with her hand and laughed.

"Finish goddamnit, fin-ish." Miranda slapped the table.

"All right already. So he started to take off his clothes, and I won't get all into that because you don't need to know all of his business, if you know what I mean. So anyway he starts kissing me and my eyes were closed and the next thing I know he was kissing and licking my thighs and you know what happened after that. End of story. *Satisfied*?"

"Kennedy, you never finish a story, so what happened next?"

"Well, after he was finished he pulled me up and carried me into the bathroom and started kissing me again and telling me how special I am to him. And then we stepped into the shower and he started to bathe me."

"And y'all didn't fuck?"

"No, I told you that earlier. He did. I didn't. Anyway he was bathing me and he made me promise that I'd come to his house tonight since I've never been there. Then he drove me to my car and kissed me. End of story. Now are you finally satisfied?"

"Hell no. Didn't you just tell me that you were at his house earlier? What do you mean that you've never been there?" Miranda asked with her hands up and perfectly made-up face twisted.

"I said that I was at his *town house,* not his house. He wants me to come to the house that he owns on the other side of Central Park. He just bought it so that when his mother visits she has a place of her own to relax in. Other than that it stays unoccupied," Kennedy said very matter-a-factly.

"Well, I'll be damned, where did you find this one at, a *Forbes* magazine party?" Miranda teased and started emptying her pockets, putting all of her money in front of Kennedy.

"No, as a matter of fact I found him at Simone's job. He's her boss. Well, he owns half of the firm."

"Get out!"

"No, seriously, he does. And *why* are you giving me your money? You don't owe me anything. Or do you?" Kennedy eyed her.

"Hell no! I don't owe you a cent. I just want in on it. I'm making an investment. If you can keep doing what you're doing and getting what you're getting and *not* have to give up the twat, I'm buying stock in your ass now, before you go public." Miranda held her stomach and laughed.

Kennedy threw Miranda's money at her. "For real, Miranda, if Simone finds out she's going to be pissed. You know how seriously she takes her career, even if she does call in all the time. She'd have a titty attack if she knew I was seeing her boss, especially the boss who hired her."

"So are you ever going to tell me his name, or do I have to wait another two to three months?"

"I'll tell you, Miranda, but you cannot tell anybody, especially Simone. His name is Michael, Michael Montgomery. As in Montgomery & Klein Inc."

Miranda jumped up and danced. "Girl, you have really done it for yourself this time. This one sounds much better than Jared. It's like comparing sugar to shit if you ask me. How come I can't find anybody like that? Someone with charm, power, good looks, and money? Rich is lacking in the charm area."

"Because you're too slick and you give it up too quick. Men can smell you coming a mile away!" Kennedy giggled and silently agreed with Miranda about Jared. Not because it was true, but because she was mad at Jared. She had painted a bad picture of Jared when she didn't tell anyone her reasons for leaving him.

Kennedy impatiently tapped her foot as she massaged Kharri's temples. They had been in the optometrist's waiting room for over an hour, and Kharri was crying. Kennedy exhaled loudly and looked at the receptionist. *Don't they know what an emergency appointment is?* she thought.

"Kharri, sweetie? Does your head hurt as bad as it did earlier?"

Kharri nodded.

Kennedy picked her up and gently placed Kharri's head on her shoulder. She kissed her temple. "It'll be okay. Mommy will take care of everything."

"Promise?"

"Promise."

Kharri walked out of the optometrist's smiling. Kennedy was relieved because she hated seeing her daughter cry.

"So how does it feel to wear glasses?"

"It's okay, I guess," Kharri shrugged. "Do you like them?"

"Sure. Pink is your color," Kennedy said, tickling Kharri.

Kennedy struggled into the apartment with her hands full. Thank God Derrick was over. She didn't want to put up with Simone and her nonsense alone. Her day had been running too smoothly and she didn't want to lose her emotional high. The house was spotless as usual. One thing about Simone, she could keep a clean house. As soon as Kennedy reached the kitchen and set down the load, Derrick came and kissed her on the cheek.

"How's it going, baby sis? Where's Kharri?" Derrick asked.

"Kharri's at Miranda's and I'm fine. Thanks for asking. How about yourself, baby bro?" Kennedy asked.

Although Derrick was her older brother she always referred to him as that because he knew how she hated when he referred to her as baby sis. His baby sis was now a certified grown woman.

Derrick leaned his tall, muscular body against the counter and ran his hand over his wavy black hair. "Everything's cool. I just came by to see how my two favorite sisters are doing."

"Your *only* two sisters," Kennedy playfully corrected him.

"Oh, before I forget, Kennedy, these are for you." Derrick held out a bouquet of flowers in a very expensive crystal vase from Tiffany's.

"Thank you very much, Derrick, but my birthday isn't for a few months. Remember, July second—I'll be twenty-nine," Kennedy added.

"Yes, I remember. How could I forget, smarty, mine is on the same day if I remember correctly—"

"Thirty-two, right?"

Derrick punched Kennedy in the arm. "Thirty-one. Don't even try it. Can you believe Simone will be thirty-three? Dang, she'll be half of sixty-six." He laughed.

Kennedy giggled. "Don't let her hear you."

"But anyway, sorry to disappoint you. The flowers aren't from me. They must be from your boyfriend. Oh, I'm sorry,

your man. I almost forgot you aren't a little girl anymore."
Derrick laughed.

"Thanks." Kennedy grabbed the vase and began to read
the card.

*Kennedy, Thank you for helping me find my heart. I didn't
realize it was missing until I met you and you showed me
what it's like to really feel. Now I'm a grateful man. I would
love to thank you in person and I'd be honored if you would
allow me to tonight.—M*

"How sweet," Kennedy accidentally said out loud, forgetting
how nosy her family was. There went that tingle again. She
was always aroused that way when around or thinking about
Michael. He was so sweet. She had to take another shower
and get dressed so she could be ready for him that evening.
Damn, it was going to be good. That was why she empha-
sized how important satisfying sex was to her, so he would
make sure he'd do the job right.

"Kennedy, are you off in lala land or something?" Simone
inquired.

"No, I'm just thinking about what kind of plans I should
make since you're having the sex fest of the year over here
tonight," Kennedy shot back with a sly look.

Derrick cleared his throat and clapped his hands. "Don't
start. I know what that look means, Kennedy. You and
Simone can try to fool me like you two have been doing for
years. But I'm on to y'all now."

Kennedy and Simone laughed.

They may have gotten smart with each other a lot, but the
three of them were like peas in a pod. Close but not close
enough to confide in one another. They called and visited.
Sometimes they indulged in the latest family gossip that
their grandmother made sure they heard. But they made it a
point not to reveal anything about themselves that they
didn't want the whole family to know. Anything that anyone
knew, their grandmother knew, because the whole family

loved their grandmother and confided in her, usually about someone else's business. And their grandmother told; she didn't believe in secrets between family. She was from another time when family stood together rather than gossiped behind one another's backs.

As Kennedy was getting undressed she could hear Derrick and Simone downstairs chatting about some new chick named Courtney that had Derrick's nose open. Kennedy knew that Simone was going to kindly throw him out soon. That was how Simone was when she had her dinner-for-two nights. Kennedy had tried on almost everything in her walk-in closet when her private telephone line rang. "This is Kennedy," she heard her answering machine start to sing before she answered.

"Hello?"

"Hello, Ms. Kennedy, I'm glad I finally caught you. Did you receive the flowers?" Michael asked.

"Yes, I did. Thank you. That was sweet. Please don't tell me that you're calling to cancel."

"Not at all, I was calling to tell you I'm looking forward to tonight and to bring a few changes of clothes because I'm hoping that you planned on staying the weekend. And besides, I'm not taking no for an answer. I won't feel comfortable letting you drive all the way home on the other side of the park," Michael teased.

"I was hoping you would say that. Oh yeah, and Michael?"

"Yes, Kennedy?"

"Thank you so much."

"For what? I haven't done anything yet."

"Yeah, I know. I was thanking you for later. Just in case I get so caught up that I forget to say it. See you soon."

"Kennedy, one more thing. You don't need to drive. I'm sending a car for you at 7:30. Is that okay?"

"That's fine. I hope you'll be in it. Bye."

Damn, he gave her the chills. She had never met a man

like him. Besides being wealthy, nice, and intelligent, he was handsome as hell, childless, never married, and had the body of Adonis. What more could a woman want? Totally absorbed in him, she knew not to let him know that. Her parents had raised a daughter, not a fool. "The more someone knows about you the more they can hurt you," she could hear her father saying.

"Kennedy, I'm out," Derrick yelled from downstairs.

"All right, I'll see you later. Page me tomorrow and maybe we can have lunch sometime later this week, okay?" Kennedy replied through her half-shut door.

"That's cool. How about Sunday?"

"Nah, Sunday's not good because I'm leaving tonight for a few days to give the H.S.I.H. some freak time and I won't be back until Sunday."

"H.S.I.H.? What's that mean, and where are you off to this time? It's only Thursday. What is it, no let me guess, no work tomorrow, right?" Derrick asked.

"Number one, H.S.I.H. stands for *hot sister in heat,* and number two, you are a genius for remembering that I do not work on Fridays. Where I'm off to is a matter of my circumference, which means my personal space, which in turn means my business and not yours, and number three, I love you always. Kiss, kiss."

"Kiss, kiss to you too. Make sure you call me tomorrow or tonight if whoever he is acts up, got it?" Derrick responded, laughing.

"Screw both of y'all," Simone yelled.

Kennedy locked her door. She had no time for any more interference and Simone, Ms. Queen of Nosiness, would be intruding soon. She was running real late. It was already six o'clock and Kennedy wasn't even close to having it together. "All these clothes and I can't even find a damn thing to wear!" she said. "A fine man will make you lose your mind."

Finally settling on a black satin chemise set and a red one

just in case, she had her bedtime ensembles together. No need for nighties and whipped cream this trip, she didn't want to scare the man. She also chose some Chanel silk lounging pajamas, a little black, knock'em-out-every-time Prada dress with matching high-heeled sandals, a couple of suits by Katharine Hamnett and Dimitri that had cost her an arm. And of course, she chose her Guess jeans that made her butt look like an angel had molded it. And she couldn't forget her Sean John shirt that she couldn't do without. She hadn't opted for anything by Liz Claiborne because her clothes weren't made for women of color and they made her butt look like an ironing board. And with a couple of pairs of shoes, one pair of sneakers, and her Victoria's Secret bras and panties (although she probably wouldn't wear the panties), and toothbrush, she was all set.

If Michael thinks he's tasted a piece of heaven, just wait till he feels what it's like to enter the golden gates tonight, she thought.

~ 3 ~

*S*imone put the final touches on the apartment. With the wine and champagne chilled and the food just about done, all she had to do was slip into her clothes and touch up her makeup, although she barely wore any. Tonight was going to be the night, with any luck. She was absorbed in work, she could never find the right man. Being the VP of an accounting firm took a lot out of a person. But she had to get her act together. She didn't want to go back to where she came from, being poor and in the ghetto, down and out and stuck for life.

Her parents had fought long and hard so that she and her brother and sister did not have to struggle as they had. Being from the South, her white mother and black father weren't accepted and therefore, denied. Her mother's wealthy family had disowned her for marrying a black man. Her father's family, regular hardworking people, didn't have enough to help out. Or maybe they just *wouldn't* help. It had never really been discussed. Simone and Derrick remembered what being poor and alienated felt like, but Kennedy was too young to be scarred. Their mother's taking ill, dying of cancer, had squeezed almost every cent that they had. When she passed away when Kennedy was just about seven, the funeral and burial had left them penniless.

A year or so later, a lawyer knocked on their door and told them that they were receiving a large inheritance. Their mother's parents had died in a car wreck and in their last will and testimony they had left everything to their grandchildren, of which they were the only ones because their mother had been an only child.

Simone snapped out of her thoughts and went upstairs to get ready. Kennedy was blasting some song by D'Angelo. Kennedy, a D'Angelo fanatic, was hopelessly faithful to him despite how many wanna-be clones came out each year. Jealous fools this and player haters that, was all Simone heard from her.

"Kennedy, turn that music down!" Simone yelled through the bathroom door.

"Girl, please, I'm in the shower getting my groove on with D'Angelo. I'll be out and out of your way in a minute, all right?"

"Yeah, you can take the girl out of the ghetto but you can't take the ghetto out of the girl. Just hurry up."

"Simone, you can't rush perfection, slow down. And that's right, sista love, I got soul in these bones and it shows. Jealous? I'm not trying to fool or impress anybody. Just because you put on a front with your colleagues, you can't fool me. I know you and you come from the same place I came from—the ghetto. Now get to know it. Get to know yourself!" Kennedy said as she sauntered, clad only in a bath towel, and walked right past Simone as if she wasn't there.

"Now here you go again trying to give me a lesson in Blackness 101. Honey, I know more about the ghetto than you'll ever know."

"Why, because you remember more than I do from child-hood? Please, Simone, you would want to get to know." Kennedy shot Simone a "yeah right" look over her shoulder. "When was the last time you were there? Because I'm always there. The ghetto isn't just some, what you would call, low-class neighborhoods. The ghetto is not just a place where black people live, all kinds of people live there. Ones with money and ones without. We may be biracial but our black side dominates. Ask a scientist or better yet, learn your history. When was the last time someone mistook you for a white woman? You can move to posh neighborhoods, think-ing you can move away from the ghetto but you can't because you can't escape yourself! Ghetto is a state of mind. That's what we are, bourgeois ghetto," Kennedy said with authority and then fell out laughing.

"Girl, if you don't get your butt out of my face preaching your ghetto seminars again, I'm going to lose my religion." Simone's laughter forced her to stop talking.

"Kisses, boo. Hope you learned something. See you Sunday and get as much as you can, like I plan to. Oh yeah, and sis, I love you so much that I hope your friend looks as good as Morris Chestnut, or that guy from *Soul Food,* um what's his name . . . you know, Bird's husband. Or even the man, D'Angelo. No, I think I'll keep that wish for myself." Kennedy laughed, walked downstairs, and opened the front door.

Simone followed, peeked around her sister, and saw a lim-ousine parked in front of the house. Obviously, it was there for Kennedy.

"Be careful, Kennedy, and be careful what you wish for 'cause you just might get it," Simone said, using one of their grandmother's favorite sayings.

"Trust me, Simone, I know. Why do you think I keep

wishing for him, 'cause if I'm lucky I just might get him."

"Bye, Kennedy."

"I got the hint, now you get the phone. It's ringing." Kennedy closed the door behind her.

"Hello?"

"Simone, it's me, Derrick. Listen, I left a small piece of paper on your bar with Courtney's number on it. Could you get it and give it to me?"

"A yellow sticky?"

"Yeah that's it, can you tell me the last four numbers because I remember the 1-800 and the first three numbers, but I forgot the rest."

"The last four numbers are 0-3-0-1."

"Thanks much, Simone, I owe you one. And as long as I owe you, you'll never go broke. Can you do me another favor and put the number away. It's very, very important and you know you guys throw everything away."

"I got you. But I have to go now, someone's at the door," Simone said as she hung up.

Nigel came through the door looking as good as ever with a perfectly even smile. Tall, but not model material, he was that rugged, handsome type of man. The type Simone was weak for because he made her feel that she was living on the edge. She was attracted to men who made her feel that way because her life was basically routine and boring. He came and then he went and he didn't bother her as other men did. She liked that because one thing she couldn't stand was someone being a pest. And Nigel was far from being a pest. For the most part, he was so unpredictable. She wasn't used to that and now it was starting to bother her. As of late, she wanted more.

"What's up, baby?" Nigel asked.

"Not much. What took you so long? You're late. You were supposed to be here at seven but don't worry about it because my little sister didn't leave until seven-thirty. But a call would've been nice," Simone answered coolly.

Nigel took off his sunglasses, wiped the perspiration from the bridge of his nose and under his eyes. His eyes shimmered flirtatiously. "Baby, I know, but you know how it is. There was an accident on the F.D.R. and you know how that traffic backs up."

"Forget it and come over here and give me my kiss and make it up," Simone said. No need to make a hot night cold. And she planned on taking Kennedy's advice—getting as much as Kennedy did. "Nigel, I made you dinner—"

"Now, Simone, you know that God has blessed you with good looks, brains, and a beautiful personality and might I add a body at that, but He did not bless you with cooking hands!"

Simone bristled. Okay, so she couldn't cook, but he didn't have to tell her that. Hell, at least she tried and the least he could have been was appreciative. What took Kennedy an hour to prepare took her at least three from trying to be careful. With the exception of keeping a clean house, she was never into domestics—one of the reasons her first marriage didn't work and why she never entertained the thought of having children. Before now.

"Yeah, well, you know what, Nigel? You don't have to eat. I know that I'm no soul-food dive like Sylvia's, but at least I'm trying."

"Take it easy, baby. I'm only kidding. Everything you do is delicious, and I love you."

"What?" Simone's heart stopped beating and her body stiffened. Nigel had stunned the life out of her.

"I said I love you, Simone, and I want for us to get serious and have a real relationship. I want us to have something special and I don't want to lose you and I won't. So let's make a commitment and move in together." Nigel grabbed her hands and looked into her eyes.

"What did you say, Nigel? Because I couldn't have heard what I thought I just heard."

"You heard me right. I said I love you and I'm saying it

again for the third time and I want you to really consider us moving in together. Now I have a question to ask you. Do you love me too?"

"Well," Simone hesitated, considering her answer before she spoke, "yes, Nigel, I do love you but I'll have to consider the part about us moving in together and living happily ever after, if you know what I mean." Simone crossed her arms and tapped her foot, shocked at herself for admitting her feelings to him—something she never did because it got her in trouble the first time with Anthony, her ex-husband from whom she was happily divorced for two wonderful years.

Nigel eased behind her and gently rubbed her shoulders. "Please, give it some consideration. I really mean it, and if you give me a chance, if you give us a serious chance, I promise not to let you down. I assure you it won't be anything like it was before with your ex, okay? So just promise me that you'll give it a lot of thought before you decide," he whispered in her ear and kissed her lobe.

"Listen to me carefully, Nigel. I will give it some serious thought, but all thinking has to wait until tomorrow. Right now, the only thing I want to think about is tonight. The only thing on my mind now is the wine that's chilling and the food I took my time to prepare. Oh yeah, and by the way, my cooking can't be that terrible because if it was, you wouldn't be trying to shack up with me, now would you?" Simone joked.

"You got me there, baby. It's not bad at all." Nigel patted her butt and winked. "So let's eat 'cause you know the best way to a brother's heart is through his stomach and his lower vicinity. I know from experience that you'll take care of that region later on though, right?"

"Nigel, not to throw you off or anything like that, but I don't know about all of that tonight. I know what you'll be trying to do. You'll be sexin' me and trying to convince me that we should live together at the same time."

"Girl, you know you need to cut it out."

"No, seriously, baby, yes you would. I know you would.

Because you know that sex is one of my weakest points and I can't think right during or immediately after. So let's just have dinner without the dessert tonight, and let me offer you some wine and stimulating conversation with a few kisses here and there, all right?"

"Whatever you want, baby, you got it."

"But, I'll tell you what, I promise to let you know my answer to your question as soon as I reach a decision and not a moment longer, okay?"

"Okay, baby. Now tell me this: What does a brother have to do to get something to eat around here? All this talking is making me hungry from moving my mouth too much," Nigel teased.

As Simone shook her head, she realized not only how much she really wanted Nigel, but how much she wanted to get serious with him. She loved him, but was she ready to share her life with him every day and every night? Living with a man was a big step. She had taken that step before. And although she enjoyed sleeping with him, it didn't necessarily mean that she would enjoy living with him. But deep down she wanted to tell him yes. Yes that she would get serious with him and yes that she wanted to live with him. She wanted to share his days, his nights, and of course, his bed. Hell, who was she kidding, she had been dying for him to ask her. She would've asked him first but she didn't want to seem desperate.

"Simone, baby, what are you thinking about over there? I'm only a couple of feet from you and you would think that my side of the table was a million miles away."

She shook her head and tilted it to the side. "I'm here, baby. I was just thinking about your question, that's all."

"And?"

"Well, I was thinking about how much I really want this to work. How much I really want us to work. You see, sweetheart, what we have is good and I don't want to mess it up. You know that sometimes people think that living together is the answer, but sometimes it's not. I love you, Nigel, I do. And I believe that you love me too. But can you honestly say that you love me that much? Can you wake up to me every day and sleep with me every night and not get too comfortable? Because that's the key—not to get too comfortable."

"What do you mean, not to get too comfortable? I'm very comfortable with you, Simone, and if I weren't, well let's just say that you wouldn't have to worry about that because I wouldn't be around."

Simone checked the manicotti in the oven and retrieved plates from the cabinet. "Nigel, listen to me carefully, baby, because you're not getting my point. When people get too comfortable they get careless. When you get too comfortable you forget that the same things you did to get the other person is the same things you must do to keep them and sometimes more."

Nigel nodded.

Simone paused for effect. "You see, it takes a lot to keep a relationship going. A relationship is like work—hell, it is work, and you have to put in a lot of overtime," she said as she took the food out of the oven, placed it on the counter, and began to butter the French bread.

"You need some help?" Nigel nodded toward the manicotti. "Maybe we should talk about this after we eat. You seem a little irritated."

"No, I got it. But you can take the salad out of the fridge." She looked at Nigel from the corner of her eye. "And why would I be irritated? You try picking it up, it's hot and kind of heavy. No need to change the subject either, I *can* walk and chew gum at the same time, you know?"

Simone fixed her plate, sat down, and gave a short silent prayer. Nigel stared at her and cleared his throat.

"So, it's like *that?*" Nigel questioned with his hands in the air.

"*What?*" Simone swallowed and laughed. "I know you didn't expect me to fix your plate. I cooked the food, isn't that enough? If you want someone to cook and serve, there's a restaurant around the corner." She winked.

"Oh boy, I can see I'm in for it."

"Mm-hmm, can you pour me something to drink before you sit down?"

Nigel shook his head and smiled. Simone had the upper hand in the conversation and took full advantage of it. She'd make up for it later. She watched him as he reached for a glass. The outline of his muscles through his shirt aroused her. Later she'd feel the hardness of his body.

"Mm-mm-mm." She patted the chair beside her. "Come on over here and sit down. I wanna be next to you."

"Oh, you can be next to me all right."

"And I will. But first let me finish what I was saying before I forget." She got up from the table a few minutes later and put her plate in the dishwasher. She stared at Nigel while he cleaned his plate. His lips were juicy. She bit her bottom lip. *Right here. He can start right here,* she thought as she ran her finger up and down her cleavage.

"Okay, babe. I'm ready. You can finish now. You were saying something about being comfortable."

"Oh, yeah." She paused, searching for her thought. "Okay, as I was saying, when you get too comfortable, you can lose the fire it requires to keep the relationship burning. Sometimes you can have the tendency to forget that the person you live with is also your friend and not just a sleeping partner. And when that happens, you'll treat your outside friends better than the one you have at home. When people get too lax and too deep, things tend to change. The long walks in the park start to disappear right along with the romantic dinners and surprises, and going out to a club or a party . . . please, you can forget that because all those things are usually replaced. The romantic dinners on Saturday night turn into a evening of boredom and take-out food. The long walks in the park turn into a casual stroll to the kitchen or bathroom, and the going out together becomes you out with your friends or me out with mine. Then the surprise comes when one of us gets fed up with the other and then decides to go out and create our own fun, for the lack of a better word . . . cheats. You do understand what I'm trying to say here, don't you?"

Nigel tilted his chair back and rested his arms on top of his head. "Yes, I understand you clearly, Simone. What you're trying to tell me is that you don't want me to turn out like your ex, right?" He studied her with knowing, accusing eyes, and when she nodded, he continued, "Now it's your turn to listen to me, baby. I love you and I'm not him and if I were, I am sure you would've recognized it by now and left me out for the dogs. You have to trust me, Simone. Better yet, trust your heart. There's no pressure here, so relax and take your time. This here is not work and you do not have a deadline that you have to meet." He kissed her hand.

Simone wrapped her arms around his neck and stood still for a moment. Finally, a man who understood her. "Thank you, Nigel, for being so patient. I don't mean to lecture you. It's just that I'm a little nervous and scared and besides, what would your daughter say?"

He grinned, showing off his killer smile. "First of all, thank you for being you. Second of all, love is nothing to be afraid of. Third of all, let us not forget that my daughter is twenty, a woman herself, and she'll have to understand. She did with her mother anyway."

Simone smiled and sat in his lap. She traced his thick eyebrows with her finger. "That's good to know, now let's go upstairs because I have an itch that needs to be scratched." Simone laughed as she took his hand and led him through the house. Her getting as much as Kennedy did, was all she could think about.

After Nigel had fallen asleep Simone silently eased up from her bedroom and walked downstairs to get something to drink. She was glad that Kennedy wasn't home because she could walk around naked. Walking around naked in one's own house felt good. Nigel could, too, although now she hoped that he'd stay asleep. She needed this time to regroup. She did her best thinking in either the kitchen or the bathroom. And right now that was exactly what she needed.

She had always known what she wanted but she now found herself a little skeptical. She wanted Nigel. He was so good to her but she was afraid of what a serious relationship would eventually amount to. After they'd spend a certain number of years together the question of children would come up.

She wanted children, but was deathly afraid. Every time she thought of Kennedy, she grew even more scared. She thought of all the single mothers and deadbeat fathers that she encountered every day at the office. If a woman wasn't complaining about how she had to raise her children by herself then a man was calling to inform one of the accountants that his child support payments were in arrears and he was being governmentally garnished. How did Kennedy do it? True, Jared was nowhere close to being a deadbeat dad, but Kennedy had Kharri most of the time. Kennedy had to take her to school, the doctor, and the dentist. Kennedy raised Kharri, not Jared. Sure, he paid child support without a court order and he spent time with their daughter every chance Kennedy would let him—mostly weekends and summer holidays—but Kennedy was Mommy and Daddy the majority of the time. Simone admired Kennedy for that, but didn't think that she could ever do it. She simply didn't believe in herself enough.

She laughed. Talk about thinking far ahead. She was too busy for a baby, but deep inside she wanted one, maybe two. Imagining a little Nigel, she laughed and headed back upstairs.

Nigel was sitting up, wide awake. Simone licked her lips at the sight of him. She had always been attracted to muscles, and he had plenty of them, but she was only interested in one of them at the moment.

"Nigel, can I ask you a personal question?" Simone asked.

Nigel jumped. "Hey. Don't scare me like that. I didn't even hear you come in. Sure, you can ask me whatever you want."

"Sorry, I didn't mean to scare you." Simone rubbed the side of her neck. "When was the last time that you were tested?"

"Tested. Tested for what?"

"You know. HIV, AIDS?"

"A few weeks ago. Remember the time I got cut on that bottle at that construction site and there was something brown on it? We couldn't tell if it was dried-up blood or not. Well, when I went to the hospital to see if I needed stitches, I had them test me. It's company policy for insurance regulations in case we get hurt on the job. You know the insurance companies want to cover their backs. It was negative. Why do you ask?"

"Because there's something I want to try," Simone replied.

"If it doesn't hurt, I'll try anything once."

Simone pulled down the sheet. She knelt down and kissed him and then climbed on top. Nigel reached to the nightstand for a condom. Simone then politely removed the condom from his hand and threw it across the room.

"Why look through the window when you can come right through the door, Nigel?" she whispered in his ear, guiding him into her quickly before he stopped her. Once he felt her, he wouldn't be able to stop her. Nor would he want to.

~ 4 ~

*B*y the time Derrick pulled into his driveway he was pissed. He had paged his new friend and didn't receive a return call. Derrick always had a "new friend," as he liked to refer to his rendezvous partners, which was the reason he was missing thirty-five percent of his check each week. Seventeen and a half percent for each of his two children, results of his long-term, on-again/off-again secret relationship with Jericha, a twenty-seven-year-old, beautiful, mean and lazy, at-home mom who did not believe in work. His son, Derrick Jr. was seven and his daughter Anjelica was almost six.

At thirty, Derrick had almost everything he wanted: two adorable children (even though he didn't get to see them very often), a condo in New Jersey across the water from his

Wall Street office, a nice and healthy bank account, a Lincoln Navigator, and to top it all off, he was in good health. All he needed to do was find someone with whom to settle down—exactly what he was trying to do. As of late, he was putting more into the relationship than he received and he couldn't take it. Courtney was gorgeous, sexy, and successful with a larger bank account than his, so Derrick couldn't complain. He, too, had played the hard-to-get role and knew it didn't usually last for long. Derrick knew the game because he played it well.

"Damn, why does it have to be the one that I'm really interested in who has to play these games?" Derrick said aloud as he entered his condo. He walked to his state-of-the-art entertainment center. Being an avid music collector, he insisted on nothing but the best of electronics, speakers, and of course, his Sony Play Station 2, of which he had become very fond. His condo, a typical well-to-do bachelor pad, was sparse of furniture and coziness, but quality and money filled the air. He hadn't paid for anything in his place except for food and clothes. The rest were all presents from his previous new friends. Well, forget Courtney. He'd just call Jericha. She was always willing to see and please him, which was exactly what he needed—some good sex and a lot of attention and someone who wouldn't want to spend the night. Just as he was about to pick up the phone, it rang.

"Hello, Derrick Jacobs speaking," he said in his best business voice in case the caller was one of his pain-in-the-butt clients who felt they had the right to call him at home.

"Hey, sorry it took so long for me to return your call. I tried your cell phone and when I didn't get through I decided to try you at home," Courtney said.

"No problem, so what's up? Are you coming by tonight or should I meet you at your place?" Derrick asked, feeling like a fool because only five seconds earlier he was mad and didn't have the nerve to say it.

"Oh, I'm sorry, I completely forgot about our meeting

tonight but I didn't forget about you. I'm kind of tied up right now. I'm in a meeting and it'll probably last a while. I'm afraid I can't get out of it, and besides it's very important, a new client and account that I'm trying to land. And tomorrow I promised my mother I'd come to her house for dinner, remember? You know I haven't seen her in weeks. I truly apologize, but I promise to make it up. Forgive me?"

"Yeah, we'll see. I'll forgive you if you promise to teach me something new, if you know what I mean."

"You got it. Oh, and did I tell you that I have a wonderful birthday surprise all planned for you?"

"That's sweet, but my birthday isn't until July, it's only May."

"I know, but I was thinking about you and I'm looking forward to making you smile. I'm also looking *very* forward to our trip to Rio next month. Unfortunately for you, you'll have to wait until your birthday for your surprise but I can assure you that it's better than Rio. On that note, sweetheart, I have to go now. My client keeps looking at me and that isn't a good sign. Okay, bye."

Courtney hung up and Derrick grinned, temporarily satisfied knowing that he was being thought of. He picked up the phone again and dialed Jericha's number. She was bound to give him what Courtney couldn't.

Derrick had not spent quality time with Courtney in weeks. They saw each other on occasion and met for lunch or dinner when the opportunity presented itself, which was not often enough. Because of their busy schedules—usually not his—they didn't have the time, couldn't find the time, and Courtney seemed not to make the time. Derrick was lonely. He silently longed for the mornings when they had awakened with their bodies entangled and their legs criss-crossed. He missed the sticky afternoons when they would sex each other until their sweat poured out like tears. He wanted the endless nights that ended way too soon. He wanted all of those things but he couldn't say it. He was a man, a man who was used to being chased, not doing the chasing.

Time to have a serious discussion with Courtney. They would have to make the time to talk, or Derrick would be forced to remove himself from the situation. How could anyone be with a person and not spend time with them? How could Courtney expect him to stay true when they were absent from each other? Didn't Courtney know how large his appetite was?

Derrick bitterly paced, pondered his current situation, then grabbed his keys from the table. He didn't know where he was going but he knew he had to clear his thoughts. His cell phone rang. Instead of answering it without thought as he usually did, he looked at the caller ID. He was too upset to talk civilly so he'd let Courtney wait on him for a change. Later they would talk. With keys and cell phone in hand, he grabbed his Palm Pilot and was out the front door.

As Derrick reached the end of the Lincoln Tunnel, Manhattan bound, his phone rang again. Damn. Must be Courtney calling again. They didn't speak as often as he would've liked them to, but when Courtney called, Courtney *called!* He refused to hide from anyone.

"Yeah?" he answered.

"Hey, babe," Kennedy said, "what's going on? I've been calling you for the last fifteen minutes and the recording kept saying that you were out of area. Aren't you supposed to have one of the best, I'm strictly Wall Street, my phone never goes out type of phones?" Kennedy teased.

"Hey, what's up, li'l sis? Nah, it wasn't the phone, trust me. I was stuck in traffic inside the tunnel. You know how it can be. Oh, I'm sorry, I forgot. You might not remember about that, considering that you never visit me anymore," Derrick said, as his aggravation turned into a smile.

"That's not true. That's why I was calling. I was on my way out there but I can see that you're here now. Any plans?"

"Nope. On my way to nowhere. What you got in mind?"

"Whatever," Kennedy said.

"Where are you?"

"Midtown, Times Square. I'm on Forty-fifth and Broadway. I'm on the way to my car, just leaving the Virgin records store."

"Meet me at Windows of the World. And yes, I'm paying. See you there," Derrick replied and hung up, anxious to see his little sister. He needed somebody to confide in and Kennedy was fair if nothing else. She wasn't always the most considerate person in the world because she had a habit of telling the truth even if it hurt. And what he needed right now was a dose of the truth to wake him up.

When Derrick saw Kennedy enter the restaurant, he waved to her to get her attention. As usual some man was trying to hit on his little sister. Even though she was now a full-fledged woman he couldn't help but feel protective. Men would always be attracted to Kennedy. She was smart, beautiful, and sexy. He hated to admit the sexy part because she *was* his sister, but he couldn't lie. He would never see her the way other men did of course, but all in all, she was definitely shapelier than a lot of his ex-women were.

When Kennedy finally saw Derrick, she dismissed her latest pursuer, who more than likely knew he didn't stand a chance in hell with her but tried anyway. They always did.

"What's up, D?" Kennedy asked, hugging Derrick, who had stood up as she approached the table.

"Apparently you, sis," he said as he kissed her cheek and nodded toward the man who had stopped her.

They both laughed when they saw the look on the man's face. The man flared his nostrils, puffed out his chest, and gave Derrick a quick nod.

"You still know how to pick 'em, huh, Ken?" Derrick teased.

"Yeah, right." Kennedy laughed. "Him, you must be crazy. As a matter of fact, I do indeed know how to pick them but them does not include him!"

"Okay, let's talk about *them.* Let's do something that none of us do. I'm talking about me, you, and Simone. Let's share, as you would say, but not too much detail, okay? I don't think that I could handle that," Derrick said.

"Sure. But you go first because I don't trust what I'm hearing. You. Wanting to share? Who'd ever believe? What is it, Mr. Jacobs? Are you in love? Did somebody break your heart? No wait, I got it. You *are* in love and you have a baby on the way, right? Because that's the only time you want to share," Kennedy said very matter-of-factly, with interest and concern, and smiled.

Kennedy left the restaurant amazed by their openness and candor. She couldn't believe how easy their conversation flowed. More important, she couldn't believe all that they'd shared. Derrick was definitely one to be proud of. Not only honest but also sincere, his smarts were never in question. Neither of her siblings lacked intelligence, just openness. All of them were that way. She couldn't remember a time when they had all been unguarded with one another. She liked being able to be honest with Derrick, well, almost honest. She couldn't tell him *everything* about Michael. And she had a feeling that Derrick had been holding back too.

———

On her way to meet Miranda, Kennedy wondered if she should've told her brother everything. She found it hard to love someone and not be able to share it, especially with family. Miranda knew. But telling Miranda was like telling herself. Miranda was one of those people who was love struck by love. She didn't care who was in love, she would still be excited.

When Kennedy pulled up in front of the hair salon she noticed Miranda's new car immediately. Although she had never saw it before, she knew because of the description Miranda had given her. It was the only bright red Mercedes SL600 series parked. As she was admiring the car up close a man's voice startled her. Immediately she turned to see Rich, Miranda's fiancé.

"What's up, Rich?" Kennedy asked nicely, pretending she really liked him.

"Like what you see? Miranda told you that I hooked her up, right? See, some of us *are* nice guys," Rich said through closed teeth as he got out of his car. The same closed teeth that made Kennedy weary of him.

"Yeah. It's nice. It's real nice."

"Maybe if you're nice, *real nice,* maybe you can get hooked up too," Rick replied.

"Hooked up? Hooked up by whom?" Kennedy snapped, not believing that the lunatic had the balls to say what he just did while Miranda was just across the street in the salon. "Are you crazy? Do you *know* who I am? I'm Miranda's best friend. We're close but not that close, not close enough to be sharing everything. You must be fucking nuts!"

Rich inched between Kennedy and Miranda's car and tried to run his finger down the side of her face. "Come on now, Ken. *You* know you wanna be hooked up. Loosen up a little bit and share the wealth. I won't tell if you won't tell."

"Fuck you!" Kennedy jumped back and mouthed under her breath as Miranda came out of the salon. She would tell her friend as soon as they were alone.

Rich followed Kennedy's eyes to where Miranda stood and immediately put on his nice-guy routine and got back in his car. This was the same routine that he used to get Miranda, Kennedy suspected. She couldn't believe that her friend couldn't see through him and she suddenly pitied her.

Too bad her friend loved too hard. Too bad Miranda loved so hard that she couldn't see the obvious. As Kennedy waved at Miranda, Rich revved his engine and honked at her.

"Go ahead and tell her if you want. Who do you think she's going to believe—a man who puts it on her at night for hours at a time and just bought her a $130,000 car, or you? If you don't believe me, test it. You know I'm right," Rich said and pulled off.

Damn, Rich was right. He knew Miranda better than she thought he did. Once Miranda was in love, that was it. She also knew from experience that Miranda was in it for the long haul. Miranda's ex tried to hit on one of their very good friends once and when she told Miranda, Miranda dropped her like she was hot. End of story. And no one had heard from the friend since. At the time Miranda was closer to her than to Kennedy, so Kennedy knew better than to tell. She didn't want to lose her friend.

"Hey, Ken," Miranda said. "Girl, do you like it?" Miranda squealed about her new car.

"Yeah, it's tight. Real tight. Rich was just bragging about it. Showing off a little bit, showing what kind of man he is," Kennedy said, trying to imply something that would pique Miranda's curiosity.

"What do you mean, what kind of man he is?" Miranda asked, crossing her arms in defense.

"Nothing really. Just that he's the man for the hookups, that's all. He said that there are some nice guys left, meaning him. Meaning him getting the car for you," Kennedy said and left it at that so her friend wouldn't think she was being jealous instead of cautioning her.

After Kennedy sat in the pedicure chair listening to Miranda carry on about how great Rich was, she drifted into her own thoughts. Michael had told her he'd be going away to a leadership seminar in China in July. Why did he have to go all the way to China to learn how to have better leadership and control of his company? She assumed it was another method of ergonomics that was more successful in China than in America. She made a mental note to research it. She planned on being one of the best business advisers New York had to offer, and had to stay on top of things.

She also knew that she had to stay on top of Michael. He was a hard one to keep up with. Her hectic schedule was nothing compared to his. He updated her weekly on his next six days, and as of late he was getting busier by the minute. But she could always catch him by cell phone, although she rarely did that. As a matter of routine, she only called him when he paged or asked her to. Other times she just paged him. She felt uneasy about the possibility of interrupting him on his phone because he always had some sort of meeting or another. Simone had told her in so many words.

"Kennedy, where are you?" Miranda asked.

"Oh, I'm sorry. I was just thinking about Michael. He's going away on business in a couple of months."

"So why don't just you go with him? You've got the summer off, so go. I would. Besides, you need it. One more semester and your master's will be completed. Hell, you earned it. Where's he going anyway?" Miranda asked as she jumped down from the pedicure chair and walked over to the nail polish stand. She returned with two different polishes and held them up to Kennedy, who took the red one.

The salon was getting crowded. Ever since Miranda had expanded and included a nail section, it was hard to get an appointment. Nosy and nosier women were everywhere.

Kennedy lowered her voice when Miranda hopped back in her chair. "China. And no, I can't go. I don't want to be that far from Kharri. Although . . . she'll be with Jared for the summer. He's picking her up next month when school gets out. But China is too far away and I wouldn't enjoy myself because I'd be worrying about her. It's bad enough that she's gone for the summer and almost every weekend. I feel incomplete when she's not around. When you have your own, trust me, you'll understand. Besides I was thinking about going out there to surprise her and take her to Six Flags or somewhere like that." Kennedy bit her lip. She hated sharing her daughter, even with Jared.

A woman bumped into Kennedy's freshly painted toes and smudged one. Kennedy sucked her teeth and rolled her eyes. The Asian pedicurist Miranda had hired put some remover on her finger and smoothed out the smudge.

"Girl, I don't blame you. Stay home in the good ol' U.S. of A with Kharri, and you and she can have your own little vacation. Anyway, as I was saying. Wait a minute, *did* you hear *anything* that I was saying?"

"Repeat it. Sorry," Kennedy said, listening intently.

Miranda threw her hands up and blew loudly. "I said that my period is late. Girrrl, I think that I might be having a baby," Miranda squealed.

"A baby! A baby by *whom?*" Kennedy couldn't contain her disappointment and stopped herself from saying, "not by that ignorant-ass fool Rich."

"Rich. Who else?" Miranda replied, crinkling her eyebrows.

"Are you keeping it?"

"*If* I am? Hell yeah, I'm keeping it. Why not?"

"So you really think that you are? Well, we can stop and get an EPT or one of those other home tests when we leave here."

"No. I don't trust those tests. I called the doctor this morning to make an appointment. They said that I can come in tomorrow morning. I'll let you know my test results when I get them."

Kennedy left the salon in total disbelief. Miranda couldn't possibly be pregnant. Now she definitely couldn't tell Miranda how conniving Rich was. It was too late. She should've told her a long time ago. But shoulda, coulda, woulda.

Oh hell, go get some cheesecake from Junior's. The cheesecake would help to soothe her and she wouldn't be able to think of anything else.

Just as Kennedy was on the FDR headed toward the Brooklyn Bridge, her cell phone rang. *Oh, don't let it be Derrick.* She was supposed to meet up with him later on but couldn't. She planned to leave a message on his voice mail, an easy way for her to cancel. But during her conversation with Miranda she had forgotten.

"Hello."

"Kennedy, is that you, baby?" her grandmother sang into the phone in her sweet voice.

"Hey, Gram. Yeah, it's me. How are you? Is everything all right down there? I miss you so much. I sent you a birthday present. Did you get it?"

"Girl, slow down. Why y'all talk so fast up there? All I heard was *It's me* and *Did you get it,*" her grandmother said.

"Sorry, Gram. I said that I missed you and I wanted to know if you received your birthday present from me and Kharri?" Kennedy replied slowly.

"Oh yeah, baby, it was really nice. But you know that you don't need to be spending that much money on me. I woulda done fine with a card, but I loved my new dress and hat for church. Thankya. Anyway, Ken-Ken, I was just calling to let y'all know that I got my airline ticket in the mail today, thankya. And I just want to see if one of y'all could pick me up from the airport. I thought I'd better call y'all now, since y'all like to run in the streets so much. I'ma be staying at y'all's house, did Simone tell you?"

"Gram, no Simone didn't tell me, but she didn't have to. You know you're always welcome to stay with us. When are you coming?"

"Thanksgiving."

"Thanksgiving? Gram, you didn't have to call so early. It's only May. She probably wanted to surprise me. You know I'll be there. What time are you arriving? Oh Gram, you're going to miss Kharri. She's going to Jared's for Thanksgiving, she's going to be so sad she missed you—"

"Ken-Ken, didn't I tell you to slow down?"

Later that night after Kennedy got home she left a message on Michael's machine. He was going to be a little irritated because she had stood him up earlier, so she made sure that she left the sweetest I'm so sorry message that she could manage. After she took a bath and ate, she sat down at her desk and wrote Kharri. She had started a journal for Kharri when she was just a baby and made a habit of writing in it. She planned to give it to her when she was old enough to move out. She considered it to be a "remember Mommy's advice" sort of journal, which Kharri could take with her through life.

Finishing, she gently closed the journal and wrapped it back up in the velvet cloth. She then sat on her chaise longue in front of the bay window and thought about Kharri, Jared, and Michael while staring out at the people crossing the street and the double-parked cars. At night her block was quiet, but during the day, New York was never quiet. Before she knew it, she had fallen asleep.

The sound of the telephone ringing startled her. She looked over at the clock across the room on her nightstand. Five A.M. She couldn't believe someone was calling her this early. Her heart started to race. Had to be an emergency. With Kharri away at Jared's, Kennedy started to panic.

"Yes," she yanked the phone, causing the base to fall to the floor.

"Kennedy, did I wake you?" Miranda asked.

"Girl, is everything all right? What happened? You scared me. I just knew it had to be something with Kharri," Kennedy said after exhaling loudly. She held her chest and mouthed "Thank you God." Glad that the call wasn't concerning her daughter but still worried. Miranda never called so early.

"No, nothing happened. I just couldn't wait until tomorrow to go to the doctor so I came here to the emergency room to have a pregnancy test. Of course I had to lie and pretend that I was throwing up just so they would see me," Miranda said.

"So, are you pregnant?" Kennedy asked, bracing herself.

"I don't know yet—my blood results haven't come back from the lab. I thought that they were going to just have me piss in a cup and send me home. I'm sorry to wake you up, but I'm *so* nervous."

"I know you aren't there by yourself at five in the morning. Where's Rich?"

"He wasn't home when I left. Look, Kennedy, I gotta go, they're calling my name." Miranda clicked off.

~ 5 ~

As Kennedy waited for Michael by the front door she checked and double-checked herself in the mirror. She always liked to make sure that she was on deck as far as appearance. She especially wanted to look good for Michael. He overwhelmed her to say the least. He always looked damn good, smelled damn good, and made her feel damn good. No one her age made her feel the way that he did. He didn't seem much older, but eight years was normally a stretch. But boy, was he classy, sophisticated, and distinguished by all means. From day one she could tell that he was an experienced man, as she had always heard about older men. He dressed in nothing but the finest, as did she, and she liked that. He was much more pleasing, and much sexier than what she was use to. All that her ex-man, Jared, had worn was the usual jeans and sneakers or boots with some shirt that had the designer's name all over it. She had learned a long time ago that often less is more, And although Michael didn't seem to have anything "less" about him, he was more than enough for her. Hopefully not too much.

As usual Michael was on time and as soon as she had stepped into the limo all else faded. She looked into his chocolate brown eyes and leaned over and kissed him. He had wonderful, perfectly full lips. Soft, succulent ones, not like an ordinary man. Michael was well kept to the point that he was almost over-kept, like those high-society women who had nothing else to do but go to spas and shop for clothes that they would probably never wear. With him, Kennedy was bold, she was herself. He brought out the side of her that she usually kept hidden. A very sexual being, she wasn't afraid to let him know. Hell, this was what older men craved, so why hide it?

"Michael, I am so glad that you decided I should spend the weekend with you again. I really enjoyed myself the last time. I think I, or rather, we need this—" Kennedy began.

Michael sat up and loosened his tie, grabbed Kennedy, and gently put her head against his chest. "Kennedy, I wouldn't have it any other way. But tell me one thing—why do you feel that we need this? I'm not saying that we don't but I would love to hear your reasons."

"Well, because we do. I've been seeing you for four months or so, since February. Remember Valentine's Day was our official first date. And although we've spent an adequate amount of time together, we don't really know each other. Earlier, you said you wanted all of me. But in order for you to have all of me, you have to know all of me. May was the first time that we ever came close to anything sexual and that seemed to be a big step in our relationship, or our friendship, I really don't know what to call what we have because we haven't discussed anything long term or anything like that. Anyway, as I was saying, we've done the dinners, the walks in the parks, the horse-and-buggy rides, movies, and so on. And yet it's not enough. Don't get me wrong, Michael, I'm thankful. You've made my life more interesting and wonderful in small ways, the ways that count. But you still don't know me and I still don't know you, not like I want to anyway. This weekened will be the turning point in my eyes. It will let us know if we want more or if we want less. I'm certain that I'll want more of you, but I'm not sure if you will want more of me." Kennedy pretended to fix her blouse.

"Why, Kennedy? What would make you think something like that? Why would you say something like that?" Michael sat up and turned Kennedy around to face him and looked her directly in the eyes.

Kennedy interlocked her fingers and rubbed her thumbs together. Nervously she cleared her throat. "Well, it's because I may or may not be the person you think I am." She shyly and reluctantly looked into his eyes. "But I haven't lied to you. I do work full time in the summer and I'm almost finished with my master's degree in business, and I don't have anyone else, and Kharri is my only child, so don't panic."

"Speaking of Kharri, how is she?"

"She's fine. She's really excited about turning four." Kennedy smiled, thinking about her daughter.

"I'm sorry about interrupting." Michael nodded for her to continue.

"Before I continue, let me ask you a few questions. How uppity and innocent do you think I am? Do you think that I'm so conservative that I don't get my boogie on? Do you even know what that means? Or do you think that I'm the classical-music type, the opera type? Wait a minute, I've got a good one. Do you know what Thug Passion is?"

"No, I definitely wouldn't have pinned you to be the classical-music type but definitely classical in another way. In your own way. And I'm from the old school, babe. Getting your boogie on means dancing, going out, etc.

Conservative? I think yes, but in your own way. And I'm sorry, I don't know what Thug Passion is."

"Part right. Getting your boogie on can mean different things. It depends on the topic of conversation. Getting your boogie on usually means that you're going to party, have sex, drink, and sometimes it's just a way of saying good-bye without saying what you're going to do. Thug Passion is a mix of Hennessy and Alizé. Not something that I'd drink in public, not even something I'd admit to drinking." Kennedy leaned back and laid her head on his lap, feeling more comfortable. Honesty had a way of doing that to her—making her relax. "Now, do you see exactly what I'm trying to get across here? You may see me as this dainty, classy type, and I am. But I am so much more than that."

Michael nodded and rubbed her leg. "Yeah, you're right about that. You are definitely more than that."

"I'm *much* more than you see because you haven't seen all of me, I haven't shown you. When I'm around I speak very polite, and usually I am, just not *all* the time. Put it like this, around you I'm very aware. Aware of how I speak, I choose my words very carefully so I won't offend you. I'm aware of how I dress, I may feel like a pair of jeans but because I know that I'll be meeting you I'll put on a dress. I'm a very down-to-earth individual, I curse, go out with my friends to clubs, and occasionally I smoke a cigarette or a joint. I'm not uptight, not saying that you are or anything like that, but I just like to have fun. You know, just be myself, and I'm not sure if you can understand that, but you need to know because if this relationship or friendship goes any farther, you need to know me. You have to know what I like to do and accept me because I'm not going to change and I don't expect you to change." Kennedy paused to take a deep breath.

"Forgive me for laughing, but I can't help it." Michael wiped tears from his eyes. "You didn't say anything funny, it's just that a lot of these things I already know. I've heard you cursing at your sister when you thought that you had pushed the mute button on the phone. I've seen you literally bob your head to rap music and recite the lyrics word for word in the car and suddenly stop because you didn't want me to see you. And just last week when we met for dinner at Jezebel's, I could tell that you had just smoked a joint because as you would say, you had the munchies and were eating everything in sight." Michael winked and patted her stomach. "You see, I don't expect you to change, and I appreciate the way you just stood up for what you believe in—yourself. So don't worry your pretty little self so much." He playfully pinched her cheek and ran his hand through her freshly done hairdo.

Kennedy grabbed his hand and nibbled on his thumb. "You sure you want to get to know me . . . all of me?" She winked.

"If anything, I'm willing to try and experience what you like. If I had a problem with you, I would have said so in my own gentlemanlike way. You may not realize this, but you excite me. You are fascinating compared to all of the women I know. You have this, as you would say it, fuck-you attitude and that alone is sexy. Strength and security are sexy as hell to me. See, baby, even I curse. You're just used to seeing me right after I finish with my business and I'm still in my business mode. I can get just as loose as you can," Michael said, laughing.

Kennedy got up and kissed him. She looked out of the limousine window. The city lights were sparkling. "Okay. Now that we've got that all cleared up, Mr. I'm Ready for the World, could you please tell me where we're going? The last time I checked your house was on the Upper East Side, not headed toward the Midtown Tunnel."

"Oh, that's easy. We're on our way to my favorite house. The other house, not my town house or the one on the West Side. I hope you don't mind because I'd like it if we became even more familiar. I trust you, believe me, I do. Not to flatter you, but I've never taken a woman to where we're going.

This house has always been my private domain. You'll see why. Now relax and sit your feet on my lap. It's going to be a long ride."

As Michael rubbed Kennedy's feet, she smiled. She was surprised that he knew more about her than she thought. That was all she needed to hear. Time to open up the shades and let the sunshine in. She could be herself.

The limo slowed as it approached Michael's house in the Hamptons. Tucked behind tall trees with a manicured lawn decorated with perfectly groomed hedges, the brick house seemed to be mostly made of windows. *Damn,* she thought, *I lucked up this time.* From the outside the house was beautiful. Tinted double glass front doors stood out from behind six white stone pillars, surrounded by an arc of windows that allowed her a glimpse of the foyer. A white-paned two-story window showed off a baby grand piano on one side. A semicircular staircase showed through the other. She knew from Michael's excellent taste that the inside would be impeccable. As just about any woman would, she could imagine herself living there.

The driver delivered the bags to the front porch and almost strategically placed them between the six pillars. Michael unlocked the door, and she knew that she was at home just from the sense of peace she felt from the warmth of the earth tones that greeted her when she stepped inside.

"Baby, your house is beautiful."

"Come on in, *mi casa es su casa,*" Michael said in bad Spanish.

His house looked like something out of a magazine. The terra-cotta marble foyer had muted sage green walls with terra-cotta and beige stripes and was as big as a two-car garage. To the left of the foyer was a beautiful cherry-wood staircase with gold leaf engravings. Kennedy turned around and acted like she wasn't impressed until she saw the white baby-grand piano sitting in the opposite room. Forgetting her composure, she walked to it and fingered the keys.

"Do you play?" Michael leaned against the piano.

"A little. Not as much as I'd like." Kennedy got up and walked out of the room. "So what's next? You're giving me the grand tour, right?"

"No, that's reserved for guests. You aren't a guest, you're home." Michael winked and rubbed her back as she walked toward the rear of the house.

Kennedy went straight to the kitchen, intentionally passing a few rooms. She would see them when alone. The house was eye candy for her and she didn't want him to know how excited she felt. Hell yes, she was home, even if the house wasn't hers. It would be one day, and she knew it.

"Michael, this house is fab—that means it's very nice. It's beautiful. I didn't know a brotha could live like this and still be considered a brotha." Kennedy laughed and playfully nudged Michael with her elbow. "No, I'm only kidding. I've seen places like this, just not this close to the city and I've only been inside one once. I don't know why you choose to live in the city instead of out here. But there's something missing, it just doesn't feel like home. You need paintings, rugs, and other little things that make a house feel like a home. Since I'm here for the weekend, I'll take the liberty of handling all of that for you tomorrow. You don't mind, do you?"

Michael grabbed Kennedy's chin and kissed her forehead, nose, and then her lips. He gazed into her eyes. "That's precisely what I like about you. Many others have seen my house, relatives you know, and no one has come out and told me what it needs. But you, you pull no punches. Make yourself at home and do whatever you like, but just to clear things up, I do have a picture of you over the fireplace in the den. It's from the time when we were at Tavern on the Green and I took it upon myself to have it oil painted, I hope you don't mind."

Kennedy breathed deeply and put her hand to her chest. No one had ever made her feel so special. Once again she was overwhelmed by this man. She closed her eyes and said a silent prayer of thanks because Michael had to be a godsend.

Michael left for the grocery store. She had given him a list, because if she didn't get the chance to do anything else, she was going to cook for him. Big Ma, her father's mother, had taught her how to cook and she liked to show off her Southern skills. She could turn a vegetarian into a meat lover. And besides, since he had shown her before that he liked to eat, she would give him his dinner and his dessert. Anybody who could taste her the way he did had to also like to eat food. She smiled, thinking of how his face seemed so at home between her legs. The way his tongue opened her door and entered as if it lived there. *Come on in,* she thought and laughed.

She went to the master bedroom to unpack. No need to feel like a guest living out of bags. She dropped her shoe and it rolled under the bed. On her knees looking for it, she noticed a brand-new big tube of K-Y jelly on the floor just under the bed. She left it there. Michael was a bigger freak than he led her to believe. She smiled.

She sat on the bed and bounced. She nodded, satisfied with the quality of the mattress. Running her hands on the chenille comforter, she licked her lips and sighed deeply. Her heart fluttered. She and Michael could do a lot of damage here, she thought.

She went into the adjoining sitting room and smiled at the barely there décor. A cream damask sofa sat opposite a matching chaise. Poor Michael. He had a beautiful house and didn't know how to furnish it. In the midst of her snooping she was startled by a noise downstairs, and jumped. She tripped over her own feet and laughed, catching her balance she fell against the wall and heard a click. The fireplace came on, then the television that hung just above it. She clicked the switches off and wiped the sweat from her forehead. Her heart was racing.

"Kennedy, I'm home."

"I'm upstairs, I'll be down in a minute," she said, gathering her composure.

Kennedy glided down the stairs in her gold chemise set, which complemented her skin tone. The silk made her look as elegant as ever. Since Michael was as unfamiliar with a grocery store as most men, she had had time to unpack, shower, and change. With a little loose powder, lip gloss, and a couple of dabs of Chanel perfume, she was all set. She knew she was a sight to behold because not only did she look sexy, she felt sexy.

Michael's eyes twinkled as he licked his lips and rubbed his hands together. "Um um um, don't we look nice. Are you sure you'll be able to cook in that?"

Kennedy spun around and bowed, taking in the compliment. "Of course. I see that you're not very familiar with the grocery store because it took you a while. But that's okay because I needed to shower and change."

"Sorry, sweetheart, but I am very, very familiar with the grocery store. Before college I went to culinary school and when I was in college I made my living as a chef. I bet you didn't know that, did you?" Michael grabbed an onion and peeled it. "The reason that I took so long is because I needed to stop at the liquor store and pick up some champagne because I don't have any in the wine cellar, and I had to pick up a little something for you. It's a surprise and I'm afraid that you'll have to wait until after dinner."

Kennedy eased between Michael and the kitchen counter, making sure to rub her lower body against his. "Michael, can I please have my surprise now? If you give it to me now, I promise that you won't be sorry—"

Michael stepped back. "No how, no way. Some things are worth waiting for. I waited for you all my life and I don't regret it. Hopefully you won't regret your surprise. It's nothing really, but it's something that I wanted you to have."

After Michael cooked a delicious dinner of chicken

smothered in gravy and onions, collard greens, baked macaroni and cheese, sweet potatoes, and corn bread, Michael
and Kennedy retired to the master bedroom, where Michael
lit the fire. Kennedy admired the outline of his muscles
through his open silk pajama shirt. She ran her eyes down to
the matching silk bottoms. He looked such the gentleman.

"Michael, you look so nice," she whispered as he led her
outside the master bedroom's double doors which connected
to the veranda.

"Shh. Don't say a word, I just want to look at you and
admire you. Kennedy, a woman has never made me feel this
way. I crave you and for the longest time I've lusted for you.
But all that can wait. We have all weekend, baby, and I don't
want to rush it."

Kennedy stood behind him. On her toes, she rubbed her
hands over his shoulders then inside of his shirt. She
caressed his chest and licked his earlobe. "Oh, believe me,
you're not rushing it or me. I've wanted to make love to you
from day one. The only reason I didn't is because I have too
much respect for myself. Not to say that I wouldn't have, but
I had to make sure that you would respect me the same. And
four months is more than enough time, wouldn't you say?"

Michael turned and held her hands. He was silent for a
moment. "I agree that four months is enough time for us to
figure out what we really want. But still, I want us to take our
time and do it right. You must first understand that although
I want you, I don't want to ruin it. You are so much more than
just a piece to me and I want to savor every moment.
Kennedy, I consider you to be marriage material—"

Kennedy removed her hands from his. She leaned against
the rail and looked out at the water. She was disappointed.
Michael had always been respectful, now he was too respectful. Tonight she didn't need a gentleman. She wanted a gentle man. Gentle in bed. She sucked her teeth.

"Kennedy, did I say something wrong?"

Kennedy tilted her head. "No. Well, I take that back," she

said, turning to face him, "you did say something wrong. Why do you always put me off? Every time I make an advance, you find a way to get out of it. Something isn't right, Michael. I just find it strange that your reason for not making love to me is because you respect me too much. If that's the case, why don't you have a problem with doing me? Every time I look down between my legs, there's your face." Kennedy rolled her eyes and huffed.

Michael smiled. "Are you serious? Do I do it that much?"

Kennedy rolled her eyes and nodded. "I'm not finding humor in this conversation, Michael."

Michael hugged her. "I'm sorry. I try to control myself, I really do. But you are just so damn irresistible. Believe me, you can't understand how hard it is for me to keep my hands off you. Please don't think that I don't want you. I do . . . all the time. I just try to be respectful because I want to keep you. It's childish, but it was my way of making you want me more. I wanted to make love to your mind and heart first."

Kennedy held back a smile. It was hard for her to be mad at him. "You're right, it is childish. I have a daughter at home. If I want to play games, I can do it with her." Kennedy crossed her arms over her chest.

Michael cupped her chin in his hands. "I told you. I told you, you're wife material. Not only are you smart and sexy, you are so much more than even you know. I like that you don't play games . . . not with your life, not with this," he said, pointing to her heart. "You are after something in life and that's very important to me. You have goals. A bachelor's degree wasn't enough for you, you had to have your master's and you're in the process of getting that. You've been in relationships before with men who were well off and you didn't try to trap them with a baby as a lot of women these days do. And you have met me—a man of considerable wealth and social standing—yet you don't see *just* that and you don't succumb to it, but instead, you stand your ground and you don't bite your tongue. You couldn't care less about my money, but about the way that I treat you. And to top it all off, you aren't easy or too difficult. You're just right. I don't think that you realize your value."

Kennedy walked into the house and sat by the fire. How could she be mad at him after all of that? She couldn't. Michael sat beside her and traced his finger along her jaw. She felt a tingle.

"Michael, don't underestimate me, I *do* know my value. It's not that I don't know it, I just know what I want, and what I want is you. I want for you and me to be together mentally, emotionally, and physically—you know, sexually."

"I know, Kennedy, and that's the reason I got you a gift. Like I said, it's nothing big, but it means a lot to me because I've never given anyone something like this before, not even my mother, and believe me when I tell you that she wants for nothing, not anymore anyway."

"Just give it to me and stop teasing me. You know that I've been waiting all night and I can't take it anymore. It's bad enough that you keep making me wait for other things."

"Okay, since you insist, Ms. Kennedy. But first let's have a glass of wine. You make the toast."

"To the future and everything it brings . . . good or bad. Because I know that you and I together can do anything, overcome all things, achieve everything, and one day, love, as we never have. *Salut.*"

"*Salut.* And for that, your personalized toast, as I thought, you do deserve this gift, a small token of my appreciation. I was right about you, I knew that I was." Michael handed her a small box.

For a moment Kennedy held the small velvet box. It was too big to hold a ring and too small to hold a watch. She had received many gifts in her time and this was one she didn't recognize. Although she wanted it and was eager for it, she was somewhat hesitant to open it. Finally she did. Inside lay two keys and a piece of paper with five numbers on it. At first she thought she knew what it was, but then the numbers threw her off.

"What is this, Michael?"

"What does it look like, baby?"

"Keys and a piece of paper."

"Keys to this house and the alarm code," Michael explained.

"Oh my God." She laughed. "You threw me off. I thought I knew what the keys were for, but I assumed that they were for your Manhattan town house, but the numbers didn't ring a bell because my alarm code for my apartment only has four numbers. Nevertheless, I'm surprised. Are you sure about this?"

Michael knelt and rubbed her thigh. "Yes, I'm sure. No woman has made me feel this way and you seem to love this house just as much as I do. You even went so far as to make plans to make it more comfortable. And I don't see why you should make it comfortable just for my benefit. You may come here whenever you like, with or without me. *Me casa es su casa,* remember? And the only thing that makes it seem as beautiful as you say it is, is your eyes. Kennedy, I truly want you to be a part of me and everything I do."

Kennedy kissed him. She couldn't believe it, and yet she knew enough not to be a fool and play coy. Hell, getting house keys before giving up the you-know-what was unusual. Please, even after that. Usually men asked for too much, they wanted too much. She was going to put it on Michael. Maybe he was ready for it all. No man had ever given her keys, even if it wasn't to his main residence. But then again she didn't really know how much time he spent in the Hamptons. At least he showed her that he wanted her.

While Michael kissed her he made his way down to her breasts. She stopped him and sank to her knees, pulling down his silk pajama pants and boxers. He knew she was quick with her tongue. Now, she was ready to show him what else she could do with it.

She pushed him on the bed and grabbed her glass of wine.

Looking at him, she licked, then seductively chewed her bottom lip, carefully pouring wine on Michael's chest and his stomach. She eased on top of him and began licking it off. She licked down to his navel and paused. She stuck her tongue in the deepness and slurped out the wine. Michael reached down and caressed her breasts, and she moaned. She gently grabbed his penis and moved her hand in an up-down motion and kissed it. She could feel Michael arch his back as she put it in her mouth. She looked up, and their eyes locked. He put his hand on her bobbing head, as she took in as much of him as she could.

Michael trembled, flipped her over, and stood. He picked her up and rested her thighs on his shoulders. He buried his face between her legs and licked, sucked, and licked some more. Kennedy put her hands on his shoulders and thrust herself forward. She shivered and felt her body drop.

Her ankles were on Michael's shoulders while one of his hands supported her back. Oh God—standing up. She wiggled as his penis parted her. Rubbing it up and down, Michael teased her. She wanted it badly and felt herself throb and melt. He worked his way inside and stayed until Kennedy climaxed over and over.

"Hello, Miranda! Girl, what's up? You'll never believe where I'm at—"

"So I see you made it," Miranda said.

"What's wrong with you, girl? Spit it out and you'll feel better. And don't dare lie, I can hear it in your voice." Kennedy was surprised by Miranda's tone. Miranda usually didn't have too many things to be upset about, unless of course she was on her period. That was when she was guaranteed to be a miserable and cranky bitch. But all in all she was like a sister, at times more so than Simone.

"Look, Kennedy—" Miranda began to cry as she spoke. "I'm having the most terrible day of my life. No, let me rephrase that, I am having the most fucked-up day of my life and I really don't feel up to talking right now—"

"Uh-uh, honey, you're going to talk about it. And you're going to talk about it to me. You know I'm the closest thing to family you have. I'll be over there as soon as I can. It depends on how crowded the Long Island Expressway is and since it's Sunday it might take a little while." Miranda not wanting to talk, it must be serious. The teeth tapper of the year, Miranda's mouth was always moving, even when she was asleep. But no one would ever know because outside of their private circle she was as quiet as a fugitive on the run from the feds.

"Just stay where you are. I'm not trying to rain on your parade. I really appreciate you being here for me. But I got myself into this mess and I have to deal with it, that's all."

"No, no. Don't even think about it. Michael and I were about to leave anyway. I'll just get dropped off at your place instead of mine. Just be cool and remember that you don't have to go through this alone, whatever it is. I'm on my way." And with that said, Kennedy hung up.

"Michael! Come on, we have to go. It's an emergency. Miranda needs me now!" Kennedy almost tripped over bags from the spree from the day before when they had gone shopping for the house. Miranda was talking crazy. She had gotten herself into this and she had to get herself out. Who was she kidding? And to whom did she think she was talking?

Kennedy made it to Miranda's house in no time flat. The huge bay window was shattered and the door was ajar. Kennedy walked in.

"Miranda, girl, are you still here?" The house was a mess. The sofas were turned over, glass was broken all over the floor, pictures knocked off the wall, and what looked like a trail of blood led to God knew where.

"I'm back here in the den," Miranda said.

"Girl, I didn't even realize that you had a den, since you hardly invite me over," Kennedy joked, trying to lighten things, until she saw Miranda's face. Dried blood and mascara left vertical streaks, masking scratches. Her friend's face was swollen from crying. Kennedy grabbed and hugged her.

"What's wrong, what happened to you? What happened to your house? And where's Rich? Miranda, you have to tell me or else I can't help you, can I?"

Her best friend broke down in her arms and cried.

~ 6 ~

*D*errick awakened to the telephone's ring. No, it was the doorbell. Man, was he tired and pissed. He did not like to be disturbed on Sunday, his only lounging day. He took his time answering the door; whoever could wait for him to brush his teeth and wash his face. When he peeked through the front window, he saw Courtney walking away from the door. He ran as fast as he could to try to catch Courtney before it was too late. He missed his baby so much that he had cheated again with Jericha the night before. Guilt set in, but Derrick knew not to be fazed by it or it would show. He was a man and he had needs, and at the moment he needed Courtney.

"Courtney, come on in, baby. I missed you. Did you come to spend the day with me or did you come to make me suffer?" Derrick teased, but in a way he was dead serious.

"Yes, I did come to spend the day with you and maybe even make you suffer a little, but just enough to make you break down and tell me you love me."

Derrick grabbed Courtney's hand and walked toward the bedroom to get what he wished he would've gotten the night before—no sex, just romance and a lot of cuddling.

Holding Courtney, Derrick remembered that he promised himself the previous month that they should talk. Even though he had every intention of getting things straight, he always found himself dumbfounded in Courtney's presence. He just couldn't find the nerve to be so forward and maybe rude if it came down to it. But he couldn't put it off any longer. They were scheduled to leave for Rio at the end of July and he didn't want to go with his hopes high just to have Courtney knock them down once they got there.

"Courtney, I need to talk to you."

———

Ever since Nigel had suggested that they live together, Simone struggled with the idea. A month had passed since they had the conversation. Nigel seemed to be getting a little anxious for her answer, and she couldn't blame him. After all, she had told him that she would get back to him about it in a matter of days, not weeks.

She thought seriously about what he wanted and what he wanted to give her. Moving in together, shacking up, living in sin, having someone to sleep with every night, kiss every day, and be there when she needed him. Having a full-time man. She wanted it, but was it going to be worth the time and effort in the long run? Was he going to prove to be all that she secretly thought he was? Was he always going to be able to last for more than an hour? She smiled as if she had hit the Lotto for millions. If he wanted to live together, he was going to have to eventually marry her. She wasn't going to be any man's full-time whore, maid, and best friend—unless the man happened to be her husband.

As Simone recleaned her already spotless apartment, the telephone rang. "I really don't have the time to talk to anybody," she said out loud, speaking to no one.

Simone couldn't remember the last time she couldn't think straight like this, except when she was promoted to VP of the firm. But even then she could think much straighter than now. She could hardly remember her own name. Talk about someone's head being in the clouds. Nigel had her messed up bad, and boy, did she enjoy it.

What to do, what to do. How was she going to tell Kennedy that she would have to move out soon? Of course, she really didn't have intentions of throwing her sister out, but Kennedy would not stay with Nigel living there. Simone was proud of her little sister, because only the Lord knew how much Simone hated having someone in the house with her and her man. Not that she didn't trust Kennedy and not that she didn't trust Nigel, she just never liked to feel as if she had to tiptoe around her own house with her own man.

Happy and confused, Simone decided to call Derrick for his unwanted but much-needed advice. He of all people would understand, because of the three of them he was the most private. But what was she going to say? That she was going to put their little sister out for a piece . . . no, she wouldn't put it in those words. But she could easily tell him that she finally thought that she had found her Mr. Right and not just her Mr. Right Now. How could anyone build a relationship with a third wheel rolling around the house? Done with all the self-induced guilt, she decided to let Derrick play mediator.

"Derrick, is that you?" Simone asked, unsure of the voice.

"No, hold on a moment, I'll get him for you. May I ask who's calling?" a familiar voice answered.

"Sure, tell him it's the big girl calling for the little boy," Simone replied in her most seductive voice. She knew better but she couldn't help it. She laughed as she heard Derrick repeating what she had just said, obviously trying to figure out who the big girl was that was calling him a little boy.

"Hello?"

"Derrick," Simone said, laughing, "it's me. I'm sorry but I just couldn't help myself."

"Simone, girl, what's wrong with you?" He laughed and explained to whomever that it was his sister. "Are we in a good mood or what? I can't remember the last time you played on my phone."

"Yes, I'm in a good mood and yet I'm not in such a good mood. Anyway, I called you to talk to you about it and get your opinion and advice. Do you have time to talk?"

"What? Am I hearing what I think I'm hearing? You want my advice? Get the hell out of here. This must be good. I'll tell you what, I really can't talk because I have company, as you already know. But as soon as I finish over here, I'll be over, because I have to hear this in person to believe that you want my advice on something. Is an hour too long for you?"

"No, that'll be just fine. It's not an emergency or anything, it's just really important to me. I'll chill some wine for us, even though it's early—believe me, we'll need it. Love you." Simone hung up as she always did. She never really waited for a reply and everyone hated it, but that was her.

An hour later, Derrick rang the bell and entered as if he lived there. He had been walking into other people's homes ever since he was a little boy. Simone never minded. The place was completely spotless, even the plants were dusted. Something was definitely wrong.

"Simone, where're you?"

"I'm in here," she yelled as she saw Derrick come through the swinging doors.

"So what's up?" Derrick asked after he kissed her on her cheek.

Simone grabbed Derrick's hand and set him down at the island in the middle of the kitchen. "Listen to me completely before you speak. I have somewhat of a little dilemma on my hands here with Kennedy, only she doesn't know about it yet."

Simone opened the refrigerator, then closed it. She got a cookie and took a bite out of it and threw it in the trash. She straightened the canisters, and then rearranged them. Derrick sat back and crossed his arms.

"You okay, sis?"

"Yes. Just listen, okay? This is my story. I have a friend, well, actually he's more than a friend, and I love him. We love each other and he wants us to live together. I want to live with him as much as he wants to live with me, but I refuse to give up my place for a man. He has to move in with me. But Kennedy's here and I don't know how to tell her that as much as I love her and she's my sister, it's time for her to be on her own. Hell, she's old enough, she's half of fifty," Simone rambled breathlessly.

Derrick got up and poured some wine for both of them. "So basically what you're saying is that you want some privacy for you and your man, and you feel that Kennedy's going to be in the way and that you would like for her to leave but you don't know how to tell her?" Derrick asked and laughed.

"Derrick, what is so damn funny? I wanted to talk to you because I thought that you of all people would understand, you know with you being all private. That's why you moved all the way to New Jersey, isn't it? So that we wouldn't be in your business." Simone slammed her glass on the table.

Derrick handed her a paper towel, nodded to the spilled wine, and checked his watch. Simone threw the wet paper towel at him. He was supposed to help, not act like he was in a hurry.

"Wait a minute, Simone, I do understand. The reason that I'm laughing is because you had no problem telling me, so how come you can't tell Kennedy in the same way? Just say it. If you want privacy for you and whatever his name is, I see no problem with that. We're not kids anymore, we're adults. You can't be responsible for Kennedy forever. She knows that. She has a job, a man who whisks her off to get-aways or to wherever it is that she retreats to for days and weeks at a time. Just tell her, but give her time. Let her know at least a month in advance and she should be okay. So tell me, sis, what's your friend's name? Anybody I know?"

After Derrick left Simone's he sped through traffic faster than he normally would. He couldn't waste a minute more than he had to. Courtney was at his condo waiting for him. He had refused Courtney's offer to accompany him to his sisters' house but secretly he would've loved for his family to meet his new love. His sisters had told him that they were tired of meeting his women because as soon as they had gotten used to one he would have a new one. This time he had to be careful and sure. He had to be certain that Courtney was going to be around for a long time—maybe even forever.

Nobody had ever made him feel this good. This love thing was new and foreign, and he didn't know how to handle it. For once in his life Derrick was insecure and jealous. It scared him. How could someone control something that he knew nothing about? He had to figure Courtney out, and fast. Derrick had to know that his feelings weren't in vain and that they were mutual.

When he wanted to talk earlier, Courtney had been sound asleep. Derrick didn't want to disturb the moment or the mood, but he had to know and hear it from Courtney's lips that they shared the same feelings. As he entered the condo, he overheard Courtney on the phone saying I love you to someone on the other end. Derrick's pulse quickened. He felt a numbing didn't-hear-what-I-thought-I-just-heard feeling. He had a lump in his throat and his heart started to race. He really was in love.

As he was about to say something, Courtney rushed toward him with the phone in hand and kissed him on the lips. "My mother wants to say hello to you, Derrick," Courtney said, handing the phone to him.

"Hello, how are you? I've heard so much about you, and I'm looking forward to meeting you," Derrick said into the receiver, being overly pleasant. Derrick's cheeks inflated as he blew a relaxed breath.

Rose petals dotted the floor, candles burned all around, and the love of his life was wearing a red thong and nothing else. Derrick hurried off of the telephone, hoping that Courtney would do the same.

As Courtney finished up the conversation, Derrick hurried off to the bathroom to shower. He was hooked. He had never imagined himself contemplating a future mother-in-law. He had never entertained the thought of marriage before. Before Courtney he couldn't even fathom it.

A cool chill came from the doorway. The shower opened and Courtney stepped in, thong and all. Derrick was helpless and couldn't have cared less. A person wasn't supposed to affect another the way Courtney did him. "There has to be a law against this," Derrick muttered as Courtney slid against him from behind and kissed his neck.

"Derrick, I need you, and I will have you. Do yourself a favor and don't try to pull that macho stuff with me. I know you've been fighting your feelings for me. It's so apparent that it's ridiculous. Just give in. I won't hurt you. Make it easy on yourself. If you want me, you have to come and get me. I'm right here and if you want me, all you have to do is spin around. But there is a catch. Once you turn around, you can't turn back. If you face me, it means you must stay in my life. So don't do it unless you really want me to be a permanent part of your life. That means there will be no one else in your life, only me." As Derrick turned, the red thong dangled in his face.

As Miranda gained her composure, she sat back and wiped her tears. "I was just thinking of that saying of how God loves babies and fools. And right now I definitely fit into the fool category—"

"Tell me what happened, please. You know you have to talk about it," Kennedy said in her best it-will-be-okay voice.

"I don't even know where to start. Well, first of all I get this call from Rich's lawyer saying that Rich had been arrested . . ."

"Arrested? Arrested for what?"

"Wait! It gets better. After the call, some heifer bangs on my door, calling me out of my name. She claimed that *she* was Rich's woman. I opened the door and she swung. I beat the living hell out of her . . . tore the house up whooping her ass—"

"No!" Kennedy shook her head in disbelief. "And Rich? I can't believe this . . ."

Miranda blotted her nose with a tissue. She rolled her eyes. "Well . . . remember when I told you that he owned a recording studio, deli, and the hair salon where I get my hair done? Well he does, or rather he did until he got arrested. What I didn't know was that they were all fronts. Rich was involved in some white-collar scheme and extortion of some stores uptown. He made a lot of money, according to the authorities, millions. That's how we've been living like this. That's how come I've never had to work. And that's the reason I have that Mercedes parked outside."

Kennedy sat with her mouth wide open. She couldn't believe what she was hearing. Miranda was smart and gifted, and all this time she had been living with a criminal. That was so beneath her.

"Miranda, I'm not going to fuss because I know you don't need that right now. But can you please tell me why you got involved with a hustler? Was it for the money?"

Miranda shook her head and ran her fingers through her tangled hair. "No. I didn't know Rich was hustling. It all came as a surprise to me when I spoke with his lawyer today. But you know we always wanted wealthy men, right? Someone who'd take care of us and buy us nice things. Well, I got all that from Rich. He was a poor girl's dream come true. I guess I just didn't realize—didn't want to realize that eventually I'd have to pay for everything I got. I pray for your sake you won't have to pay in the end for what you have with Michael."

"I don't think I will—Michael's legit. He'll always take care of me."

"Hmm, I said the same thing about Rich. But look at me now. Just remember that illusions aren't meant to be revealed . . . things aren't always what they seem to be. I mean, look at me. I'm not even supposed to be here. The authorities are seizing the house and the lawyer says I have until tomorrow to remove my things. Where am I going to go?"

Kennedy bit her lip and stared at the floor. "You can come and stay with me and Simone if you like and put all the furniture in storage."

"Kennedy, that's really sweet of you, and you know that if I had anywhere else to go I wouldn't burden you two. Are you sure that it's going to be alright with Simone? I wouldn't want to put you two out or anything like that. I just don't know what else to do."

"Girl, don't be so silly. We're your family. You won't be putting us out. First let's get your things together and make arrangements to have them moved," Kennedy said as she put her arm around her friend and led her through the house.

———————

Simone picked up the telephone on the first ring. She had been waiting for Kennedy to call her back for more than an hour. She hated pagers. Why did people have them if they weren't going to return calls? She had been mentally practicing what she was going to say to Kennedy all day. And now finally she would get the chance to talk to her sister woman to woman.

"Kennedy, what took you so long to return my call?"

"Listen, Simone. Miranda's in a bit of trouble . . . not trouble exactly but she has just gone through one of the worst days of her life. I'm bringing her home to stay with us for a little while until we can figure out something. She has nowhere else to go."

"What happened, Ken? Is she all right?"

"She's fine now, I guess. Listen, we'll tell you about it when we get there. Hey, did anybody call?"

"Yeah, some guy called. I could overhear him on your machine but I don't know who it was, you know I don't answer your phone."

"All right. See you later then."

Simone didn't know what she was going to tell Kennedy but she had to come up with something. Although she loved her sister and Miranda, they couldn't stay. When she said what she had to say to Kennedy all hell was going to break loose. So she decided to prepare herself for round one.

~ 7 ~

*W*hat was Simone going to do? She couldn't turn Miranda away, she was like a sister to them and she had always been there for them. But something had to be done. Hell, she had a life too. They would just have to make do, as they always did. With the two of them together, it was no stopping them. She would just have to give them a month to move out and get on their feet. Neither one of them was broke. Kennedy had plenty of money and she never spent it.

Simone's temples began to throb, she was pissed off. She decided to run some errands. Shopping always made her feel better, and she hadn't been out to the outlets or the mall in New Jersey in a while. She grabbed her coat and headed out the door and ran right into Nigel.

"Hey, baby, where you going?" he asked, bending down to kiss her on her lips.

"Oh, Nigel, you scared me. I didn't know you were coming over. I was about to do some shopping. I've got a lot on my mind and I need to deter my thoughts for a while."

Nigel stuck out his lips, pretending to pout. "I hope it's not me. It is, isn't it? I hope you don't think I'm moving too fast."

"Nigel, please give it a rest because it's not you. You're not the problem, believe me. So, would you like to join me? I know how much men hate to shop with women but I'd like it if you came. You might enjoy it."

"Sure, baby, whatever you want. And since you hate fighting traffic so much, I'll drive *and* it's my treat."

"So what are we standing here doing all this talking for? It's Sunday, the mall closes at six-thirty," Simone teased.

When they arrived, Nigel gave Simone all of his cash and then he headed for the ATM to get more. He told her to go ahead and start shopping and he would catch up because he had a little shopping of his own to do.

When he walked away she counted what he had given her. Seven hundred dollars. What was she supposed to buy with that? It wasn't enough. Didn't he realize that she was shopping as a means of therapy? She put the money in her pocket and decided to use her life-saver—her credit cards.

Five stores and three hours later, Simone started looking for Nigel. Her previous experience with men had taught her that he was either sitting or eating somewhere. Men didn't usually enjoy a full day of shopping and only God knew why.

After scouting out all the benches and sitting areas, Simone tried all the restaurants. No Nigel. Where could he be? She walked past Victoria's Secret and decided to pick up something sexy to wear for Nigel that night. Fredrick's of Hollywood would've been better because they had the sluttier stuff men loved so much, but Victoria's had the quality. All Simone cared about was getting something slinky and going home.

Entering Victoria's, she noticed Nigel in the back of the store by the perfume and body spray. She was about to surprise him when she noticed that he was with a younger woman—a pretty younger woman with thick shoulder-length hair, flawlessly shaping her over-made face. She was dressed in almost nothing. Simone decided to take in as much as she could before she interrupted them. They talked, laughed, and talked some more. Innocent. *He could just know her.* But then she saw the woman in the mirror. Nigel stood beside her and whisked the hair out of her eyes.

Simone cleared her throat but got no response.

"*Uh-umm.* Nigel, aren't you going to introduce me to your *friend?*" Simone managed to hide her feelings behind a professional voice that she used on pain-in-the-butt clients.

Nigel turned around with bulging eyes. The young woman turned around and faced Simone with a Kool-Aid smile. She was the spitting image of Nigel.

"Hey, Simone. I didn't expect to see you here. My, today is full of surprises, having my two favorite women in the same place. Simone, this is my daughter, Kaisha."

"*Oh,* I was getting jealous there for a minute. Hello, Kaisha, it's nice to finally meet you. Nigel speaks highly of you," Simone replied, hoping she didn't look as foolish as she felt. She was ashamed for being too judgmental and jealous.

Kaisha glared at Nigel and turned to Simone and looked her up and down.

"Hi, Simone, or should I call you Ms. Jacobs? Daddy and I were just talking about you. It's nice to meet you too," Kaisha coldly replied.

"Call me Simone. That's usually how people refer to me, considering that *is* my name," Simone answered very matter-of-factly to let Kaisha know that she wasn't the least bit intimidated by her. Nigel had warned Simone of Kaisha's childish behavior toward any woman other than her mother.

After her little run-in with Nigel's daughter, Simone told

him to meet her by the exit. She was not one to stand around and make small talk, especially with a little heifer who was dressed like a stripper, even if she happened to be Nigel's daughter.

Simone shook her head in disgust. That could never be her child. For some reason she pitied Kaisha. Why did she walk around in public the way she did, as though she were allergic to being fully dressed? And if that wasn't bad enough, she was a little too overweight to be revealing anything. Simone would teach Nigel's daughter how to dress. If she wanted to be serious with Nigel she had to get to know his daughter. Possibly even like her.

After an eternity, Nigel finally came out of the mall carrying more bags than Simone had credit cards—and Simone had every credit card that any woman would want. Kaisha followed, smiling as if the world belonged to her. And if all the stuff in the bags was hers, it did. Simone cringed. By the smirk that Kaisha wore on her overpainted face, Nigel had bought everything. As they got closer to the car Simone noticed that some of the overstuffed bags were from baby stores. *What in the hell?*

Simone sat in the car, refusing to help Nigel with his load. For a brief moment she questioned disliking Nigel's daughter but that soon subsided. She could hear her grandmother saying, "Ya betta listen to that woman inside ya, 'cuz she's tryin' to tell something to ya soul, child." Simone laughed. Her grandmother was right. First impressions did matter. She also knew that eventually she'd find out why she disliked Kaisha.

After Nigel closed the trunk Simone frowned. Why was he putting that stuff in *her* trunk? True, he had driven, but in *her* car. All of that stuff wasn't his. She knew she shouldn't care because Kaisha was his daughter. *Fuck it. I feel how I feel and that's all to it,* Simone thought. She turned up the air conditioner and sat back as if she didn't have a care in the world.

"Simone, we're going to take Kaisha home, if you don't mind," Nigel said as he and Kaisha were getting in the car.

Turning to face Kaisha, Simone asked, "Where do you live, Kaisha?"

"In Flatbush—"

"*Brooklyn?*" Simone asked. The girl had traveled all the way to New Jersey and didn't have a ride home?

Nigel sighed loudly.

Kaisha tilted her pretty face and nodded. "Yep."

"Really, baby, it's not a problem, right? I told her that we'd be more than happy to take her home," Nigel said with an edge of irritation in his voice.

"You're driving, not me. So what are all the bags for? Seems like someone is going to have to serve some hard time wrapping gifts," Simone said, correcting her own attitude.

"*Gifts?*" interjected Kaisha. "What gifts? *Ohhh,* you saw the bags. Those aren't gifts. Daddy didn't tell you? I'm having a baby. I *hope* you didn't think I was this fat for nothing. I'm four or five months. I'll know for sure next week," Kaisha said and beamed like the sun.

"A baby? You mean to tell me that you don't know how far along you are? Four or five months . . . that's irresponsible." Simone snapped, unable to contain herself no matter how hard she tried. At that point she didn't care how petty she looked.

"Sorry, babe. I forgot to tell you that Kaisha's pregnant," Nigel apologized.

"Obviously," Simone said, doing a full 180 degree turn to face Kaisha and look her in her defiant eyes. "Why haven't you gone for prenatal? You did know that you were pregnant, right?" Simone asked, knowing how stupid it sounded. The girl had to know.

"Yeah," Kaisha said point-blank.

"It's not like it sounds, baby. Kaisha's just being silly. I taught her better than that. She's going to do the right thing by that baby, and she knows it. *Right,* Kaisha?" Nigel said in a disgusted tone, looking at Kaisha through the rearview mirror.

Kaisha just rolled her eyes.

Simone had Nigel drop her off first and pretended that she needed to go somewhere so that they could switch cars. She didn't want to be anywhere near Kaisha, and she didn't want the girl in her car. Outside was baking. The temperature had to be more than a hundred. New York was definitely having a heat wave. Simone stood watching as Nigel unloaded her trunk and loaded his. Kaisha stood fanning her face, complaining that she was thirsty. Simone smirked, told Kaisha to take care of the baby, and loudly added that she was going to get something to drink and walked away.

After she entered the house Nigel knocked on the door and walked right in.

"Sorry, baby. I don't know what's wrong with Kaisha. I guess the idea of me having a new woman in my life . . . or maybe because she's pregnant . . . I don't know. I told her to apologize. I'm really sorry. I wanted you two to hit it off. I want us all to be a family—"

"No need for you to apologize. No need for her to apologize either. I'm okay, trust me. *But,* I'll tell you what. She better not *ever* speak to me in that tone again. I know she's your daughter but she is *still* a woman just like I am and I won't have it—"

Nigel rubbed his head and pressed his fist against the bridge of his nose. Aggravation showed on his face. "Simone, no need to get hostile. I'll handle her. You gotta remember, baby, that Kaisha's a part of me. I love her *and* I love you. Not in the same way but still . . . you know what I mean."

"No. I don't. Her being your daughter doesn't excuse her attitude. If she wants to play the part of a woman, I'll treat her like one—"

Nigel's chest heaved as he raised his voice. "What does that supposed to mean? Is that a threat?"

Simone crossed her arms. "Look, Nigel. I don't know why you're in here getting huffy-puffy with me. I'm not the one who was rude."

Nigel banged his fist on the wall. He flared his nostrils, blew and closed his eyes, evidently trying to gain composure. "You're right, and again, I apologize. Anyway, she's thirsty. Do you mind if I get her something to drink? The temperature is a hundred and hell outside and I don't want her to dehydrate, you know . . . with the pregnancy and all."

"All I have is wine. *Sorry,*" Simone lied. She felt giddy because she got the last laugh that day, and worried because she had never seen Nigel so upset.

As Simone was putting her new things away she heard her front door slam, then Kennedy and Miranda's loud voices. Talking loudly when they thought no one was listening had been their trademark for years. Simone decided to stay put and listen. Kennedy and Miranda could be so close-mouthed. They, especially Kennedy, would tell only what they wanted you to know, which was not much, and usually half truths.

"These no-good motherfuckin' men get me so sick. I don't know how he could've done that to you. I never liked him from jump but I couldn't tell *you* that. Your head was so deep under the water, all you could hear was the fish talking. Rich was the fish. The barracuda."

"Ken, not right now, please. I'm tired, stressed, and all this drama has my stomach turning. I just need to lie down—"

"Okay, I'm sorry. It's just that I am *so* mad. So you go on upstairs and lie down. You can go in my room if you want, the door's unlocked. I'll be back tomorrow—call me if you need anything."

Simone closed the door to her room loudly behind her to let Miranda know that she was home. The last thing she wanted was to scare her by sneaking up on her. When Simone got downstairs and looked into Miranda's eyes, she was startled. They were red and swollen, staring into space. Immediately she went over and hugged her.

"Are you okay?" she asked, knowing full well that she wasn't.

"No, not yet. But I will be. I'll be fine, trust me."

"Can I get you anything?"

Miranda shook her head.

"Okay. Where's Kennedy?"

"She had a date with her friend. She'll be back tomorrow. I'm just glad someone is happy," Miranda said and started to cry.

"Ssh, Miranda, don't cry. Just go upstairs and lie down, it'll make you feel a little better. When you're tired everything seems worse," Simone said. She would have to wait to talk to Kennedy.

––––––––––––

The next afternoon Kennedy walked through the door and saw Simone sitting in the chair.

"Well, good afternoon. Don't we look all dolled up and nice," Kennedy said.

Simone stood and put her shoes on. "Thanks. Listen, Kennedy, are you busy today? I mean do you have plans for right now? Because I need to talk."

"Sure, sis, anything for you. Besides I need to talk too. I can't wait to tell you about last night, and if I don't tell someone quick I'm going to burst. How's Miranda?" Kennedy's smile faded.

"She's fine. She's upstairs sleeping now. She was up half the night crying. But let's talk about that in the car. I don't want her to overhear us talking down here and take it the wrong way. She's so fragile right now. What happened?" Simone grabbed her bag and keys.

"I'll tell you about it when we get to where we're going. Where are we going anyway?" Kennedy asked.

Simone pulled Kennedy's arm and led her to the front door. "Don't worry about it, just come on. You know we're going to eat. That's what we Jacobs women do, eat and talk."

After Simone and Kennedy sat down at a table, Kennedy was somewhat amazed that her sister had managed to secure a table for them. Justin's was a known spot owned by Sean Combs a.k.a. P. Diddy, so the reservation list was long.

"Simone, I didn't know you had it like that."

Simone smiled. "Not really. I'm just lucky enough to handle major clients with major power."

Kennedy knocked over the salt shaker. "You handle P. Diddy? Why didn't you tell me? Do you know how long I've waited to come here? Can you get me on the guest list for one of his private parties—"

"Slow down. I didn't say that I handled him. You know we have a confidential rule that we don't break—we don't tell unless they want us to—"

"Okay, I got ya. So do you think that you can get me on the guest list for Kennedy plus one?"

"Stop being a groupie and I'll see if I can pull some strings. *But* mind you, I *didn't* say that I'll pull strings with Mr. Combs. Because we don't publicize who we represent. *Okay?*" Simone winked and chewed on a breadstick.

"Cool. So what's up? What did you want to talk to me about?"

"You go first, mine can wait. So who was playing in your garden of love last night and got you smiling ear to ear?" Simone playfully asked.

"It's not a matter of who. Because you know it was my mystery man. Maybe one day I'll tell you who he is but one day isn't today."

"I'm listening," Simone said and rolled her eyes.

———

For the first time in a long while Kennedy confided in her sister but never revealed Michael's name. She told Simone how Michael had taken her for a helicopter ride over the city and then out to dinner where he fed her. Simone thought the feeding thing was a little over the top but Kennedy loved it and thought it seductive, which apparently it had been because it landed her in his bed. Kennedy told her how he bathed her and then massaged her with some aromatherapy oils and then placed steaming hot towels on her back to relax her muscles and release all of her tension. Kennedy squealed and squirmed in her chair as she shared how it felt when he brushed her hair and massaged her scalp.

Simone fanned her hand in Kennedy's face. "Damn, Kennedy. This man must really care for you, or he's just *extremely* good." Simone giggled like a schoolgirl sharing her first sexual story.

Kennedy squirmed in her seat. "No, wait a minute, girl. I haven't gotten to the good part yet. Let me finish. You ain't heard nothing yet. This man, this wonderful man, God bless *him,* gave it to me in a way that I ain't had in long, long time. I mean he sucked my toes, my knees, my elbows, and every-where else that requires extra Vaseline to prevent the ashy look that's *never* in. Then he went down South—"

"Down South?"

"Down South. Come on, Simone, you ain't that old yet. He went down South. You hear me? He went to the Y." Kennedy pointed between her legs.

Simone nodded and Kennedy continued, "Girl, I thought I was going to have to call an ambulance. The brotha wasn't coming up for air. I thought maybe he had drowned or some-thing." Kennedy laughed and slapped her leg. "And after that . . . pure heaven. Simone, he had me climbing walls like they were ladders. I couldn't believe it. After all of that I was drained and I woke up this morning with a semi-hangover. I had to take Alka Seltzer to settle my stomach."

Simone sat back and dabbed her forehead with the linen napkin. "Damn, Ken. That's all I can say is *damn.* So are you serious about this guy? I mean I know you've been seeing him for a little while now," Simone asked, using the question as an introduction for the real reason they needed to talk.

"Serious is an understatement. Simone, this man even gave me keys to his house *and* the alarm code."

"So are you going to move in with him?" Simone asked.

"No, I don't think so. Not yet anyway. I can't just up and move Kharri in with another man. That would confuse the hell out of her."

"Oh, because I just thought that it would be a good idea. It would be good for everyone."

"Did you not just hear what I said about Kharri? And who else would it be good for?" Kennedy asked.

Simone straightened the salt and pepper shakers. "Yes, I heard you. I just thought that with you and this guy being so serious that Kharri would know him by now."

Kennedy rested her elbows on the table and spoke slowly. "No. I don't think it's healthy for a parent to introduce a child to someone too soon. Children have to get adjusted, and Kharri hasn't adjusted to me and Jared not being together yet. I'll know when she's ready."

"Oh, I see. The reason I said that is because I need to discuss something with you, and I hope you'll understand," Simone said with a pleading look.

After Simone explained that she wanted Nigel to move in and Kennedy to move out, Kennedy sat in disbelief. Her sister was asking her to move out. And not only her but Kharri. Miranda could take care of herself. Kennedy hardly heard Simone when she said how much she loved Nigel and even had entertained the thought of one day marrying him. Kennedy didn't hear anything except that her sister was throwing her and Kharri out of *their* house.

"Simone, let me stop you there. Quite frankly I don't need to hear anymore," Kennedy said in a tone so cold that it could make ice shiver. "So you're saying that you want me and Kharri out? Well—"

"Not like that, Ken—"

Kennedy reached across the table and pointed her slim finger in Simone's face. "No, you had your say. Now let me have mine. Not twice, Simone," Kennedy shook her head. "Not twice. You pulled this before with your ex. He popped the question and then you put me and Derrick out. Then you begged me to leave *my* own place and move back in. Promised me that it would never happen again"

Simone reached across and grabbed Kennedy's hand. "Ken, I'm sorry. What else can I say—"

"Sorry? Please, Simone." Kennedy waved her hand. "That's what you said last time. If you want me and my daughter out, we'll leave. And it won't be in a month either, I'll tell you that." Kennedy flared her nostrils and bit her lip. "*But* if you want *us* out, I suggest you take your sneaky ass to the bank and come out with a shitload of money. If you want us out, you're going to have to buy me out. Simple as that! Remember, you didn't buy that house with just your money, baby. You bought it with *our* money. Mommy and Daddy left me money too. And another thing, if you want the house that bad, you're going to have to pay me more than half of what the house is worth. Got me?" Kennedy sneered across the table.

Simone looked around to see if anyone was listening. "Kennedy, wait. I didn't mean for this to get nasty. You're a woman too. Would you have wanted someone in the house with you and Jared when you two were together? And why on earth would I have to pay you? Hell, I took care of you all these years."

"First of all, *you* didn't take care of me. You may have contributed, but you contributed with my trust fund and the Social Security checks. Remember the checks after Mommy died? I wasn't that dumb. You didn't think I knew about the checks, huh? Well, I did. And the reason you have to pay me more than half is because you used my inheritance that wasn't supposed to be touched, which could've been sitting in the bank collecting a hell of a lot of interest. *You don't believe me?* Well, we can just take this to court. No problem. The SSI checks were what you were supposed to use to take care of me, not my trust fund. Anyway, I've said all that I need to say. You just have my check—make that my cashier's check—ready. And don't you ever, and I mean *ever* breathe in my direction or my daughter's direction again," Kennedy instructed.

"Not Kharri, Kennedy. That's not fair—"

"Fuck fair and fuck you! If you cared about your niece so much you wouldn't be kicking her out." Kennedy rose, grabbed her purse, and walked out.

~ *8* ~

*A*s Kennedy pulled up to the front of the house to pick up Miranda, her phone rang. At first she wasn't going to answer but then she decided to since she had paged Michael.

"Hello," Kennedy sang into the phone.

"Ken, it's Jared. Listen, Kharri just fell off her bike and we're at the hospital—"

"What do you mean, at the hospital? Is she all right?" Kennedy's heart beat faster by the second.

"Yeah, she'll be all right. We just don't know if her ankle is fractured or sprained. The X-rays haven't come back yet. She's not in pain, the doctors gave her something. But her ankle swelled up pretty fast—"

"Okay. Miranda and I will be on the next flight out."

"No, I'm capable of handling this and she'll be fine," Jared said.

"If *you* were capable, Kharri wouldn't be lying up in the damn hospital, now would she. I said I'll be there. And keep your girl out of my way," Kennedy snapped.

"She's not here—"

"Good." Kennedy hit the end button on her cell phone and paged Michael again.

Kennedy walked into the house without knocking. She was pissed. How could Jared be so careless?

"Miranda, it's me, so don't get scared. You need to start locking the door too. If I walked in anybody could." Kennedy sat down.

Miranda came downstairs. "When did you just start walking into houses? I thought the door was locked."

Kennedy rolled her eyes. "Last time I checked I lived here too."

"I was just joking, Kennedy, damn."

"I know, I'm sorry. I'm just upset. That *damn* Jared, I tell you. Anyway, I need you to take a trip with me. Kharri's had an accident so I need to be on the next thing smoking—"

"Oh no. Is she okay?"

"Yeah. According to Jared, she'll be fine."

Miranda hurried back to the stairs. "Okay, just let me get my stuff. Do we have time?"

Kennedy shook her head. "Just grab your purse and a jacket. Planes can get a little cool."

When Miranda went to get her things Kennedy called the airline to make reservations. She had to get to Kharri. She picked up an *Essence* magazine and absently flipped through it before finally throwing it on the table as she waited for her reservations to be confirmed. "Come on, Miranda, we gotta go," she mumbled.

Miranda ran in the living room. "Okay, I'm ready. But do we have a few?"

"Our flight isn't for four hours, why?"

Miranda smiled. "Well . . . I gotta go somewhere—"

Kennedy put her hands on her hips. "Miranda, don't you realize this is an emergency?"

"It's on the way to the airport." Miranda pulled Kennedy out of the house.

On the way to the airport Kennedy and Miranda stopped by the bank. Miranda insisted on paying for the trip despite Kennedy's protests. She told Kennedy that she went to visit Rich twice but the guards wouldn't allow her in. When Miranda asked why, the C.O.'s showed her the visitor's list, on which another woman's name was signed. Apparently Rich had a few women because Miranda had seen the woman's signature twice, and she wasn't the one who had come to Miranda's house. Miranda was pissed but went to see Rich a third time because she knew Rich had a stash of money somewhere. Convincing Rich that she'd hire a lawyer for him, he told her where the money was. Miranda had gone to get it and never spoke to him again.

After Kennedy and Miranda got to Virginia Beach and Kharri was released from the hospital with a sprained ankle, they checked into a hotel located on the beach. The hospital had kept Kharri overnight for observation because no one was sure if she had hit her head when she fell. Kennedy took Kharri to the hotel and Miranda instructed Jared to pack some of Kharri's things and bring them over.

When Jared arrived Kharri was sound asleep and Miranda was halfway asleep herself, or at least it looked like it. Jared walked through the door and looked around. He nodded as he opened curtains and cabinets.

"Jared, who or what are you looking for?" Kennedy asked.

"I'm not looking for anything, just checking the place out.

It's pretty nice. Where are your bags, in the car? I can go get them for you if you want me to," Jared said, flashing the same smile that made Kennedy fall for him.

"I didn't bring any luggage. I didn't have time. I'll just pick up what I need while I'm here."

"Big time, huh. It must be nice," Jared teased, showing his dimples.

"Yeah, right, Dr. J. How much money are *you* making now?"

"None really. I won't see anything until I'm done training."

"Training? Is that what they call it? Oh, I see, you're using laymen's terms with me. So how much do geneticists make nowadays, a billion or so?" Kennedy nudged Jared as she passed him and walked out to the balcony.

"Please, I'm sure *you* know, Ms. Research. So, how's school coming along and when will you be done?" Jared asked, following her out onto the balcony.

"I'd be done by now if I hadn't taken two years off to stay home with Kharri. You know that. But I'll be done after this semester. I already got a job offer, beaucoup money and perks too. That's what you get when you graduate among the top of the class." Kennedy beamed.

"Well, all right for Ms. Kennedy." Jared applauded. "How about we go celebrate?"

"What will Tasha have to—"

"Nothing. I can go and celebrate with my daughter's mother if I want to. Please, a step in the right direction for us is a step in the right direction for her, right?" Jared said as he placed his arm around Kennedy's back in a friendly manner.

"You're right, but I can't leave her now. She just got out of the hospital, Jared."

"Ken, trust me. The hospital monitored her all night. Kharri's fine. She'll be okay, she's with Miranda. If not as her father, take my word as a doctor. We'll only be downstairs . . . in walking distance."

Kennedy was reluctant but needed the air. She'd been through a lot lately and she still hadn't talked to Michael.

"Okay. But I will be checking on her."

After they checked on Kharri and Miranda told them to have a good time, they headed for the beach. They walked hand in hand, laughing and playing like two old friends. Jared took Kennedy to an outdoor restaurant where they could see the beach from their table.

Kennedy admired the whiteness of the sand and couldn't wait to feel it between her toes. Her nose tickled from the salty smell of the water. All beaches smelled the same. She smiled as the couples walked by. She and Jared had once left their footprints in the sand.

They ate, drank, talked about Kharri, and drank some more. Kennedy couldn't remember the last time she saw Jared drink. She decided not to mention it because she liked this side of Jared. When he talked, his dark brown eyes smiled. Did they smile for his fiancée too? Kennedy wondered about Michael and why he hadn't returned her page. She decided to page him in China and let him know where she was. It wasn't like him not to get back to her, and she was worried. She missed him already.

"Penny for your thoughts, Kennedy," Jared said.

"Oh, nothing. I just need to make a call and check on Kharri, that's all."

"We haven't been gone long, Kharri's fine. Can't the call wait? Is he that important?"

"Don't be silly. I was supposed to analyze a friend of mine's company and make some suggestions tomorrow. I just need to call and tell her that I won't be able to make it, that's all," Kennedy lied without thinking.

"Oh. Sorry, I was just prying. I know that it's not my place to but I still can't help but wonder about someone else in your life."

"I understand, believe me. So let's go back to the hotel so

I can leave her a message. Her number's in the room," Kennedy said, warming up to the lie.

At the hotel Jared told Kennedy that he would wait for her outside on the beach. Although she was going to call Michael, she still felt butterflies in her stomach knowing that Jared was waiting for her. She decided that she wouldn't have any more alcohol.

She eased herself into the hotel suite so she wouldn't wake Kharri or Miranda, who was holding Kharri like a protective mother. She eased the door shut and headed for the phone to page Michael. Out of habit she left her cell number instead of the hotel's and immediately regretted it. Her cell phone was in the room with Miranda and Kharri. After she eased back into the darkness she found her phone and tried to ease back out. Instead she stubbed her toe and yelled, "Damn."

"Mommy, is that you?" Kharri asked.

"Yes. I didn't mean to wake you with my yelling."

"Are you okay?"

"Yeah, baby, just fine. Are you okay?" Kennedy stepped to Kharri's side of the bed and held her and played with her hair.

"Yes. Where's Daddy?" Kharri asked.

"He's downstairs waiting for me. Do you want me to tell him anything?"

"Tell him hi and that I'm okay. And tell him to be extra nice to you, that way he can get you back like he wants to."

"Is that what he told you?" Kennedy asked, smiling.

"Yes, a long time ago. Just tell him to be extra nice because that's what I do and most of the time you give me what I want when I'm being a good girl. So tell Daddy to be a good boy," Kharri said.

"Oh, is that right? Well, I'll tell him for you. Now you be a good girl and get some rest," Kennedy said between laughs.

As Kennedy walked out of the bedroom her cell phone rang.

"Hey, I was wondering when you'd call. I'm in—"

"I can't talk right now. Let me call you back," Michael said.

"Michael, is someone at your door? I hear knocking. Who's at your door at three in the morning?" Kennedy asked.

"Kennedy, it's not three here, and this is really not a good time. I'll call you back," Michael said as he covered the mouthpiece of the phone.

A woman's muffled voice told Michael to hang up the phone.

Kennedy said, "I see why you can't talk. Well, tell her when she kisses you that she's tasting me!" Kennedy hung up, threw her phone on the sofa, and left to meet Jared.

Kennedy kicked the elevator door. She couldn't believe that Michael had fooled her. She thought that he was one of the good guys, but he wasn't. He thought he was slick by covering up the mouthpiece, as if she wouldn't be able to hear the woman in the background. She couldn't let Jared see her in this state. She couldn't let Jared know that her love life had turned to shit and his was roses. When she saw Jared waiting for her she quickened her step and smiled like everything was gravy . . . all good.

"Let's get a drink," Kennedy said, abandoning her no-more-drinking policy.

"That bad, huh?"

"No, I'm just enjoying myself with you. Is that a problem?" Kennedy asked as she playfully nudged him with her elbow.

"No problem. We're friends, right?" Jared winked.

"No problem at all. So where to now?" Kennedy asked and winked back.

"Well, I bought some wine earlier. Some very good wine," Jared said, looking at his watch, "and since it's officially your birthday, I guess we could take a walk down the beach and drink a couple of bottles like some winos," Jared teased. "Happy Birthday, Ken Ken." Jared kissed her on the cheek.

Kennedy beamed. Worrying about Kharri and Michael, she'd forgotten her birthday. *Michael didn't even wish me Happy Birthday,* she thought. "Thanks, Jared. So you have a couple of bottles? I don't know if I can handle that, but I'll try. I've had a long couple of days and I need it."

Jared took Kennedy's hand in his and they went in search of a place on the beach where they could be alone. Kennedy smiled as she felt the sand ooze between her toes. When she wasn't looking, Jared dropped his bag and tickled her. Kennedy laughed until her stomach hurt and fell in the sand. Jared picked her up and carried her until he found a spot. He pulled two crystal flutes and a bottle of wine from his backpack that he'd carefully wrapped in two towels. He confessed that he went to the liquor store before he had came to the hotel and had the wine in a cooler in his car trunk. He also admitted that he had hoped that they could get together and talk. Kennedy's stomach fluttered.

After a few glasses of wine Kennedy loosened up and stared at Jared. She couldn't believe that he was engaged to some other woman. She couldn't picture him with anybody else. He spoke of things she couldn't hear because she was lost in her own thoughts. While he was talking, she got up and walked to the shore. He followed.

"Kennedy, what's wrong?" Jared asked.

"You used to love me, remember?" Kennedy whispered.

"Of course. I still do and will always," Jared said as he grabbed Kennedy's face and held it gently, gazing into her eyes.

"It's not the same, Jared. You love me because I'm Kharri's mother. Now you love *her.*" Tears welled up in her eyes. She was definitely letting the alcohol get the best of her.

Jared dusted the sand from his hands and wiped her tears.

"Ken, don't start. I don't want to fight. I thought we were enjoying ourselves. Aren't you enjoying yourself?"

"I'm not trying to fight, Jared. I'm just being honest. Honest with you . . . honest with myself. Do you realize that you never asked me to marry you? Hell, I gave birth to your child. I just don't understand. No matter how hard I fight it, it hurts. I wasn't really mad when you told me. I was more hurt than mad . . . jealous, I guess. But I have no right—"

"You do have a right. We had a lot of good years between us. They will always mean something. And if it makes you feel any better, I didn't ask her, she proposed to me. When we were together I *did* want to marry you. I was just waiting for the right time." Jared stared in Kennedy's eyes, refusing to blink.

"Okay. Let's just let this go. Let's just enjoy the moment," Kennedy said as she felt a lump starting to form in her throat.

"No, Kennedy. Let's not. That was always our problem. We didn't talk enough and that's why it was hard for us to get along after a while. You used to flip out and not tell me what the real reason was, and I used to just tune you out. We used to be good together. I just don't know what happened or when. It was like all of a sudden we were two different people." Jared paused to open another bottle of wine and refilled their glasses.

"I was mad because you were never home. I don't know why but I just couldn't handle the doctor thing. I felt like a single mother. You were never home, and you were always with that woman," Kennedy finally admitted.

Jared spit out the wine he was drinking. Kennedy had caught him off guard. "What woman? *Amanda?* Are you serious? Kennedy, she was my lab partner and also a genius. She was there to help me on my shortcomings, and I did the same for her. If it weren't for her I wouldn't have graduated. And she's married. Just last month she married a member of our study group. They were together all during medical school and college, I might add. They were even living together at the time," Jared explained.

"Oh, I'm sorry. More sorry than you'll ever know." Kennedy closed her eyes and cried on his shoulder for throwing away a man she once considered her future.

Jared held Kennedy until her cries subsided and then he pulled her face up to his and kissed her. The feeling was warm and inviting. He seduced her like he used to, as though he were all hers and she, all his. Then he brushed his lips against her face where the tears had been and apologized for making her cry. She had never cried in front of him. She always held her head no matter how difficult the situation. As Jared was running his fingers through Kennedy's hair, she stopped him.

"Jared, I can't. You're involved with someone and someone just hurt my feelings."

"Don't worry, I just wanted to kiss you, that's all. I didn't mean to. I wanted to kiss you ever since we came out here," Jared said quietly. "And who hurt you, Kennedy? Tell me."

Kennedy told Jared the whole story, even Michael's name. She also told him about Simone and their argument. Kennedy and Jared talked for hours and finished all the wine. By the time they left they were both drunk and they knew it. Kennedy suggested that Jared stay over on the sofa because she didn't want him to drive. They headed back to the hotel and Jared pushed the wrong floor button on the elevator.

"Jared, you know you shouldn't drink. You pressed the wrong floor."

"Ssh, just trust me. Have I ever steered you wrong?"

The elevator doors opened to the top floor. Jared took her hand and guided her to the left penthouse suite and took out his key card and opened the door. Kennedy opened her mouth but Jared grabbed her, leaned her against the front door, and kissed her before she could utter a word.

Kennedy kissed Jared with a passion but felt the same

butterflies she had the day she had given him her virginity. It had been a long time since they had been that intimate. Her nervousness soon disappeared when she felt his bulge rub against her. She reached down for it as they entered the doorway. Kennedy closed it with her foot.

Jared lay Kennedy down on the floor and looked into her eyes, and she nodded.

"Are you sure?"

"Yes, I am," Kennedy said as she grabbed his head in both of her hands and kissed him.

When Kennedy woke up the next morning her head was pounding and she was very disoriented—definitely hung over. At first she hadn't the slightest clue as to where she was. She hadn't gotten drunk in years. She had made it a point not to ever drink that much outside of the house or while Kharri was home. She had heard stories of what happened to other women when alcohol controlled them and thought it disgusting.

Kennedy eased herself up, ready to get out of bed when she realized that she wasn't on the bed but still lying in the foyer. *Jared's* foyer. Kennedy shook her head in disbelief. Oh God. She was startled out of her quiet hungover daze by Jared's loud snores. He was sleeping with his mouth open, which meant that he was in one of his comatose-like states. She smiled because from their history she knew that she had knocked him out.

When she pulled herself together and got up from the floor, she was very sore and her back was burning. The foyer was marble but Kennedy remembered that somehow they had managed to start on the marble and ended up on the carpet. Eventually, when she couldn't take the sting of her back rubbing against the plush fibers, they had scooted back onto the marble. She laughed. She had a carpet burn like some silly young girl.

Kennedy tiptoed to the bathroom. Although she wanted

Jared to get up, she couldn't bring herself to wake him. He was so peaceful and his sleeping gave her a chance to admire him without his knowing. In the bathroom she looked in the mirror and was glad that she woke up before he did. All the alcohol, sweating, panting, and scooting had done her in. Her eyeliner resembled mud and gave her raccoon rings around her eyes and her wild hair was a shorter version of a troll doll's.

After staring in the mirror because she just didn't have the strength to move, she located one of the complimentary toothbrushes and brushed her teeth as though she were trying to get red wine out of white carpet. Eventually she made it into the shower. The steaming water felt like heaven. Her hair would be a mess, but thank goodness she didn't relax it as her beautician had suggested. She nodded in silent approval of her smart decision to keep her natural curly hair in its original state. She still felt a little disoriented and her stomach felt queasy. She needed to eat.

She was greeted by Jared as she dried off. She immediately grabbed her towel and covered herself.

"Good morning, Ken," Jared said and smiled. "What's with the towel thing? Don't tell me you're getting shy. I saw all of you last night. *Every* nook and cranny."

"Shut up. And how did you get dressed so fast? Don't tell me that you didn't wake up with dragon breath because I know I did," Kennedy teased right back.

"Hell yeah, I did. But I took care of that. This place has two bathrooms. Glad I bought it."

"Bought it? How?"

"I bought it. Some of these hotels around here sell suites, kind of like a time-share thing, but I don't share my time. This is where Kharri and I stay when we visit my parents. She even has her own little room on the other side."

"Oh, that's nice. I didn't know—"

"That's because after we broke up, you stopped visiting my parents. They miss you, you know." Jared massaged her scalp.

Before Kennedy could answer him, Jared grabbed her and kissed her, and the towel fell to the floor.

"You still got it, you know," Jared said as he looked her naked body up and down.

"Yeah, I know," Kennedy responded in her best sexy morning voice.

"So are you still in a yes mood?"

"Yes. A sober yes mood." Kennedy nodded.

"Let's do it right this time, okay. No more hard floors—"

"Well, I was thinking that since we're already here in the bathroom . . ."

~ *9* ~

*A*s Derrick sat at his desk he thought about how great the last couple of months had been. Courtney had been very attentive and wonderful. The trip to Rio had done them good, and Courtney had even taken some time off from work to make time for them.

Derrick picked up his phone and called the florist. He ordered two dozen irises—he was tired of the rose thing. Every man ordered roses, and Courtney deserved something different. Because Courtney *was* different.

As Derrick looked at the clock on the wall, he drummed his fingers on his desk. One more hour and he would be free. Free to go buy that ring he saw in the diamond district. He rubbed his palms, which sweated more by the minute.

All morning he practiced in the mirror and all he could

come up with was the same three words that he used to take for granted, I love you. He had no idea how to propose but knew that he'd do it that night. It was their five-month anniversary, and he hoped that Courtney wouldn't think that he was rushing. Under normal circumstances—namely someone else's relationship—he would think it was too soon. But he had finally found an irreplaceable love, one that he wanted to wake up to every morning.

The sound of the telephone ringing woke him up from his daydream, and immediately his gaze shot up to the clock. Five on the dot. Time to go. Whoever would have to wait until Monday because Derrick was on salary—a nine-to-five salary, and he didn't do nine to 5:01. He didn't get paid for that extra minute, so he didn't work it.

After purchasing the ring he headed straight home. The traffic was hell but Derrick was in heaven. He had the key to his new life in his pocket, the ring. He had the night all planned—for the most part anyway. All except the words. He knew that when he looked into Courtney's comforting eyes the words would come. All he had to do was tell the truth and expose his heart and his love.

As soon as he got his foot in the door the telephone was ringing. He looked at his caller ID and picked it up.

"Hey," he cooed into the receiver.

"Hey, yourself. Thanks for the flowers. You caught me by surprise—I really didn't expect them. Everyone was wondering why I was laughing. Rio, huh. That's your new name?" Courtney laughed.

"No, I'm still D. I just had the florist put Rio on the card to make you think about our wonderful time there. And besides, I know you don't want your office whispering about us. I know how nosy people can be."

"Oh, how thoughtful of you. You remembered."

"Thanks."

"So are we still on for tonight?"

"Yes. What did you have in mind, or is it another one of

your surprises? You know I like your surprises, right," Courtney flirted.

"Yes, it's a surprise. But remember that you have to drive, because my Jeep is in the shop. Something is wrong with the navigation system." Derrick laughed.

"Yeah, *something* is wrong with it all right. Did you tell them that *you* spilled coffee on it? No, never mind, I'll see you at eight. Gotta go. Love you." Courtney laughed and hung up.

———

Derrick sat on the sofa and quickly got up and walked to the bedroom, then the kitchen, and then the front door. Finally he found a comfortable spot on the sofa where he could easily look out the window. It was almost nine, and Courtney hadn't showed up or called. He checked the phone's dial tone. Why hadn't Courtney called? As of lately Courtney was always punctual and had showed up every time.

At midnight the sound of the "This is a test of the emergency broadcast system" on the television woke him up. Derrick knocked the phone off the nightstand. He couldn't believe that none of his calls or pages were returned. Courtney had really hurt him. This time was the worst, and he felt like a fool because he was going to offer the rest of his life to someone who obviously didn't care.

———

Kennedy sat on the sofa and wiped the sweat from her brow. Tired, exhausted, and relieved all at the same time, she reached for her bottle of water and thought that she had done a pretty good job. Other than the delivery guys, Kennedy had no help in getting the apartment together. Miranda had gone down South and wouldn't be back for days. Kennedy couldn't wait on her. She had decided to go ahead without Miranda. Even if Miranda was there, she probably wouldn't have been able to help because she lacked creative skills, so Kennedy was forced to decorate the apartment alone. She swore that she would never wallpaper, paint, or move a heavy piece of furniture again.

As Kennedy sat back and surveyed her work she was glad that she had decided on two sofas and two wing-backed chairs. She couldn't stand the standard group furniture. A sofa, loveseat, and chair weren't for everyone, and they definitely were not for Kennedy. Who really even used the chair anyway? It never really fit, or it always seemed like the odd one out.

Kennedy moaned and sighed loudly as she forced her tired and aching body from one of the matching overstuffed, oversized damask sofas facing the other. She nodded at her decorating skills as she walked around and fingered the two chairs, which also faced each other. Taste and flair were in the air.

Just as she finished pouring Epsom salts in her bathwater the phone rang. On instinct she was about to run and answer it but stopped. It could only be Michael or Jared. Michael had been trying to catch her for weeks, but she refused to answer or return his calls or pages. Actually she hadn't spoken with him since a month earlier in July, when he was in China and Kennedy heard that woman in the background.

Kennedy turned off the water so she could hear who was talking on her answering machine. Just as she heard Jared leaving a number for her to call him back, she rushed and answered the phone.

"Jared, I'm here. Don't hang up," Kennedy answered in one breath.

"Ken, don't tell me that you're still screening calls. I know you can't still be hiding from Big Mike," Jared teased.

"Oh please, Jared, stop it. You know I don't want to talk to him, and you better be glad that I picked up for you,"

Kennedy responded, pretending not to be bothered by his mention of Michael.

"Kennedy, explain something to me. Why on earth would you give him your new number if you didn't want to talk to him?"

Kennedy shook her head. "But that's just it, I didn't give him my number. I don't know how he got it, because it wasn't from Simone. She doesn't even have it."

"Oh well, I don't know what to tell you then. But be safe, Kennedy. He doesn't sound wrapped too tight to me. If you've been avoiding him like you say you have . . . just watch yourself and Kharri. Call me if you need me. I don't care what time it is, okay. Anyway, are you dressed?"

"No, why? Jared, look, don't start that. Don't think you can call over here and start trying to talk dirty. I know we have had a couple of terrific nights since I was out there—"

"Correction. We've had a *few* terrific nights. Hot, sweaty nights. And no, I'm not calling to talk dirty, even though I know you want me to. I'm calling to see if you're hungry."

"Hungry?"

"Yes, hungry. I'm about a mile away and I wanted to know if you wanted to go get something to eat, maybe catch a movie."

"Jared, have you lost your mind? What are you doing here, and where is Kharri?" Kennedy asked, smiling.

"Kharri's still at my parents. I just thought I'd sneak up and visit you for a day or two. Actually, I have a couple of offers here, and I just thought it'd be nice to see you. So, you up for some company?"

When Jared arrived, Kennedy was still in the bathtub. The bell chimed and she jumped up, grabbed a towel, and ran to the front door, dripping water all through the house. When she cracked open the door Jared was standing there with sweat streaming down his forehead.

"Kennedy, are you gonna let me in or what? It's hot as hell out here," Jared said and smiled.

"Okay, let me run and jump back in the tub first. Count to ten and then come in. All right?" Kennedy closed the door and took off running toward the tub.

Jared walked right in. He grabbed her towel from the toilet and sat down.

"What are you doing?" she asked.

"Visiting." He smiled

"I know that, Jared. But what are you doing in here?"

"Visiting. Now stop it. I've seen you naked before. Please, I saw you give birth before. So *I* even saw something that *you* didn't," Jared joked.

"Well, do you mind turning around or something? I need to get out. I was supposed to be soaking so I can relax. I just arranged and rearranged all the furniture in the house."

"Looks good too," Jared said, nodding.

"It should. I tore down wallpaper, put up new paper, painted, stripped floors, stained and waxed floors, put in a new chandelier in the dining room, *and* a carousel ceiling fan in Kharri's room. Please, I did it all by myself too, I might add," Kennedy informed, smiling.

"Sounds like you needed me. You do, don't you." Jared licked his lips slowly.

"Yes, as a matter of fact I do. Here, take this and wash my back." She handed him the towel and grabbed her stomach, laughing as if she were being tickled.

Kennedy and Jared talked for hours. They reminisced about their time together in Virginia Beach. Both agreed that it had complicated their new relationship. They enjoyed being just friends. One night had taken them back to a time when they were really great friends, right before they had gotten serious.

After a couple of cappuccinos they decided that they wanted the real thing and headed to the local Starbucks. Kennedy liked the feeling of walking with Jared. At times she would stop and pretend to adjust something so she could view him from behind. Once or twice she had to give some strange woman a dirty look, a what-are-you-looking-at look.

She had to remind herself that Jared was as handsome as he was. Over the years she had seen him so much that he just grew on her, like a relative or something. He really was fine; she was just used to it. The only time she used to really appreciate his looks was when he was mad at her and refused to speak, or when she thought that he might've been tipping out on her with his lab partner.

Sitting on a barstool in Starbucks, Kennedy sipped iced caffé mocha and rested her chin in her hand and just stared at Jared and smiled. He was on his cell phone, scheduling a meeting with a local hospital. After he caught Kennedy watching him, he blushed.

"What is that all about?" Jared questioned as he hung up.

"Oh, nothing. I was just sitting here thinking about how cute you are. Damn, J," Kennedy flirted.

"Cut it out." Jared blushed again, exposing his dimples. "I should be the one saying *damn*. You're the cute one here, not me. Besides, men aren't cute."

"Sorry. Handsome then. But I still say you're too cute. It's a woman thing, Jared. We call handsome men cute." Kennedy playfully kicked him under the table.

"Enough already. Could you please stop looking at me like that. You're going to make a brotha nervous."

They played footsie under the table for a couple of minutes and then the conversation took a turn. Kennedy took advantage of Jared's welcoming ear and trusting mouth. She knew that she could confide in him and he would never tell. They talked about Michael and Tasha, taking turns looking solemn as the other talked about the their new love. Jared admitted that it hurt him that Kennedy had moved on and was loving someone besides him and he understood her feelings toward Tasha.

Kennedy asked if he loved Tasha, and he acknowledged that he did.

Kennedy sucked her teeth, "Well, why did you sleep with me then?"

"Because I love you too. I love her, Ken, I do. But my love for you is different."

"Different how, Jared?"

"Well, before I answer, let me ask you something first. Do you believe that a person can love more than one person at a time?" Jared's eyes sparkled like an eager child's on Christmas morning.

Kennedy nodded.

"Now answer me this, do you believe that a person can be *in* love with more than one person?" Jared asked and mimicked Kennedy by resting his strong chin in his hand.

Kennedy shook her head.

"Okay, last question. Do you think it's possible for a person to love one person and be in love with another person at the same time?"

Kennedy chewed on her bottom lip. "I think it's possible. Because I think that it's possible to love more than one person at a time. There are many types of love and several different levels of love. But, and I said but, I think a person can only be in love with one person. In love is for life, love isn't necessarily for life and even if it lasts that long, it isn't on the same level and doesn't possess as much depth as being in love," Kennedy answered and sat back, folding her arms.

Jared nodded. "I couldn't have said it better myself. So you understand then."

"Understand what?" Kennedy asked, frowning.

"How I can love you both."

"I guess." Kennedy shrugged and took a sip of her drink.

"But I don't exactly love both of you—"

"Make up your mind, Jared—"

"I will if you give me a minute. I was trying to say that I love her, but ever since I was twenty-one years old, I've been in love with you. You don't know how hard it was for me to lose you. I didn't only lose my woman, Kennedy, I lost my best friend. I lost the one person who understood me, or at least I thought you did . . ." Jared stared into his coffee cup.

"Me, Jared," Kennedy said, pointing at herself. "I'm the one who lost. I left and I lost."

"No, Kennedy. We both lost. We lost each other and our family." Jared grabbed both of Kennedy's hands.

Kennedy sat in Starbucks with tears streaming down her face. She made no attempt to hide or dry them. She had waited forever for Jared to open up and tell her how he felt about her. She knew he cared, but she wanted to hear it from him—had to hear it from him to let go of the anger. She had forced herself to dislike him because she was hurt. But she couldn't force herself to stop loving him.

"Why didn't you say this before . . . before Michael and *her?* Why now, Jared? Is it because I'm not seeing him anymore? Because you could've said something a while ago. We broke up almost two years ago. I've only been seeing him for six months." Kennedy palmed her forehead and rubbed her temples.

"I just wanted to be able to tell you without us ending up in an argument. I don't like to fight with you, Ken, because we end up hurting each other. We were together long enough to know how to really hurt each other. It's like over the years we programmed the words into our minds that we knew would hurt the other. Can you understand me not wanting that?"

Kennedy nodded, once again at a loss for words.

"But as much as it hurts me to say this, I think that you should at least hear him out. From what you tell me he seems like an okay guy, not the psychopath that I envisioned. And you still speak of him in present tense—you said we've been seeing each other for six months, and that says something right there. You still love him, don't you?" Jared said as reached across the table and gently turned Kennedy's face toward him, and then grabbed her hands again.

"I don't know, Jared. He hurt me. But I guess I'd have to be honest and say that I do love him. I just don't know if I can trust him. Anyway, how can you tell me that you're in love with me in one breath and then turn around and tell me to hear him out in another? That doesn't make sense to me." Kennedy stared at Jared.

"I just want you to be happy. I *am* in love with you, but then . . . there's Tasha and our situation."

"What situation?"

Jared's eyes widened. He rubbed his face with his palms and looked out the window.

"I asked what situation?" Kennedy repeated.

"Tasha's pregnant." Jared hung his bald head.

"That's nice." Kennedy smiled and nodded. "I wish you two the best of luck."

"You're not mad?" Jared's eyebrows shot up.

"Uh-uh, baby." Kennedy shook her head and continued. "But I'll tell you what, you're not as smart as I thought you were. We broke up what . . . only two years ago? And you've been with her for how long, six months? Hell, you don't even know her. She caught you, Dr. Reid. Just remember, when it was me . . . at least you knew I wanted you for you. It wasn't any doctor business back then. Hell, at first you didn't even know what you wanted to do with your life. I took you in baggy jeans, decorated shirts, and Timberland boots, not suits." Kennedy politely pulled her hands from his, walked outside, and jumped in the first available cab.

Kennedy thought about what Jared said during her cab ride home, and although she would never admit it to him, maybe he was right about her hearing Michael out. And that was exactly what she planned to do when she walked through the door.

She was glad Miranda was gone. She would've had to go through one of Miranda's interrogations about why she looked so terrible. She looked that way because she felt horrible. Jared had definitely caught her off guard with the new "situation," as he called it.

Shrugging off thoughts of Jared, Kennedy reached for the phone. She dialed Michael's office number and then hung up when it started to ring. She knew that he'd be gone since it was after six. Probably still in his car stuck in traffic. Traffic was always horrible on Fridays. So Kennedy did something that she never did—she called his cell phone.

"Hello? Hello?" Michael answered.

"Michael, this is Kennedy."

"Kennedy! I'm so glad you finally returned my call. I never thought I'd hear from you again. Kennedy, you don't know how much I miss you. I wish you would hear me out."

"That's why I'm calling," Kennedy said dryly. "I'm listening."

"Not over the phone, please. I want you to see me when I explain. I want you to see that I'm telling the truth. Just look into my eyes and you'll know."

"I guess I can do that. When and where?"

"How about I come and pick you up. What's your address?" Michael asked.

"Nope. I don't think so. I'm not so sure that I want you to know where I live."

"Okay. Fair is fair. You don't know if you can trust me, right? I understand. So do you mind meeting me at the town house?"

"Okay. But you have to leave the front door wide open. I'll stand there and listen. Twenty minutes, that's all you get."

"Twenty minutes? Come on, Kennedy, don't do me like that," Michael pleaded.

"Michael, do you realize that a person is capable of saying more than a thousand words in a couple of minutes? Now I'm giving you twenty minutes. Can you calculate how many words you can say in that amount of time? Anyway, if you tell the truth, it shouldn't take any more than a minute. When people make up things or beat around the bush, that's what takes so long."

When Kennedy rung Michael's bell an hour later, she

wanted to change her mind about the whole situation. She didn't know if she wanted to hear Michael out or not, but Jared had been right about her giving Michael a chance to explain. Besides, Jared had hurt her and she didn't want to be alone while his life seemed so full.

Michael opened the door and smiled. Kennedy stepped into the opening so Michael wouldn't try to close it. The town house had changed since the last time she had been there, or at least what she could see from the foyer. The white walls had been repainted a smoky gray color, and were trimmed in off-white. The natural wood floors were replaced with a rich ivory-and-gray marble. Burgundy-framed paintings adorned the walls. Someone had decorated. A mix of flour, cooking oil, and seasonings drifted through the air. Fried chicken. Kennedy's stomach started to growl. She prayed that Michael couldn't hear it too. She hadn't eaten all day, having only coffee with Jared earlier.

Kennedy looked good and she knew it. She put on one of her best knock'em-out dresses to make Michael suffer even more. Michael just stood there and looked her up and down, licking his lips. Damn, she had missed him. Why did he have to go and mess things up? He was so handsome. He and Jared were total opposites, but both could make a nun's head spin like in *The Exorcist*.

"Michael, your time is running out," Kennedy said, pointing to the Cartier on her wrist.

"I see you still have the watch. Thank you for wearing it. It suits you. So . . . are you ready?" Michael said as he rubbed his hands together.

"No, are you ready? I'm not the one with the explaining to do. Fifteen more minutes," she reminded him.

Michael put his hands up in defense. "Okay. But it's going to hurt a little bit."

"Not as much as you hurt me, I guarantee. Just go ahead, I'm listening."

Michael looked Kennedy directly in her eyes. He told her how much he loved her and that he never wanted to hurt her. He explained that he tried to call her back but she didn't answer.

Michael paced and eventually went in another room and grabbed a chair. After Kennedy declined his offer to sit down, he sat and continued. He told her that he didn't make it to China for the seminar but instead wound up in Brazil and stayed there with his brother, who was ill. It turned out that Michael's brother, James, was gay and the family had disowned him, even in his time of need. Michael was the only one still proud of him who still claimed him as family.

The day that Michael was supposed to leave for China, he received a telephone call at his office from a hospital in Brazil, saying that James had passed out and Michael's business card was found in James's wallet. Michael was called because they had the same last name. James had passed out because he was weak from some sort of cancer that Michael didn't even know he had. So Michael decided to intervene with James and their mother and took her on a surprise vacation to Brazil. Michael's mother had been the woman in the background who was flipping out because James was knocking on her hotel room door.

"Michael, if that's true, I'm sorry to hear that. I don't know if it's just me, but it sounds a little melodramatic," Kennedy confessed.

"Kennedy—"

"Michael," a woman's voice called from somewhere in the house. Kennedy knew the voice, she just couldn't put a face to it. She thought about it and then knew where she had heard it before.

Just then an older attractive gray-haired woman walked into the foyer. "Kennedy, I presume," the woman said and hugged Kennedy as if they were old friends.

"Hello," a startled Kennedy managed to say.

"I'm Mrs. Montgomery, Michael's mother. You can just call me Ma like everybody else," she said and turned toward Michael and smiled.

"Nice to meet you, Mrs. . . . I mean, Ma," Kennedy said and swallowed.

"Kennedy, my, you are a beautiful young lady. Michael sure struck gold with you. I wish my other son would do the same but he's funny, if you know what I mean."

"Ma, don't start." Michael pulled her arm.

"Well he is, Michael, and you know it. Fruitier than a Christmas fruitcake, that Jimmy is. And don't you try to hush me. You don't want to get embarrassed in front of this nice young lady, now do you?" Ms. Montgomery glared and turned back to Kennedy and said, "Now you and Michael cut this mess out. Michael is something else I know, that's my son and I raised him but I didn't raise him to be a fool and that's why he's in love with you. Now you two go on and make up. Cause y'all just fighting over James. Michael had that fool brother of his knock on my hotel door. This just doesn't make sense to me. Now Kennedy, you go on over there and get your man. Oh yes, sweetheart, thank you for the compliment."

"Compliment?" Kennedy said with a smile. Michael's mother was a trip. Sweet, but a trip.

"Well, sure. You thought that I was some other woman, right? Well, that's a compliment. I knew that I sounded young but not that young." Mrs. Montgomery playfully hit Kennedy on the arm with the kitchen towel and chuckled.

Michael whispered, "See, Kennedy. I told you. Now will you forgive me?"

Kennedy stood with tears in her eyes. She had been rash in her assumptions and almost lost Michael because she thought he cheated. How could she have been so stupid? She rested her head on his chest as the tears ran down her cheeks. She never should've slept with Jared.

"Well . . . there's one more thing. We didn't celebrate your birthday—"

Kennedy closed her eyes and swallowed hard. Michael hadn't forgotten her birthday. She turned to hug Michael, but before she could, he dropped to his knee.

"Ms. Kennedy Jacobs, I love you with all that I am and I'd never known love until I met you. I almost lost you once, and I refuse to let that happen again. Will you make me the proudest man on earth by becoming my wife?" Michael held out a black velvet box that housed the most beautiful engagement ring Kennedy had ever seen.

~ 10 ~

Simone sat on the edge of the tub and looked at her watch's second hand as she tapped her right foot in unison with the clock ticking on the wall. Nigel was due home from work any moment, and she was pressed for time. She needed to hurry up and get herself together but she had a slight headache, which was slowing her down. Simone kept looking down at the tiled floor then up at the wooden medicine cabinet, like a spectator at a tennis match. Finally she got up and riffled through the medicine cabinet until she found a bottle of Tylenol.

Holding the bottle, she thought for a second, read the label, and took two pills with the water from the faucet. Again she stared down at the floor. Something couldn't be right. As she stood silently, lost in her own disbelief, the bathroom door swung open and Nigel walked in, smiling.

"Why aren't you dressed yet, baby?" he asked as he grabbed the back of her head and kissed her forehead.

"Hello Nigel, and how was your day? I'm not dressed because I'm not feeling particularly well. I have a terrible headache," Simone answered.

"Oh, I'm sorry, baby. Hi, and how was your day? You have to excuse me because the guys at work weren't . . . wait a minute, what are those on the floor?" Nigel asked as he pulled back and looked into Simone's face.

"Pregnancy tests," Simone answered as she backed up in front of the tests scattered on the floor to block Nigel's view.

A smile spread across Nigel's face, "How many tests did you take, Simone?"

"Ten, because I knew that the first one couldn't be right, and then it was the second one and so on and so forth."

"Well?" Nigel's eyes lit up.

"According to those," Simone said, pointing to the floor, "we're having a baby."

Nigel picked up Simone and spun her around, careful not to bump into anything in the fairly small bathroom. He stopped and held her in the air and stared into her eyes and kissed each one of them as a tear streamed from one of his eyes.

"You have just made me the happiest man alive. And I'm going to give you two the world, just wait and see," Nigel said as he smiled.

"You've already done that, Nigel," Simone said as she reached up and wrapped her arms around his neck and attempted to hug him, but he pushed her back.

"What were you doing with these?" Nigel asked, picking up the bottle of Tylenol.

"I told you that I had a headache."

Nigel growled, "Did you take these before or after you knew that you were carrying my baby?"

"After, why? The label says that it's—"

Nigel slapped Simone so hard that she saw white spots. She stood dazed for a moment and started to swing back at him, but Nigel was too strong and he grabbed her arms and pinned her up against the wall.

"What are you trying to do . . . kill the baby? If you ever take another aspirin or have a drink or do anything that might harm the baby, I'll kill you. You hear me, Ms. High-and-Mighty? I'll beat the living shit out of you."

"What the fuck is wrong with you? Are you crazy? It wasn't aspirin, it's okay to take Tylenol. Call any doctor and he'll tell you. You just pack up your shit and get the fuck out of my house. Get out!" Simone screamed at the top of her lungs as Nigel walked out of the front door.

———————

Derrick pulled up in front of Simone's house and saw Nigel closing the front door. Derrick blew his horn but Nigel didn't look, so Derrick blew again and rolled the passenger side window down.

"What's going on, Nigel? How ya been, man?" Derrick yelled from the open window as Nigel came over to the jeep.

"Hey, man, nothing much. How about you?" Nigel answered as they slapped hands and gave each other a brotherly handshake.

"Not much here, either. Same ol', same ol'. Just working. So how's living with my sister?" Derrick joked.

"Aw, man, I can't complain. She's just moody, but I'm used to it. You know you're gonna be an uncle, right?"

"No shit, man? Look at you. You've been here . . . what, a couple of months now? And already you've knocked my sister up. Boy, you better be glad I ain't a teenager no more." Derrick laughed as he playfully punched Nigel in the shoulder.

"Right, right. But you better get your sister, man. You

know how these women are now. We don't have to do nothing and just like that . . . hey, you know. Well take care, D, I gotta go back to the site and make sure these knuckleheads finish this drywalling. Take care, man, and talk to your sister. She's on a rampage, so I'm outta here," Nigel said as he shook Derrick's hand.

Derrick entered the house and sat on the sofa, waiting for Simone to finish talking on the phone. He noticed that her face was a little swollen.

"So, Derrick, what brings you over?" Simone asked as she hung up the phone.

"Just thought I'd drop by. What happened to your face?"

"Nothing. Oh, you mean this," Simone said as she rubbed her hand in the spot where Nigel had slapped her. "I used some kind of new skin cream and evidently I was allergic to it. You should have seen it a couple of days ago, the whole thing was swollen." Simone lied and was happy for her dark skin because if she had been lighter she knew her face would've been red.

"Oh, okay. I just ran into Nigel outside. You got something you want to tell me?" Derrick asked with a smile.

"Oh, that stupid ass. It was nothing, we just had a little argument, that's all," she lied again.

"I wasn't talking about you two's mess. I been sitting here wondering when you were going to tell me that I'm going to be an uncle." Derrick laughed as he patted Simone on her stomach.

Derrick and Simone talked for a couple of hours. He constantly teased Simone about her pregnancy, and Simone constantly teased him about being in love. They were both at a place in their lives about which they'd only dreamed. Simone admitted to Derrick that she missed Kennedy and that she had tried to page Kennedy but she wouldn't call her back. They hadn't spoke since they had the argument in the restaurant in July, more than two months ago and Derrick promised that he would talk to Kennedy for Simone.

After Derrick left Simone's house he paged Kennedy. He didn't really want to get in the middle of his sisters' fight but if someone didn't intervene, Kennedy would never speak to Simone again. Kennedy was just made that way.

When Derrick pulled up in front of the Disney store in Times Square, his phone rang.

"Hey, Derrick. What's up, bro?" Kennedy sang into the phone.

"Nothing much. Just getting ready to go into this Disney store to pick up something for our niece or nephew."

"What are you talking about? I know you're not talking about Simone." Kennedy asked.

"Jackpot," Derrick said.

"Oh well, good for her. I hope her and her little family have a nice life."

"Ken, come on now. You still mad at her?"

"If someone threw your kids out of their house, wouldn't you be?" Kennedy asked.

"I guess you got a point. But come on now, Ken, that's our sister."

"Your sister. Listen, D, I gotta go. I'm with my man right now. We're getting ready to work on our own baby. Love ya," Kennedy said and hung up.

Derrick woke up Monday morning and stared at his ceiling as his alarm clock buzzed. He reached over and grabbed the phone and called in. He didn't feel like going to work. He had called Courtney the night before to come over and once again was stood up.

Derrick got up and got himself together. He wasn't going anywhere but still he got dressed. As he walked out of the foggy bathroom his doorbell chimed. He wondered who it could be at that time of the morning. No one knew he was home.

When he opened the door, Courtney was standing there. Derrick stood debating whether to give in or not. He wanted to see Courtney but he was still mad. Ever since he'd been stood up on the night that he was going to propose, things hadn't been quite the same. One minute everything was okay, and the next Courtney was pulling disappearing acts again.

"So are you going to invite me in?" Courtney asked.

"Yeah, come in. You're going to have to excuse the house. I wasn't expecting company. How did you know I was home?" Derrick asked as he moved slightly out of the way for Courtney to pass.

Courtney walked by slowly and plopped down on the sofa. "Actually I didn't know. I just rode by to leave you a note and I saw your Jeep parked outside and I decided to give it a try."

"Oh, you can just give it to me since lately you seem to have a hard time expressing yourself. Lately, you seem to have a hard time making yourself available. I mean, just two days ago I called you and you said that you had to get back to me." Derrick paced and threw up his hands. "What was up with that? Are you seeing somebody else because if you are, just let me know, and hey—"

"Hey what? Hey, and it would be over like that?" Courtney asked softly. "Well, you know that I have a lot of issues that I'm dealing with right now. And I don't even know what you're giving me a look like that for. We couldn't even have an uninterrupted vacation. You were right there, so you know I'm telling the truth." Courtney walked to the door and paused.

"Listen, I don't mean—"

"Forget it."

"Listen, you're the one who's wrong here. When we left Rio, everything was fine. You couldn't get enough of me, but then about a month later you started messing up again. And what do you want me to do? Sit around here and wait for you? Don't you know that's not how you treat people?" Derrick said as he looked Courtney up and down in disgust.

"Okay, Derrick, you got a point. But it's just hard for me.

I've been struggling with work, that's true. But I have to admit, it's you too. I've never experienced anything like this before. No one has wanted me as much as you do. It scares me." Courtney's eyes glistened.

Courtney explained being hurt before and confessed to loving Derrick. Derrick empathized with Courtney's over-cautious behavior, and understood the playing hard-to-get game that he, too, had once played.

After Derrick and Courtney made up, they ordered Chinese food and lounged in bed, watching a couple of movies and listening to some "oldies but goodies." Derrick put on "Before I Let Go" by Frankie Beverly and Maze and the two of them started dancing. Courtney danced out of the bedroom to the kitchen to grab a bottle of wine and a couple of glasses.

"Derrick, is it hot in here or is it just me?" Courtney yelled and disrobed.

"Turn the AC up. It is a little warm in here," Derrick yelled back.

When Courtney got back in the bedroom the front doorbell rang. Derrick told Courtney to hold on a moment, that it was probably UPS delivering a package. Courtney stayed out of sight just in case.

Derrick opened the door without checking to see who it was, expecting a delivery person. Kennedy stood on his doorstep with flowers in her hands.

"What's up, Ken? What're you doing over here?" Derrick asked as he held the door semi-open.

"I just need to talk to you," Kennedy said as she pushed open the door and walked in.

"Ken, I'm kind of busy."

"It'll only take a moment," Kennedy sang as she looked around Derrick's place. "I'm just his sister," she announced, smiling.

"Stop it, girl. Now what's up?" Derrick said, still standing.

"It's about Simone."

"Five minutes, Ken. As you already know, I got company and I don't want to be rude."

Derrick had convinced Kennedy that she needed to talk to Simone herself. He couldn't help her. They both missed each other, so it would only be right that they hash out the problem themselves. Kennedy agreed and started to walk toward the back of the condo.

"Kennedy, where are you going?"

"Oh, I just need to use your bathroom before I leave. Is your friend Courtney back there?" Kennedy asked innocently.

"Yes, but she's asleep. Just go ahead and hurry up."

"Forget it, I can hold it. Damn, you're rude. You better not ever come to my house and expect to have a pleasant visit because you won't get it," Kennedy said as she leaned on the dining room chair. "You know what? I bought my man a shirt just like this one," Kennedy said as she held up the shirt that Courtney had given Derrick.

Derrick just nodded and hoped that Kennedy would hurry up and leave. Kennedy finally got the message and picked up her purse when a crash came from the bedroom.

"Oh, she's up now, I guess I can go back and meet her," Kennedy said as she made a beeline to Derrick's bedroom as he chased behind her.

———

When Derrick left Simone's, she had thought about all the lies she had told him. Why didn't she just tell him the truth? Maybe she knew what would happen. Derrick would lose his mind and either he or Nigel would he hospitalized.

Simone hated lying, and she also hated what had become of her and Nigel. She didn't understand Nigel lately. He was getting moodier by the day. She never thought he'd hit her. But he did, and she hadn't seen it coming.

After they had moved in together, Nigel changed. He

became Simone's heaven and hell—caring and attentive one day, and grumpy and isolated the next. Lately his moods had shifted from bad to worse. He expected Simone to look her best at all times and he wanted her to do everything around the house although Simone worked too, sometimes longer than he did. But he didn't see that as a problem because he never came straight home from work. Simone didn't know where he went and he wouldn't tell her. Tired of arguing, Simone found things to do to avoid being home when Nigel got there. Although Simone hated to admit it, she feared Nigel. She feared and loved him at the same time, and knew that he'd come back. She shook her head because she also knew that she'd let him back in as she had done before.

Simone wondered if she was becoming a statistic like so many other women she knew. A tear ran down her cheek. She knew she should be stronger, but Nigel was her weakness. She picked up the phone to call a locksmith to have her locks changed, but before she could dial, the doorbell rang. Simone cringed because she knew it was Nigel. Every time they had an argument he would ring the bell instead of using his key. The door burst open and in sauntered Kaisha. Simone rolled her eyes. Just when she thought the day couldn't get any worse.

"Where's Nigel?" Simone asked Kaisha, who struggled with a large duffel bag.

"I don't know. He's not here?" Kaisha asked very nicely as some guy walked in and set some boxes down.

"What do you mean, you don't know? And what's all this stuff and how did you get in? The door was locked." Simone asked, getting madder by the second.

"Daddy gave me a key. I'm moving in. Don't tell me you didn't know. *Please* tell me that you knew." Kaisha's bag dropped as her arms fell to her sides. She closed her eyes and blew out a long breath as she sank on the edge of the sofa.

Simone shook her head and leaned over and threw up.

~ *11* ~

*A*s much as Kennedy hated to admit it, she missed her sister. *Someone has to be the bigger woman,* she thought as she picked up the phone. She knew Simone would never call her first because everyone assumed that Kennedy held grudges. And she did, but not against family.

Simone picked up on the first ring.

"Hey, Simone. You got time to talk?"

"No, but I'll make it for you, little sis." Simone laughed.

After they apologized, Kennedy and Simone talked for hours. They laughed, cried, and made plans for Simone's baby.

Miranda walked into the bathroom as Kennedy sat on her knees with her face in the toilet, holding onto the sides of it for dear life. Miranda laughed. "Kennedy, I told you about drinking so much."

"But . . . I . . . wasn't," Kennedy said between heaves.

"Uh-oh," Miranda said as she wagged her index finger at Kennedy. "I betcha you caught the bug too."

"What bug?" Kennedy asked as she got up and went to the sink to rinse her mouth, brush her teeth, and wash her face.

"The same bug that Simone got caught by. The pregnancy bug."

"Forget you. No, I didn't, not me."

"Well, why not? You're having sex, right? So who's to say you're not?" Miranda crossed her arms. "Who's the daddy?" Miranda teased.

"Forget you. I'm not pregnant. I better not be, and if I am, Michael's the daddy, who else?" Kennedy answered seriously.

"Hmmm, let me see." Miranda put her index finger up to her lips and stared up in the air. "Jared?"

"Impossible. Why would you say that?"

"Well, you two did stay together when we went to Virginia Beach. Are you trying to tell me that y'all didn't screw? Wait, I don't even want to hear your answer because I already know the answer."

"We used a condom," Kennedy said. But she couldn't remember whether they did.

"Whatever. Anyway, I have to finish packing while I have the energy to do it. The movers will be here bright and early in the morning," Miranda said as she headed out of the bathroom.

"Miranda, wait. Where have you been?" Kennedy asked.

"Here. Where else would I be besides work?"

"Here? Right, apparently not. Go look in the dining room." Kennedy pointed to the door and followed Miranda out.

"Kennedy, where is all my stuff?" Miranda looked around the dining room. All her boxes were gone.

"Michael and I moved the boxes last night while you were in your room snoring up a storm. The rest of the things we moved at about three this morning, so now everything is taken care of, that is of course, all except the things in your room," Kennedy said.

Miranda stood with tears in her eyes. Miranda hadn't wanted to leave but said it would be best for everyone. Kennedy and Michael were getting more serious by the day, and Kharri seemed to like him after Miranda convinced Kennedy to finally introduce them. "Kennedy, thanks. I would say that you didn't have to, but I won't. God knows that I didn't feel up to it," Miranda said as she hugged her friend.

"Girl, don't start me crying up in here. I don't know why you don't just stay here. You should've seen Michael this morning. He was moving furniture and trying to console me at the same time. It's like with every other box I sat down and cried. So when you see him, thank him. He did most of the work," Kennedy said as she went over to the sofa and plopped down.

"Well, thank you for being there for me when I was going through that thing with Rich. I don't know what I would've done without you," Miranda said as she sat down on the sofa opposite Kennedy with tears in her eyes.

Kennedy threw one of the sofa pillows at Miranda. "Girl, don't start. Don't start crying over him. You have to get over it. End of story. So do you really have to move to Connecticut?"

"Yeah. The job was too good to pass up. Besides, it'll be good for me to start over somewhere new . . . to have my own apartment." Miranda scratched her head.

"You know that I don't want you to. But if you feel that you have to, then I guess you have to."

"I'll be less than two hours away. Anyway, I can't stay here. What if Rich gets out? Girl, you know that I took all his money. But really, and seriously, I'm going to miss your crass ass though." Miranda hugged Kennedy and cried.

Kennedy jumped up and clapped her hands three times. "Okay, enough. We gotta stop crying."

"Yeah, you're right," Miranda said, wiping her eyes, "But can I ask you a serious question?"

Kennedy nodded.

"What if you are pregnant?"

Kennedy shrugged. "I don't know . . . I'd keep it, I guess."

"Not to offend you, Kennedy, but don't you think it's a little too soon to be having Michael's baby? I mean, you haven't even been with him a year yet. How much do you really know about him, besides the obvious?"

"I know enough. I know that I love him. And if I were pregnant, which I'm *not,* he'd be a wonderful father—I know he would."

"Okay, let's say I'm right and you are pregnant. How would you know *who* the father is? I'm serious, Ken. How? I mean if you think about it, when you got pregnant with Kharri, you and Jared were using protection. So who's to say it can't happen twice?"

———————

Kennedy smiled as Kharri covered her eyes, awaiting her surprise. She could see the excitement on her daughter's face as she patiently waited to see what was in store. They'd played the game for two years and every time they played it, Kennedy loved it more. She loved the way Kharri would dance around and giggle, happy to receive Kennedy's gifts.

"Okay, Kharri. Try to guess what this one's for?"

Kharri held her small finger to her mouth in thought. "I got it, Mommy. It's because I have glasses, right?"

"No. I already gave you something for that."

"Okay. It's because I learned my ABC's backwards."

Kennedy grinned. "Nope. I took you to the movies for that."

Kharri stomped her foot, exhaled, and shrugged her shoulders. "Well, I don't know then. I haven't done anything else."

Kennedy removed Kharri's hands from her eyes. "You can look now."

Kharri looked at the cake that Kennedy held, bulged her eyes, and licked her lips. "Is it ice cream cake?"

Kennedy nodded.

Kharri jumped up and down and danced as Kennedy knew she would. Kennedy set the cake down on the table and served it.

"Mommy, so why did you get the cake? It's not my birthday and I haven't done anything."

Kennedy kissed Kharri on the forehead. "Sure, you did. You do it everyday . . . you smile, Kharri. That's worth a surprise, wouldn't you say?"

Kharri grinned from ear to ear, exposing all of her teeth. Kennedy laughed, pinched her cheeks and dabbed frosting on her nose. Kharri stopped laughing and wrinkled her eyebrows.

"Uh-oh," Kennedy said, getting up from the table.

Kharri screamed: "Cake fight!"

Kennedy walked Kharri outside to meet Jared. She hated to see him but refused to let Kharri go out of the apartment alone even if Jared was waiting in front. When Kharri was looking, Kennedy smiled and when she wasn't looking, Kennedy glared. As usual Jared was being overly polite, which irked Kennedy to the umpteenth degree.

When Kennedy was hugging Kharri good-bye the cordless phone in her hand rang. It was Michael, and Kennedy made sure she said his name very loud so Jared could hear it.

"Take care, baby. Call Mommy as soon as you get there, if your eyes bother you again, and every day. Have a good weekend. Now come over here and give me my kiss," Kennedy said after she told Michael to hold on. Kennedy just stood there and glared at a now pissed-off Jared as he got out of the car to strap Kharri in her seat.

"Hey, baby, sorry. I just had to see my little princess off," Kennedy said to Michael as she got back on the phone, waved bye to Kharri, winked at Jared, and headed toward her apartment.

She felt victorious. She still had the power to make Jared jealous, which had been her intention. She looked at her ring and smiled. He wasn't the only one with someone else. She had moved on too. What she and Jared shared in Virginia Beach had been nothing more than a fling, she reminded herself. She loved Michael—only Michael. So why did she tingle when she saw Jared?

Kennedy was glad to finally get to Michael's house. The ride had been terrible because she felt nauseated all the way there. She kept thinking about Miranda's tease. But she wasn't pregnant, so something else had to be wrong. She just didn't know what.

As soon as she found a place to lie down, she did. Michael wasn't home yet, so she decided to get some rest before he came in and wanted to go out. Kennedy always teased Michael about their outings because they never stayed in one place for too long, and they were always running into someone famous or important. She never really minded because she knew that she was his trophy. But hell, he was hers too. Their relationship was convenient for them both.

Kennedy woke up on the sofa and quickly sat up. Something didn't feel right. She looked up and she saw Michael sitting across the room, watching. It was then that she knew why she felt uncomfortable. She didn't know why he liked to watch her sleep, but he did. The whole idea of being watched scared her at first but she was getting used to it. Michael claimed that he was watching beauty rest and that was why he stared at her while she was sleeping.

Before Kennedy could mutter a hello, she felt her stomach turning and raced to the nearest bathroom. Michael must've been wearing new cologne because it was making her sick, and she could smell the woodsy aroma all the way across the room. She could taste it in the back of her mouth.

"You all right, babe?" Michael asked as he rubbed her back when she emerged from the bathroom.

"Yeah, it must've been something I ate earlier," Kennedy lied, not wanting to hurt his feelings about his cologne.

"Let me get you something for that. What do you need? I got some 7Up in the fridge. I hear that's supposed to be good for queasy stomachs."

"Yeah, that'll be good. I'm just going to head up to the shower. You coming?" Kennedy asked as she kissed him on the cheek, hoping that he would say yes so he could wash off the cologne.

After Kennedy showered and got dressed she sat down on the chaise in the bedroom and stared out of the window. She thought about how good Michael was to her and about what she would say when the topic of marriage came up. She had said yes to his proposal because his mother was standing there, but later she explained that she needed time to think about it. She loved him but didn't know if they knew each other well enough for marriage. They'd only been together eight months and Kennedy didn't believe in rushing, though she wore the ring from time to time.

"You ready to go, babe?" Michael asked as he came over and kissed her on the cheek.

"Not really. Do you mind if we stay in tonight? I'm feeling a little better now, but the way my stomach's been acting lately . . . I'd feel better if we stayed indoors. You wouldn't want me losing it all over the restaurant, would you?"

Michael stretched and took off his jacket. "No problem. As a matter of fact I really don't feel like it myself. I just thought you might want to. I'm going to go downstairs and light the grill."

Kennedy watched from the deck as Michael prepared the

food. Her stomach was turning again and she wasn't going to last long before she had to run into the house. Even though she wasn't feeling her best she still found the energy to yearn for Michael. She looked at him from head to toe and admired his every feature. She loved his legs and how she could run her gaze up and down every curve of his muscles. She loved the thickness of his arms. He wasn't too muscular like those body builders on television, nor was he too lean. His arms were the type that flexed every time he picked something up or bent them at the elbow.

Kennedy walked up behind him. She rubbed her body against him and kissed her way up to his ear and nibbled on it. Michael turned around and Kennedy reached up to kiss him. But she couldn't. She turned around and ran into the house, covering her mouth with her hand.

"Kennedy, are you all right?" Michael asked from outside the bathroom door.

"Yeah. Now I'm better," Kennedy said as she came out.

"How long has this been going on?"

"I don't know. It comes and goes."

Michael scratched his chin and paused. "Kennedy, have you been to the doctor yet?"

"No, for what? I'll be okay. I just have a stomach virus that's all. I'm just going to lay down for a couple of hours and I'll be okay," Kennedy said and headed for the bedroom.

Kennedy woke up and felt terrible. She'd known hangovers to feel better. She couldn't believe that her nap had turned into a whole night's sleep. Although she needed the rest, she felt bad because she came to spend time with Michael. She smiled. He had been so caring and attentive. The last thing she remembered was him coming in with a thermometer to check her temperature.

Kennedy drowsily walked down the stairs and was greeted by the smell of a familiar pungent aroma. It was a scent she hadn't smelled in a long time and to her surprise it didn't turn her stomach. As she walked into the kitchen Kennedy heard Mrs. Montgomery's voice.

"Hey, Ma, I didn't know you were coming over," Kennedy said as she kissed Mrs. Montgomery on the cheek.

"Hey, yourself. Do you feel any better? Michael called me and told me that you weren't feeling well, so I decided to come on over and take a look at you myself. I also came to cook y'all some decent food—"

"Ma, I can cook," Michael said as he entered the kitchen from the laundry room.

"That chef-school cooking don't count. That's not home cooking, boy. That's textbook cooking. Anyway, Kennedy, as I was saying before I was so rudely interrupted"—Mrs. Montgomery cut her eyes at Michael—"I think you need to go and see if the rabbit died."

"The rabbit died? Ooh, is that gumbo I smell?" Kennedy asked as she walked over to the stove and took the lid off a pot, looked into it, and gave Michael a sideways glance.

"Yes, child. Don't act like you don't know what I'm saying. And get outta my pot."

"Kennedy, that's her way of saying she thinks you're pregnant. It's some saying she picked up down South," Michael explained with a grin.

"Pregnant? Why does everyone keep saying that, because I'm sick? I wasn't sick with Kharri."

"Child, I had five kids and every last one of my pregnancies was different, so that doesn't mean nothing," Mrs. Montgomery said, poking out her lips and raising her eyebrows.

"But I'm not pregnant—"

"Oh yeah, so you won't mind going to take a test then, huh? Just to make your sweet ol', soon-to-be mother-in-law feel better. I called Dr. Milford's office this morning and they can getcha in today." Mrs. Montgomery smiled and gave Michael an I-told-you-so look.

———

As Kennedy and Michael sat outside Dr. Milford's office she silenced him with a look. She had to go in for her test results. All of a sudden she was scared. She hadn't been scared to take the test. That was easy, except for them drawing blood. She had been livid with Michael for suggesting that they take urine and blood. "Just to make sure," he said.

The overfriendly nurse called her name.

She got up to follow the nurse and Michael got up and tagged along.

She stopped and asked, "Where are you going?"

Michael just nodded for her to keep going and smiled.

"Okay, Ms. Jacobs, just climb up on the table for a second and lift your shirt halfway. I don't normally do this before a complete checkup but since you're with Michael, well, just consider yourself a part of the family now," Dr. Milford instructed as he patted the table and playfully threw an air jab at Michael.

"Family?" Kennedy asked as she did as instructed.

"I forgot to tell you that Dr. Milford is my uncle, my mother's brother," Michael explained as he rubbed his hand up and down Kennedy's back.

"All right, Ms. Jacobs, this is going to be kind of cold, the warmer wasn't on, sorry."

"Wait. Wait. What's going on here? I get the feeling that you're going to give me an ultrasound," Kennedy said.

Dr. Milford laughed. "I am. Don't you two want to see how the baby's doing?"

"Serious! Thanks, Unc. I gotta call Ma. Do you mind if I tell her, Kennedy?" Michael asked as he beamed like a kid on Christmas and hugged and kissed Kennedy over and over, with tears in his eyes.

"Don't thank me, boy. I didn't sleep with you. You need to be thanking this pretty young lady right here. Oh yes, please call your mother because if she calls here one more time . . . do you know she called here twice today to see if she could talk me out of the results? I'm surprised that when your father was alive she didn't get his medical license pulled from him," Dr. Milford joked.

Kennedy just lay with her mouth open.

Before Kennedy and Michael could make it into the house, Mrs. Montgomery ran up and hugged Kennedy. Happy tears ran from her eyes as though they were racing one another. Kennedy looked up to Michael for assistance to calm his mother down, but he had his own tears. Before Kennedy knew it, she was crying herself.

"It's an epidemic around here," Kennedy said.

Mrs. Montgomery smiled and brushed imaginary lint off Kennedy's shoulder. "Oh, it's going to be alright. I used to feel a little nervous at the beginning of all my pregnancies too."

"I'm not talking about the pregnancy, I'm talking about all this boo-hooing that's going on around here." Kennedy laughed as Michael and Mrs. Montgomery joined her.

Pregnant? Dr. Milford, or Uncle Millie as he liked to be called, said that she was thirteen weeks. At first Kennedy didn't know how to feel but then she thought about Kharri and remembered how much of a joy she was to raise and to be with in general. She closed her eyes and sent up a great big thank-you for her new blessing.

———

Simone stood at the stove and stirred the gravy as she watched Nigel from the corner of her eye. She couldn't believe he was fool enough to invite Kaisha to live with them, and that she was fool enough to let her stay. It was bad enough that she accepted Nigel's apology and let him walk back into her life as if he never walked out. She guessed being pregnant had made her either more sympathetic or stupid.

Nigel explained how Kaisha's baby's daddy had left her to go live with some other woman and how Kaisha couldn't afford the rent on her own. He said he couldn't pay it—they'd need it for their baby. He convinced Simone that Kaisha could learn a thing or two about being a lady, being around her. He even said that Kaisha was going to go back to school after the baby was born. Simone could understand all of that and even accept it, but what she couldn't understand or accept was Kaisha walking around her house with a chip the size of Denver on her shoulder.

As Simone and Nigel sat down to dinner, Kaisha stomped into the kitchen and opened the refrigerator and slammed it shut. Simone looked at Nigel, waiting for him to react. He didn't. Then Kaisha went to the glass cabinet and did the same thing.

"Kaisha, what is your problem?" Simone asked with a frown.

Kaisha turned her rounded body around and flared her nostrils. "Ask your man what my problem is. Because—"

"No, I'm asking you. What the hell is *your* problem? Don't walk around my house like you pay rent here and start slamming cabinets and shit. Quite frankly, I'm tired of your attitude, like someone did something to you."

"Simone. Kaisha. That's enough. Can't we all just act civil around here?" Nigel asked and continued eating.

"No, Daddy, you be civil. You're the one who told me to come here. But you didn't tell me that she's pregnant too!" Kaisha yelled.

"Yes, I'm pregnant too. And? So that's what's bothering you? That I'm pregnant? Well, check this out Kaisha—news flash . . . it happens. What, you don't expect Nigel to move on? I guess that you expected to be the only child forever, right? Well sorry, babe, too late," Simone said, patting her stomach.

"News flash for you, Simone. I come first and you betta believe that, and the only baby that Daddy's going to take care of is this one, his grandchild, bitch," Kaisha said as she patted her stomach.

Simone jumped up.

Nigel jumped up and stood between them.

"Nigel, you can take this raggedy bitch to a shelter for all I care. Take her wherever you want, just get her out of my house!" Simone yelled.

Nigel picked his teeth and shook his head. "Kaisha isn't going anywhere, Simone. She's my daughter . . . I can't allow you to put her out on the streets. We can all just sit down and talk this out—"

"Oh no? Is that what you think? Well, I'll tell you what, you can get your ass out right along with her, and if not then I guess I got to call my buddies at the NYPD," Simone said as she picked up the telephone.

Nigel grabbed it from Simone and slapped her with it. "Now you got a reason to call them," he said as he strode out with Kaisha on his heels.

~ *12* ~

As Kennedy sat at the stoplight waiting for it to turn green, she couldn't get Simone out of her mind. She had a feeling that something was wrong with her sister. At first she had dismissed it because of Simone's pregnancy, knowing that some women shut themselves in, not wanting to be seen after they started to show. But Kennedy knew that wasn't the case with Simone. Happy to be pregnant, Simone was beautiful. She was one of those pregnant women that others loved to hate. Simone didn't have morning sickness, her nose didn't spread, and she was all baby, meaning that the only weight she put on was that of the baby. Simone could've been on the cover of one of those pregnancy magazines.

Earlier Simone refused to go to breakfast with Kennedy

and Kharri. Strange. Simone told Kennedy on the phone that she was hungry enough to eat the whole house, but when Kennedy suggested that she meet them at IHOP for an early-morning breakfast, Simone made up every excuse in the book. But what really startled Kennedy was when Simone told her that she had to check with Nigel when he got up. Kennedy knew her sister well. Something wasn't right, even if Simone didn't want to admit it.

An angry New York cabdriver lay on his horn. She didn't know how long she had sat there but assumed it wasn't long because the cars in the next lane were just starting to pull off. After shaking her head she politely rolled her window down, stuck her head out, smiled, and flipped him the bird and pulled off at a snail's pace. She laughed at her own version of road rage as she drove just under five miles per hour, which would piss off the cabby because the streets were crowded and he couldn't go around her.

After searching fifteen minutes for a parking space she finally gave in and parked in an overpriced garage. She couldn't understand why garages charged so much, but then again she did. They could charge whatever they wanted to. That's why Kennedy usually took the subway to NYU after walking Kharri to school. But because she had moved far from Kharri's school she had to commute to both. Kennedy refused to take Kharri on the overcrowded subways, which usually didn't have an empty seat.

After Kennedy finally graced the class with her late presence she found her seat and nodded at her professor. Dr. Randell cleared his throat and stared. Kennedy shrugged. She was at the top of her class. Besides being the only straight-A student, she was the only one who participated and showed a general interest in his boring class.

After the stare-down, Dr. Randell finally continued. Just as he posed a question, Kennedy's cell phone rang.

Dr. Randell stopped the class, took off his glasses, and

threw them on the podium. "Ms. Jacobs, need I remind you that this is an institution, not your home. You are in my class and on everybody's time."

"Hello?" Kennedy answered her phone in the middle of Dr. Randell's speech as she began walking out to take the call. It had to be an emergency for someone to interrupt her during her classes. Everyone knew not to call before noon unless it was a matter of life or death, and if not someone was going to get cursed out big time. As Kennedy made it to the front of the class Dr. Randell cleared his throat, and she mouthed "I'm sorry" and walked out.

"Ms. Kennedy Reid?" an unfamiliar woman's voice asked on the other end of the line.

"Kennedy Jacobs." Kennedy corrected and then asked in a very shady tone—she hated when someone called her by Jared's last name—"What is it?"

"This is the nurse from Kharri's school. I'm afraid that Kharri isn't feeling too well and someone's got to pick her up. She doesn't have a temperature, but she says she has a headache. We usually tell the students to lie down until it passes but Kharri came in the office in tears holding the sides of her head and is crying uncontrollably."

"I'm on my way. Could you do me a favor and take her glasses off? They're new and the eye doctor said that it could take her a little while to get adjusted to them. She complained about it this morning but was fine after I gave her a children's Tylenol. Thanks," Kennedy said as she walked back into class to retrieve her things, again interrupting, but she didn't care.

As Kennedy was about to leave class without saying a word, she thought better of it and stopped at the front of the class. She didn't want to piss off any of her professors during her last semester before graduation.

"Dr. Randell, can I speak to you for a moment. It's very important," Kennedy said as she walked out of the room, knowing that he would follow her. Although she pissed him off earlier, she knew that he would understand because he had flirted with her in a very careful way once although staff was not allowed to date students. But when she didn't take the bait he was nothing but professional.

Dr. Randell crossed his arms. "Ms. Jacobs, you know the procedure. You are to speak to me after class or during office hours."

"Listen, Dr. Randell, the only reason that I interrupted was because I have to go. That was the nurse from my daughter's school, and my daughter isn't feeling well. In fact, she's crying uncontrollably. I just wanted to apologize for earlier and for my disturbance with the phone thing."

"I understand. But at the beginning of the semester I informed you, all of you, that there was a no cell-phone policy in my class and I mean it. Do you comprehend?"

"Yes. But I can't follow that policy. I have a child. And any respectable mother who cares about her child would do the same. What if I did follow your policy? Then my child would be at school sick, crying uncontrollably, apparently in a lot of pain. Do you comprehend what I'm saying, I'm not your conventional student, Dr. Randell. I'm not some twenty-two-year-old, I'm a grown woman with a child, an intelligent four-year-old daughter who happens to already be in kindergarten. So please do not scold or chastise me like I'm here because my mommy and daddy pay for me to be here. *I* pay for me to be here. And just like I respect you, please respect me. Like I said, I apologize and hopefully it won't happen again," Kennedy said and walked off, leaving Dr. Randell standing in the hall alone.

After Kennedy had strapped Kharri into her booster seat in the back of the car she smiled at her through the rearview mirror.

"Are you okay, baby? Do you feel a little better?" Kennedy asked Kharri for the third time since they walked out of the school.

"Yes, Mommy. My head doesn't hurt anymore. I'm just a little tired and I want to lay down," Kharri whispered.

"Are you sure? Well, I'm taking you back to the eye doctor anyway, and then we can go home and you can lay down. Okay? Mommy's just a little worried about you. Ever since you got those glasses your head still seems to hurt and by now it shouldn't. Does it hurt more with or without the glasses on?"

"I don't know, about the same . . . I guess."

"That's what I thought," Kennedy said as she picked up her phone to call Jared.

Kennedy was put on hold while Jared was paged. At times like this, Kennedy was glad that he had pursued medicine instead of some sport like everyone else seemed to do.

"Dr. Reid speaking," Jared answered after about two minutes.

"Jared, it's Kennedy. Could you do me a favor and have one of your colleagues refer Kharri to an eye specialist here in the New York area?"

"What's wrong, Ken? I thought she was doing better."

"I thought so too. But I just had to pick her up from school because her head was hurting again and she was crying uncontrollably—"

"No, I wasn't. I'm not a baby," Kharri said in a sleepy voice.

"Well, the nurse said that she was holding the sides of her head and crying uncontrollably," Kennedy said as she turned and nodded at Kharri. "This morning Kharri said that she had a headache again, so I gave her some children's Tylenol and she felt better by the time we sat down to eat. So I took her to school thinking that she was okay," Kennedy explained as she looked back at Kharri, who was leaned against the window asleep.

"So what did the eye doctor say? Go kind of slow because I'm taking this down. I don't know any eye doctors here but we have some specialists on duty and I'll just give them all the info. They'll refer her, don't worry."

"Well, they just said to bring her in. The last time they checked her she still had the same vision. She just isn't adjusting to the glasses, and I know why. It's the wrong prescription. It's got to be, otherwise she wouldn't still be having headaches and she wouldn't still be getting dizzy from them," Kennedy blurted in one breath.

"All right, Ken. I got it even though you did a Speedy Gonzales on me. Give me five and I'll call you right back," Jared said and hung up.

Thank God for Jared. He was always better at handling these type of situations than she was and he always made her feel better. Just after she drove through Central Park to the east side where the optometrist was located she decided to stop at a local deli and pick up some Oreos for Kharri to have after the appointment. The cookies wouldn't make her feel better but at least they could help get her mind off the pain, for the moment anyway. Just as Kennedy made a right on Eighty-sixth and Third she spotted a mini-market.

"Kharri, wake up, sweetie. We're at the store. I feel like having some Oreos, how about you?" Kennedy said, knowing that just the mention of Oreos would make her daughter smile.

Kharri didn't say a word. Kennedy turned around and smiled at Kharri's smooth pecan skin, which was flawless, almost angelic. Her thick eyebrows complemented her long eyelashes. She was a real beauty. Kennedy really hated to wake her. Earlier she had said that she was tired and Kennedy guessed that the day, although short, had been a long one for Kharri. Kennedy smiled again as she remembered almost having to pull Kharri out of bed, which was unusual because Kharri was always up and ready to go. She loved school. Just as Kennedy was about to try and wake her again her cell rang.

"Jared?" Kennedy asked.

"Yeah, it's me. I have the doctor's info and from what I hear, he's excellent. He's affiliated with NYU and Cornell. I called his office and spoke to him personally. He's booked solid but he said that he'd see her after hours, today. He said to go ahead and take her to the other appointment and get a copy of her records faxed to his office. I know that you're driving so I called and left his information on your answering machine."

"Thanks, Jared. I don't know what I'd do without you. I don't know what *we'd* do without you."

"Hey, no problem. She's my daughter, too, you know. Is she right there? Let me speak to her before we hang up," Jared said.

"Okay. I just tried to wake her up but she's sound asleep. We're in front of the store, so she has to get up anyway. Can't leave her in the car. I'm picking her up some Oreos for later to lift her spirits," Kennedy said as she turned and gently shook Kharri.

"Khar-ri!" Kennedy yelled at the top of her lungs.

"Kennedy, what happened? Why are you yelling at her like—"

"Jared, she won't wake up. I shook her and she fell over. Oh-my-God. Kharri, please wake up. Please!" Kennedy begged, sobbing and dropping the phone.

Kennedy lurched over the backseat to wake Kharri. With her upper half in the back and her legs and feet in the front she reached for Kharri's head and put her ear up to her mouth and nose to see if she could hear or feel her breathing. She shook her by her shoulders and held her, and then Kharri exhaled a loud breath similar to a moan. Then she started to twitch. Kennedy cried and tried to keep holding Kharri but couldn't.

Kennedy pulled herself back up front. She threw the driver's door open and bumped her head. She rushed around to the back passenger door next to the curb and wrenched open the door. She grabbed Kharri and started to pull her up to a sitting position. Kharri slipped from her grasp and fell over in a forward slump.

Kennedy knew.

She had just lost her daughter.

Kennedy jumped from the car and screamed. Passersby stopped and looked as Kennedy slumped down on her knees on the cold cement that was covered with litter and dirt. Kennedy grabbed the sides of her head and pulled her hair as tears and snot streaked her face. Looking skyward she screamed, "Why God, why?" She pulled herself up just enough to grab Kharri and pull her halfway out of the car. Kennedy held her daughter in her arms and squeezed her as she cried, as though trying to squeeze the life back into her.

She sat there for almost twenty minutes, unaware of the time. All Kennedy saw was Kharri, as she grew colder and stiffer in her arms.

Kennedy sat and rocked as she held Kharri and rubbed her fingers through her daughter's hair. "Wake up, baby, please wake up. Kharri, please, baby!" Kennedy pleaded. "God please. I will do *anything*. Please give my baby back. She's my baby. Just give her back. Take me . . . take me," Kennedy begged as a pair of hands tried to pull her up from the ground.

Someone had called 911. As the paramedics attempted to release Kharri from Kennedy's grasp, Kennedy held on even tighter. She wasn't letting her daughter go. The harder they tried, the harder Kennedy held on. Eventually the paramedics managed to release her right arm and Kennedy held Kharri even tighter with the left one.

"Ma'am, we have to check her out to help her," a voice with a blurry face said.

"No! You can't have her. Why *my* daughter? Please don't try to take my baby," Kennedy said as she pulled the rest of Kharri's limp body out of the car into a standing position and tightened her grasp with her left arm and punched the paramedic with her right.

Kennedy kept swinging and lost her balance. She fell hard on the cold, dirty ground and Kharri fell on top of her. Kennedy wrapped both of her arms around Kharri, who was facing her. Kennedy just lay there and cradled Kharri's head on her shoulder.

Closing her eyes, she just cried like a baby for her baby. Kharri would always be her baby. Her first baby. She heard someone tell the paramedics to just leave her for the moment and then she felt Kharri being pulled from her embrace and she couldn't overpower whoever it was.

When the police pulled Kharri off Kennedy, Kennedy curled up into a fetal position, feeling as if she were going to die. She wanted to die. She begged to die. She *was* dead—on the inside. Two people pulled her up from the ground. She buried her face in someone's shoulder and sobbed. She whispered, "Why did He have to take my baby. Could you please ask God for me? He wouldn't answer me. She didn't do anything, so it must've been me, what did I do? Can you please tell me."

When the officers were putting Kennedy in the ambulance she stopped and turned around and looked at the dirty sidewalk that she and Kharri had just lain on. New York had never looked dirtier to her. How could everybody who stood there just go on with their lives as if nothing happened? As if her daughter didn't just die.

Kennedy opened her eyes and saw a very swollen-eyed Jared looking down at her. She just stared at him, hoping that he would tell her that she just had a bad dream. She went to speak to him but something was covering her face. Jared reached down and removed the oxygen mask. He put his fingers to his lips as tears rolled down his face. She had not dreamed that Kharri had died.

Jared sat next to Kennedy and ran his big fingers through Kennedy's short hair. When he saw her tears start to form he doubled over on her chest and cried loud, uncontrollably. Kennedy went to reach for his head but a pain shot through her arm.

Jared looked at Kennedy and tried to pull himself together and wiped his eyes and then his nose with his sleeve. "You okay, Ken? I mean I know you're not okay, but are you okay? You passed out," he said.

"What happened to my arm, Jared?" Kennedy asked, refusing to believe that Kharri was dead.

"Well, some kind of way you broke your fingers and managed to pull a couple of your nails completely from the nail beds—"

"The car door . . . I was trying to open Kharri's door . . ."

"And you fractured your wrist when you hit the ambulance driver—"

"But Jared, he was trying to take Kharri from me," Kennedy whispered as tears started traveling from her eyes down to the pillow.

"It's okay, Ken . . . I know, I know." Jared nodded, not able to look at Kennedy.

"Where is Kharri?"

Jared looked away.

"Jared, did you hear me? Where is Kharri?" Kennedy asked loudly, on the verge of losing control again.

"In the mor—she's gone, Kennedy. They have our baby in the morgue, Ken," Jared said as his voice cracked. Tears streamed down his face and he didn't try to stop them.

"No, Jared! That's not true—"

Jared just nodded.

"Jared, I said it's not fucking true. Because if it was, it means that Kharri's dead. And Kharri *can't* be dead. She's only four and a half years old, Jared!" Kennedy yelled.

"Kennedy, please . . . please," Jared said, wiping his tears.

Kennedy turned her head and looked out of the hospital window at the overcast sky. The room seemed so cold. What could she do for Kharri so she wouldn't feel cold? Jared touched Kennedy's arm, rubbing her skin with his fingers. Kennedy turned around and they locked eyes.

"Jared, now what am I supposed to do? What am I going to do. She was . . . *is* my baby, Jared. I carried her and felt her move inside of me. She used to kick me—she was so strong, so beautiful. She was perfect. Jared, please help me. What am I going to do? Now, what can I do? I love her, Jared. Do you think I loved her enough? Do you think she knew how much I loved her? Because I did . . . I do. I carried her for nine months, held her when she was born and held her when she died. Oh God, why?" Kennedy sobbed.

"I know, Kennedy. Yes, she knew. We all knew," Jared reassured her.

Kennedy sat dazed for a minute and then said, "What about my other baby, the one I'm carrying now, is it going to be okay?"

Jared just stared at her.

~ *13* ~

*K*harri was buried on a cold but serene November day. The sky was a pale robin's egg blue and not a breath of a breeze blew. New York seemed to be at peace and still for a beautiful little girl who left the earth too soon. The funeral had been a harmonious celebration of Kharri and her short life. Jared had insisted that no one wear black. Black was too depressing, but mainly because Kharri had been afraid of the dark.

Kennedy sat in the front of the large church in a chair placed right in front of Kharri's soft pearl-pink casket. She refused to sit in any of the pews and look at her daughter from a distance. Instead, she sat right there with Kharri, holding her hand and kissing her. But she didn't break down like everyone expected her to. For the moment she was all cried out and in a state of shock.

Kharri's little body was dressed in pink silk pajamas and surrounded by white rose petals. In fact, Kharri had received so many flowers that the huge church had to use the balcony to help house them all. After the services, Kennedy asked everyone to take flowers home to remember Kharri by.

When leaving, she saw Michael standing in the back pew. His coming meant a lot to her. She stopped, and their eyes locked. Tears streamed down her face. He had been good to Kharri, and she knew he was going to be a good father to their baby too. She wanted to reach out and hold his hand—she wanted his comfort. But her whole family was there, and Kharri's funeral wasn't a place for controversy. She wiped her eyes, handed him a white rose, and exited the church.

After they left the cold cemetery, the family and visitors went to Simone's house to eat and socialize. Everyone was supposed to be there to comfort the grieving family and assist them if they needed it, but of course that wasn't the case. The evening had started with everybody eating and drinking and talking about how sad it was for Kharri to go as soon as she did. But by the time the food was almost gone and the alcohol started, it seemed more like a reception than a post-funeral get-together.

Jared and Kennedy arrived at Simone's hours after everyone else. Kennedy just couldn't leave Kharri's gravesite. When the cemetery workers lowered Kharri's casket into the ground and someone threw the first shovel of dirt on it, Kennedy lost her mind and jumped in the grave and started throwing the dirt back out.

When Kennedy walked into Simone's house she stood still for a moment and surveyed the surroundings. How could these people seem happy and at peace?

"Jared, how could they do this?" Kennedy turned to Jared, who was holding her hand.

"Do what?"

"How could they just forget that fast? Do they realize or even care that we just buried Kharri? Our baby just got lowered into that cold-ass ground and these greedy motherfuckers here act like they're at a Fourth of July cookout!" Kennedy said as her voice grew louder and louder.

"It's all right, Ken. They're just here for us—"

"No one is here for us!" Kennedy yelled at the top of her lungs as everyone in the room turned toward her. "Y'all aren't here for us, right? Everyone just brought their greedy asses over here to eat for free and drink for free, isn't that right? You know, all of you, family and friends alike, got a lot of nerve coming over here to take advantage of us in our time of grief. You knew it would be food here. You knew someone would have liquor and beer here. And I bet if I asked for a show of hands as to who brought something besides the immediate family, I wouldn't see none. And somebody turn that damn music off! This isn't a party. My baby is dead, do you hear me? Dead!" Kennedy said as she broke down in tears and Jared grabbed her and held her as the house started to clear out.

Simone and their grandmother, Big Ma, cleaned the house after everyone left. Big Ma flew in early for the funeral and had held everyone and everything together since Kharri's death. They had just finished the dishes when Jared came into the kitchen.

"Is Kennedy all right?" Big Ma asked.

"Yeah, I guess as well as can be expected," Jared said as he sank down into the kitchen chair.

"Jared, how are you holding up? Can I get you anything?" Simone asked as she came up behind him and patted his shoulder.

"No, I'm okay, thanks. I'm just really messed up behind all of this. I should've known," Jared said as he rested his head in his hands.

"Jared, baby. You should've known what?" Big Ma asked.

· "I just should've knew. I mean, I'm a doctor and I should've insisted that the hospital perform an MRI. But I wasn't thinking. When nothing showed up on the head X-rays, I didn't think anything of it. I just figured, hey at least we know Kharri didn't hurt her head when she fell off the bike—"

"But how could you have known, Jared?" Simone asked. "The doctors said that it was a subdural hematoma, and that it could take weeks or months to even show any symptoms."

"That's right, baby. Don't go blaming yourself. It's not your fault." Big Ma bent down and kissed Jared on top of his head.

"Yeah, but when she started having headaches, and eye problems . . . Kennedy said she was sleeping a lot. I should've guessed that something was wrong," Jared said as tears started streaming down his cheeks.

"No, not necessarily," Big Ma said. "I remember when Kennedy's daddy was going through something similar. He was having headaches, he was tired a lot, and his eyes hurt, too, and you know what cured him? Glasses. You and Kennedy did the right thing. How were you supposed to know that Kharri was bleeding?" Big Ma held him.

Jared stared up through tear-filled eyes at Simone. "Simone, when were you guys going to tell me that Kennedy's pregnant?"

"Pregnant? Boy, what you talkin' 'bout? You must be jesting." Big Ma laughed.

"Kennedy's pregnant? How far along?" Simone asked in disbelief.

"Who's the daddy, you?" Big Ma sat down at the table.

Jared shrugged.

"Get out of here. So you're the one she's been sneaking around with for all these months?" Simone sat down at the table next to Jared.

"No, she's seeing this other guy. What's his name . . . I

can't recall right now. But it's an easy one," Jared stared up at the ceiling.

"Well, never mind him. Seems to me, you think you the daddy, huh?" Big Ma crossed her hands and waited for an answer.

"I don't know, Big Ma. Me and Kennedy . . . well you know. I'm not a hundred percent sure, but I'd bet money that there's a possibility."

"Well, you . . . him. What's that they say, Simone? Oh, I got it. Momma's baby, daddy's maybe." Big Ma got up and chuckled, shaking her head.

Kennedy rested her head in Michael's lap as he massaged her scalp. She knew he was worried about her but was too afraid to say anything. For the past month she had been more than fragile and didn't want to be reminded of her pain. Michael had reminded her anyway. After Kharri's death, she went into overdrive and didn't even take a break from school, but instead had received a 4.0 grade point average. Michael told her that a psychiatrist friend told him that was Kennedy's way of coping and eventually she would slow down. She had to. But how could they expect her to get over the death of her child?

"So, how do you feel?" Michael asked as he bent down and kissed Kennedy's forehead.

"Much better now. I'm so glad the semester's over. Can you believe that I finally did it? I am officially done." Kennedy forced herself to smile and wiggle a little dance on the sofa.

"I knew you could do it. I told you that you could. Now don't you feel better, like a weight has been lifted off your shoulders? Now you can rest and take care of both of you," Michael said as he patted Kennedy's protruding stomach.

"Yeah, I guess I can do that. I have to . . . God's giving me a second chance," Kennedy said as she offered a smile that Michael hadn't seen since Kharri died.

Kennedy watched as Michael placed the star on top of the tree and couldn't believe that Christmas Eve had come already. Time had flown by so fast and Kennedy began to feel better when she felt the baby move. She knew that she would grieve and hurt for Kharri for the rest of her life but she also knew that she had to find strength to hold on, for the sake of the baby. She thought of Kharri, and ached. Nothing had ever hurt so much. She knew everyone worried about her, so she pretended to heal. She never would.

Michael had been there for her every step of the way and she was at a point in her life where she had begun to grow. She was no longer mad at Jared, but instead, wished him well and meant it. She would always care about him. He had been so supportive, and she couldn't have asked for a better father for her daughter. Jared had grieved as much as she did, but he put his hurt aside to help her cope with hers.

Kennedy sat on the bare floor next to the huge tree as she put the myriad Christmas gifts under it. She looked down at the gift she held and a single tear ran down her face. She had forgotten all about the gift that Kharri insisted that they buy for Jared. Kennedy stared at the blue-and-silver box that Kharri had so carefully wrapped, using almost a whole role of tape, and kissed it. Kharri had been adamant on wrapping Jared's present herself. Kennedy smiled. What a little lady Kharri had been. She had done some good for the world, even if only for four and a half years.

Stealing a candy cane from the tree, Kennedy got up and saw Michael waving his finger at her. She laughed.

"How about a little music? Turn the radio on to 107.5 because they always play Christmas music at this time," Kennedy said as she tore open the candy cane wrapper.

"I got one better," Michael said as he went over to the stereo and popped in a CD.

"Donnie Hathaway, huh? I knew you'd learn a thing or

two from me," Kennedy joked and started to sing at the top of her lungs.

Michael cleared his throat.

"What? Boy, you know I can sing, cut it out. You like my singing, admit it," Kennedy said as she put herself in a boxer's stance in front of Michael.

Kennedy and Michael started to play-fight and Michael pulled her close and they began to dance. Michael felt so good. He was big and strong, and Kennedy felt safe and protected in his arms. She could've stayed there forever but the doorbell interrupted them.

"Who is it?" Kennedy yelled on her way to the door but no one answered.

She peeked out of the peephole and saw Jared standing there. At first she didn't know what to do, but then, why should she be nervous? She didn't have anything going on with Jared. And he was having a baby and getting married himself. Kennedy turned around and looked back at Michael and opened the door.

"Merry Christmas, Ken," Jared greeted as he kissed Kennedy on the cheek and walked into the apartment.

"Merry Christmas, yourself. I was just thinking about you," Kennedy said nervously.

Jared looked past Kennedy and saw Michael. Jared nodded. Michael nodded. Kennedy looked from Michael to Jared and back to Jared again. Jared's eyebrows were drawn together as he stared coldly. What did he expect? He knew that she was pregnant and in a serious relationship.

"Kennedy, I was on my way over to your sister's house and decided to come over here to drop this off," Jared said as he handed Kennedy a bag and went into the kitchen.

"Thanks, Jared, but I didn't get you anything," Kennedy said and shrugged at Michael.

"No problem," Jared said, returning with a glass of soda. "It's not from me. It's from Kharri . . ." Jared sat down on the sofa facing the one on which Michael sat.

"Oh yeah, you got one from her too. That's why I was thinking about you. I just finished putting the presents under the tree." Kennedy smiled as she began to pull the gift from the bag.

"I don't think you want to open that right now. Why don't you wait until you're alone—"

"Why is that?" Michael asked.

"Because it's something private from *our* daughter. You're Michael, right?"

"Yeah. Kennedy told you about me, right? I'm the father of the baby she's carrying," Michael answered and patted Kennedy's stomach.

"Oh, is that right? You think so?"

"Jared, what is that supposed to mean? Where do you get off, coming over here with a chip on your shoulder? Respect my house," Kennedy snapped.

Jared sat up, twisted his face, and cut his eyes at Kennedy. "All right. I may be wrong, but if that's your man, your baby's daddy, where was he when Kharri died? I didn't see him there comforting you. I comforted you—I comforted her, man, not you," Jared stood. Michael stood and put up his hands.

"Let me talk to you for a minute." Kennedy grabbed Jared's hand and pulled him into the kitchen. Any minute Jared and Michael would be fighting like two schoolboys. Kennedy stood against the counter with her right hand over her face before finally glaring at Jared.

"Jared, what is your problem? We were sitting here enjoying ourselves and you had to come in starting shit. And what in the hell did you mean by that remark about the baby?"

"Just what I said. Tell me, Kennedy, how far along are you?"

"Five months, *why*?"

"So that means you got pregnant in July, huh? So how do you know that I'm not the father?" Jared asked.

"Ssh! What the hell are you talking about?" she whispered harshly. "Are you crazy or something?"

"Well, we did have sex in July, remember? Don't tell me that you—"

"So what? We used a condom." Kennedy rolled her eyes and crossed her arms.

Jared shook his head.

"What do you mean, *no*?" Kennedy shuffled from one foot to the other and pounded her fist on the counter.

"Do you remember when you nodded and I asked you if you were sure? Well I meant if you were sure about . . . you know . . . without a condom. I didn't have one and you must've known, I mean you were right there just like I was. It wasn't planned—"

"So what are you saying, Jared? That you think this is your baby? Please."

"Why not? I mean we had sex in July, what? Five times. All the while we were in Virginia Beach I didn't use a condom," Jared pointed out.

Kennedy just shook her head. But Jared was right. How could she have been so careless, so stupid? What if Jared *was* the father?

"I can't believe that I let you . . . and I knew that you were with that chick. I can't believe I let you inside me unprotected, and ugh . . . you were doing the same to what's-her-name."

"Wrong. I never went in her raw and that's how I knew that wasn't my baby. I never had unprotected sex with anybody but you. Honest." Jared held Kennedy's chin and stared in her eyes as he spoke.

"What? What is this, some kind of game?" Kennedy asked. *The baby wasn't his?*

"I said the baby wasn't mine. I doubted it from the beginning but you know how much I love children. Well, she knew that too. But I never had unprotected sex with her, and I know you don't want to hear this, but the condom never broke and it was always in place afterward. She had the baby and it wasn't mine. The DNA test proved it. And that's what you're going to have to do, Kennedy. I'm not playing. I think you're carrying my baby and I want you to take a DNA test. If not, well, just say the courts love men like me, men who want to take care of their children," Jared said and kissed her on her cheek and walked out.

———

Jared sat on Simone's sofa and told her and Derrick the whole story about him, Kennedy, and Michael. Simone and Derrick kept asking who Kennedy's man was. They had been trying to find out since after the funeral. Simone guessed the man was married, and Derrick thought Kennedy was just embarrassed.

Jared stood and waved his arms in the air. "Are you two even listening to me? Did you hear a word I said? I can't believe that you are more concerned with who he is than what I'm saying."

"Sorry, man." Derrick nudged Simone and put his finger in front of his mouth. "We just want to know who this mystery man is. If it were your sister . . . man, you know what I mean."

"So what are you going to do?" Simone asked, giving Jared her undivided attention.

"I'll take her to court if I have to," Jared said.

"Good for you. That's what we men need to do, we need to take them before they take us," Derrick joked and slapped Jared five.

"Please, Derrick, you know you need to hush. Just because Jericha has you in court every time you get a raise—forget it. Jared, look, I don't know, but if you are certain that this baby could be yours, I guess you're going to do what you have to do. But you know Kennedy is going to have a fit," Simone said and crossed her legs.

Derrick's cell phone rang and he walked out of the living room.

Jared paced and loosened his collar. "Simone, I don't know what to do. I just lost my little girl and I can't bear the thought of having a child out there and not being able to raise it. Do you understand what I'm saying? And Kennedy needs to let him go."

"You still love my sister, don't you, Jared? I know you do. I see the hurt in your face, and this is about more than just the baby."

"That's not the point—"

"Well, what is?"

"Simone, look. Kennedy and I had a beautiful time together, and she said that she was through with this Michael person and she went right back to him."

They talked for a long time. Simone offered to run interference with Kennedy for him. Her sister was stubborn, but she wasn't stupid. Kennedy would never lie about the paternity of her child. What decent woman would?

Derrick came out of the kitchen and started searching the living room for something. He removed the pillows from chairs and dug his hands down in the grooves. He flipped through the magazines and then shook them.

"Derrick! What are you looking for?" Simone stood and placed her hands on her hips. "I wish you'd sit down. You're making us nervous."

"Yeah man, you need help or something?" Jared asked.

"No, I'm just looking for my keys," Derrick said and put his hands in his pocket and smiled.

"I guess that means you're going to see Courtney?" Simone said.

Derrick froze. "Why would you say that?"

"Who?" Jared asked.

"Courtney, Derrick's new flame that has him spinning on his head. Isn't that right, Derrick? That's how come he has that big Kool-Aid smile on his face." Simone laughed.

"Yeah, that's right. But I'm going to see her later on

though. Her brother is picking me up so we can meet up with Courtney later," Derrick said as he grabbed his coat and scarf.

"All right then, D, take care and have a merry Christmas if I don't see you tomorrow," Jared said as he and Simone walked Derrick to the front door.

"You too, J, and don't worry about Kennedy. She'll do the right thing. And between me and you . . . I hope it is yours. See you tomorrow, sis, I promise," Derrick said as he opened the door and kissed Simone on the cheek.

Jared looked outside and then to Derrick. "Is that your friend's car right there?"

"Yeah, you know him?" Derrick asked, raising his eyebrows and rearing his head back.

"Looks like my boss Michael's car to me," Simone said.

"Michael? Wait—I might be wrong but it looks exactly like the car that was parked over at Kennedy's apartment," Jared added.

"Nah, couldn't be. Maybe it was a car like his but it wasn't him. I know it wasn't him," Derrick added as he started walking down the steps.

"How can you be so sure?" Simone asked as she shivered from the cold.

"Trust me, I know. He just bought the car today and he wouldn't be interested in Kennedy—he's on the other team." Derrick nodded and paused before he walked away.

Jared and Simone walked back into the house and were quiet for a moment.

Finally Jared asked, "Are you buying that?"

"I don't know. I think Derrick knows something and isn't saying anything. He and Kennedy have been rather close lately. But I can tell you one thing, I know my boss's car." Simone paused and pursed her lips. "Wait a minute, you saw him, right? I mean, you saw Kennedy's man, right? What did he look like?"

Jared and Simone exchanged details. Kennedy's Michael was Simone's boss. Simone was pissed.

"Simone, why are you so upset?"

"Because I have a rule about my brother and sister dating any of my coworkers. The rule is: don't."

"Why? What's the big problem with that?" Jared asked, sitting up.

"Well, I don't know if you are aware of this or not, but a long time ago Derrick had a fling with one of my bosses. Anyway he dogged the poor woman out and I had to hear about it every day at work. And one day I just got tired of hearing this woman dragging my brother's name through the mud and I flipped out, then she flipped out, and I slapped her. She was being rude, and not just about him, she pointed her finger in my face. I just lost it . . . job and all. So ever since then I just told them, Derrick and Kennedy, to stay away from anyone that I work with or I'm friends with. I do the same for them," Simone explained as Jared nodded.

~ *14* ~

*D*errick and Courtney were sitting in BBQ's in the Village having lunch. Derrick sat across from Courtney, waiting for Courtney to stop beating around the bush. Courtney had called Derrick at the office earlier, saying that they needed to talk about something important. Derrick didn't know what it was but he had a good guess. Courtney had been very attentive since the holidays and also very, very generous. On Christmas morning Derrick woke up to find himself by himself. He was angry at first because he hated when Courtney disappeared. But when he went into the bathroom he found a note taped to the mirror.

"What are you smiling about?" Courtney asked, smiling too.

"I'm just thinking about Christmas. That was so sweet of

you." Derrick smiled, reached over, and politely patted the top of Courtney's hand.

"The car or the note?" Courtney asked.

"Both. I loved both of them equally. I mean, the car is great, believe me. It's not every day that I wake up to a new Jaguar XKR parked in my driveway with a big bow wrapped around it. But the note topped it all off." Derrick beamed.

Courtney smiled. "Why the note? What was so nice about it? I'm just curious."

"Because it was special. I was raised to believe that a person's worth is based upon how much they have in their heart, not in their pocket. In the note you made it very clear that you love me and that you want to be with me forever. No one has made me feel that way. I've heard it before, but never have I felt it," Derrick said, squeezing Courtney's knee under the table.

"Well, I only said what I meant."

"I appreciate—" Derrick's phone vibrated loudly on his waist. "I better get that. I snuck away from work," Derrick explained as he answered his cell phone.

"Derrick Jacobs speaking."

"Derrick, sorry to interrupt you while you're working. Are you busy?" Kennedy said.

"Hey Kennedy, don't worry about it. I'm taking a long lunch, what's up?" Derrick asked as he smiled at Courtney.

"I just wanted to know if you wanted to do some shopping with me. I was going to pick out some baby things for Simone."

"Sorry, sis. I have to get back to work. I'm real proud of you, Kennedy, I am. You've come a long way."

"What do you mean?"

"Just that I'm proud of you, that's all. Love you," Derrick said and hung up.

Courtney sat still, staring out the window. Derrick drummed his fingers on the table. Courtney seemed just fine a couple of minutes ago, but Derrick thought it best to ignore it because he was getting used to Courtney's mood swings.

"That was my sister, Kennedy, as I'm sure you could figure out from our conversation," Derrick said.

"Oh, Kennedy." Courtney nodded.

"Yes, Kennedy. You remember her . . . the one I stopped from running in the bedroom," Derrick said.

"Oh, okay. Good thing you stopped her. I wouldn't have wanted her to see me half-dressed."

Simone looked in the mirror and shook her head. All day she had been unsuccessfully trying to find something to wear. The clothes weren't the problem, the shoes were. She had difficulty trying to find something to match the only pair of shoes into which she could squeeze her feet. She was almost six months pregnant and her feet were starting to swell, and her ankles looked like an elephant's. After an hour of fighting with herself, Simone settled on an outfit that she hated and called it quits. She had to be at Kennedy's in an hour. Seeing as though she would already be late, Simone took her time. She walked downstairs into the kitchen, grabbed a glass, and got some water from the water cooler that Nigel had had delivered. She didn't want anything from Nigel, and at first told the Poland Spring men that she didn't want it but then decided to keep it. It was his dime, not hers.

Simone grabbed her coat and car keys and called Kennedy to let her know that she'd be late. She checked herself in the mirror and got ready to leave. But when she opened her door to walk out, Nigel was standing there with roses in his hand.

"Oh, I'm glad I caught you. I wasn't sure if you were here," Nigel said, not budging.

"You knew I was here. My car's parked right there,"

Simone said, pointing to her car directly in front of the house.

Nigel stepped back and held his head down before he looked up. "Can I talk to you for a moment?"

"I was getting ready to go. You can call me later. I'll answer this time," Simone said as she put her hands on her hips and huffed.

"I won't take long, I promise," Nigel said with misty eyes.

"Talk."

"Well, can we at least go inside? It's pretty cold out here."

"Trust me, Nigel, it's going to be even colder in there."

"That's okay."

"Okay. I see you're not going to give up, so come on. But you have to hurry up, I have somewhere to be and I'm already running late." Simone turned around and walked back into the house.

Nigel followed and lay the roses on the coffee table. Simone stood, even though her feet were hurting. She didn't want to sit because she didn't want Nigel to feel comfortable, and she didn't want him to sit down either. She knew she had made a mistake letting him in after what happened the last time.

"So how have you been?"

"Fine, Nigel. Is that what you came here to ask me?"

"No. It's just that I haven't seen you in three months and I was wondering about you."

"Well, I'm fine and the baby's fine too. I just thought that I'd tell you that, since you didn't ask. So what do you want, Nigel?" Simone asked as she crossed her arms and tapped her right foot.

"I just want another chance, that's all. I want to be here for you and the baby. I love you and I miss you, can't you understand that? Don't tell me that you don't miss me, because I know you do." Nigel stepped closer to Simone.

"Uh-uh, Nigel, don't. I can honestly say that I haven't missed you. Why should I miss you? You became demanding, abusive . . . too many negative things to list. You weren't the man you pretended to be in the beginning. And just to think, I almost lost my sister because of you and your lies."

Nigel stiffened. "What lies? I never lied to you," Nigel defended.

"Are you kidding me? *Please.* You lied. Yes, you did. You lied about loving me. You didn't love me. How could you love me and hit me? That's not love, Nigel. And if it is, it's not the kind of love I need."

The veins in Nigel's forehead popped out and his voice deepened. "So what kind of love do you need, Simone, huh? Tell me that. Is it the kind of love you get from that white guy at work?"

"See, that's what I'm talking about. You come over here with your corner-store flowers, talking about how much you love and miss me, and then you accuse me of . . . never mind, that doesn't even deserve an answer. You can leave now, Nigel. I think I've heard enough." Simone opened her front door.

"I'm not going anywhere and you're going to answer my question. I've seen you and him together, and on more than a few occasions. You two looked pretty cozy to me," Nigel said as he kicked Simone's front door closed and grabbed her by her coat collar. "So that's your new man now, huh?" Nigel threw Simone against the wall.

"Get out! And I'm not playing, Nigel. You don't want me to call the police again, do you?" Simone yelled and then bent over and grabbed her thighs. Her legs and back were cramping.

"Are you okay? I'm sorry, Simone, I am. I don't know what got into me. When I call the office you won't take the call. When I page you, I don't get a call back and you changed your number here at the house. So occasionally I come by your job, hoping that I'll get a chance to see you and talk to you. But every time I come by, I see you with him walking hand in hand."

"Nigel, just leave and go get yourself some help. I work with that man. He's my *boss,* you know, Mr. Klein, as in Montgomery and Klein, and I don't mix work with pleasure. You know that. I take my job very seriously, thank you very much. And when you do see me and him walking hand in hand, as *you* say we do, it's only because I'm pregnant and he doesn't want me to slip on the ice. In case you haven't checked outside, it *is* winter. And we don't walk hand in hand, he supports me by my arm. He waits for me every morning to make sure that I'm okay. We're the first two people to get in the office every day. He's just being considerate, like you should be doing. After all, it's your baby that I'm carrying, not his," Simone said between deep breaths.

"How do I know that it's mine?" Nigel yelled.

"What? What did you just say? How could you sit here in my face and say some stupid mess like that?" Simone said as she briefly forgot about her pain and her anger.

Nigel pounded his fist on his chest. "I said, how am I supposed to know that the baby is mine? I mean, it could be someone else's. Look how long it took me—"

"Took you to *what,* sleep with me? I think you better get your women sorted out because it took you a long time. Maybe you slept with someone else quick but it wasn't me. I made you wait, what was it . . . five months or so. Get your women right, Nigel. You're blowing up your own spot. And I'll tell you what, if you don't know then I don't know," Simone said as she walked toward him despite the terrible pain.

"What did you just say?" Nigel asked. Simone could see his temples throbbing.

"You heard me. I said, if you don't know if this baby is yours, then I don't know," Simone said and then held her stomach and moaned in pain.

Derrick sat behind the wheel of his new car, feeling like trash and looking like a million dollars. He was supposed to be at Kennedy's with everyone else for her get-to-gether, but he didn't feel like being around a bunch of happy people. He didn't want to depress them with his own funk.

Courtney had really gotten to him in the worst way the day they had met for lunch. As hard as Derrick tried, he just couldn't understand Courtney who was confused with a capital C and wasn't trying to remedy the problem.

After they left BBQ's, Courtney convinced Derrick to call in sick and then they went to Derrick's place. They watched television, played truth-or-dare, and made love. Derrick slept like a baby that night and awoke to find Courtney gone and a Dear John letter.

Derrick sat and stared out the front window as two beautiful women walked down the street carrying a liquor store bag. He guessed that they were going to Kennedy's. They saw Derrick and smiled and he smiled back. Months ago, before Courtney, Derrick knew he would've talked to at least one of them. He smiled at himself and his past ways and waved at one of the women, who kept looking back at him. She was definitely beautiful and worth talking to but he couldn't do to her, or anybody else, what Courtney was doing to him. He refused to complicate someone else's life. Derrick knew where his heart was.

He rolled down the driver's side window and called to the woman who kept looking back and flirting with him. She whispered to her friend and walked back to his car.

"Hello. Would you happen to be going to Kennedy's?" Derrick asked.

"Yes. How did you know?" The tall shapely woman smiled as she shifted from one foot to the other.

"That," Derrick said as he pointed to the wine bottle sticking out of the bag. "Oh by the way, I'm Derrick Jacobs, Kennedy's brother. What's your name?" Derrick asked as he extended his hand.

"Crista, Crista Reid. It's nice to meet you, Derrick. Aren't you coming in?"

"Crista, Crista Reid, huh? I guess you're one of Jared's relatives."

Crista drew her head back. "Yes, how did you know?"

"By the last name. Jared has . . . had a daughter with my sister, Kennedy." Derrick stopped smiling.

"Okay. Now I know who you are. I remember you from Kennedy's baby shower. Small world. Jared's my brother."

Derrick smiled. "I can see the resemblance. Sorry but I'm afraid I won't be able to attend. Could you do me a favor and give this cheesecake to Kennedy for me? Tell her it's from Junior's. I'd really appreciate it." Derrick said as he handed the woman a bakery box.

"Sure, but are you certain that you don't want to come in, at least for a few minutes? It's going to be real nice. And I think Jared's supposed to be here. Just for a few minutes?" Crista bent over and ran her long fingernail over Derrick's hand.

"Wish I could, Crista, but I have to get home."

Derrick pulled up in his driveway as Courtney crossed the street. He wished that Courtney would just leave him alone and go home. He couldn't take the pain of this up-and-down merry-go-round. It wasn't fair. And Courtney didn't seem to care.

"Listen, Courtney, today isn't a good day. I'm not even sure if I want to see you right now."

"Let's just go in and sit and talk about this for a while. I'm really sorry for all that I've put you through. You really deserve better," Courtney said seductively and rubbed Derrick's shoulder.

"Just come on in. I don't want my neighbors knowing what's going on over here," Derrick said as he unlocked his door and walked in.

Derrick listened as Courtney apologized, talked, and apologized some more. Courtney was incredible but not in a good way, at least not that day. Derrick couldn't believe the things that he was hearing, but he finally figured out what Courtney wasn't telling him.

"So there's someone else?" Derrick asked.

Courtney was silent for a moment. "To be honest, no . . . not now. There was someone else but I ended it before I met you, but he wasn't willing to let it go. He started following me, calling me. You name it, he did it."

"And that is supposed to explain the letter—the reason you disappeared? I'm not buying it. One minute you love me and the next minute you can't be with me. Courtney, pick a time and stick to it."

"Derrick, don't be so harsh. I wasn't playing with your emotions. I just didn't want to drag you into the middle of my mess. Don't you know how much I love you? Do you understand that if I could marry you tomorrow, I would?"

"Would you?"

~ *15* ~

Kennedy leaned against the kitchen counter and rested. She knew that she should sit or lie down because her body needed a break, but she didn't have time to give it one. Jared was in the other room waiting for her and she didn't want him treating her like she couldn't pour two glasses of orange juice. If he saw her in this stance, that was exactly what he would do. Other than a couple of minor aches and occasional swelling, Kennedy's pregnancy was going rather smoothly.

She turned on the faucet to rinse the glasses. She stood in a trance and watched it flow out. Kharri had always loved the water. Tears streamed down Kennedy's face.

Why did Kharri have to die? The wood floor creaked and snapped her out of her thoughts. Jared was coming toward the kitchen. Wiping her eyes, she rushed from the sink to the refrigerator. By the time Jared walked in, she was pouring the orange juice and smiling as though everything was fine. Jared poked his bald head into the kitchen and Kennedy handed him his glass. When he turned around to walk out Kennedy rolled her eyes. She didn't know why she always did this to herself. She had a habit of making promises that she didn't want to keep. "Might as well get this over with," she mumbled as she walked out.

Kennedy pulled out the dining room chair and sat down. "So what was it you wanted to talk about?" she asked.

Jared stared at Kharri's pictures on the wall, then walked over to the fireplace. He picked up Kennedy's diploma and nodded. He set it back down, stared at Kennedy, and shoved his hands in his pockets.

Kennedy cleared her throat and crossed her ankles. "Well?"

Jared sat down. "The baby, remember?" he said as he circled his index finger around the rim of the glass.

"What about the baby? You still think it's yours?"

Jared jumped up, paced, and waved his hands in the air. He shook his head. "You know I do and I think that somewhere in that stubborn mind of yours, you suspect it too."

Kennedy got up and stared at Kharri's picture. "Maybe, maybe not. Are you sure you're not doing this because of Kharri? Because if you are, then I don't think your intentions are right."

"Hell yes I'm doing this because of Kharri, and there is nothing wrong with my intentions. I'm doing this because I already lost one child, so why would I want to lose another? If you are having my baby and I don't know . . . then that means that I'll be losing that one too."

The room was silent. Kennedy hung her head and thought about what Jared said. What if it was his baby? She didn't know what she would do. She couldn't deny him his own child. She shook her head. She wouldn't allow Jared to confuse her. She knew who fathered her child, and it wasn't Jared.

Kennedy wouldn't look up. "Well, I don't know, Jared—"

"Look at me, Kennedy. Look at me and tell me that I'm wrong, that there is no possible way that I can be the father. See, you won't because you know that there's a chance."

Kennedy rubbed her hands up and down her face and then rested her forehead in both of her hands. She finally looked up with tears in her eyes. "I can't believe that this is happening. I've never been that type of woman."

Jared looked in Kennedy's eyes, walked over to her, and wiped her tears. He held her hand and kissed it. His touch was the familiar comfort she needed and she couldn't pull away. "What type of woman? The type of woman who sleeps with two men at the same time? It's not your fault, Kennedy, and I don't look at you any different than I used to. When you were with him, you slept with him, and when you weren't with him, you slept with me. How were you supposed to know that you were going to get pregnant? The only thing that I question is why you were doing it unprotected." Jared knelt in front of her.

Kennedy snatched her hand away. "Me, what about you? You're just as guilty as I am."

"Ken, the only thing that I'm guilty of is loving you like I always did and trusting that you were the same as you were when you met me. When we first started out having sex you made me wear a condom for almost a year. I assumed that you were making him do the same."

"Jared, I really don't want to discuss this anymore, not about me and him or me and you. None of that matters now, it's irrelevant. You want some more juice?" Kennedy rose.

Jared stood in front of her and she put her hands on her hips. She refused to give in and give him a straight answer. She knew he wanted to hear that he was the father. But she couldn't tell him that if she wanted to. She was sure Michael was the father.

"Hold on a second, the juice can wait. So will you take the DNA test, for me . . . for the baby? We can have it done right in the hospital, no one has to know and you can avoid the embarrassment of going to a DNA clinic," Jared said as he held Kennedy's hand to prevent her from walking away.

"I don't know. What about Michael? He doesn't know about us. And I—"

"Forget about Michael, Kennedy. He's not what's important here, the baby is. But if it'll make you feel any better then I can speak with someone and just you, me, and the baby will be tested. Kennedy, I know that you won't let me down. I know that you don't want the baby growing up not knowing who his or her real father is. You're not that type of person, not that type of mother. You're not grimy like that. So will you?" Jared put his palm on the side of her face.

Kennedy put her head on Jared's chest and cried. Too much had happened to her in a short period of time. She missed Kharri.

"What's wrong, Ken? Don't cry, baby. Don't cry." Jared held her tight.

"I—I can't help it. I just miss Kharri so much. I try to be strong . . . I try to get over it. I can't, Jared. I was the best mother to her that I knew how to be. But how much of a good mother was I? I mean look at me . . . look what kind of mother I'm being to this baby now—"

"Ssh, it's okay. You were a great mother, and you will be again. Go ahead, Ken. Get it out. I'm here, baby." Jared rocked her in his arms.

Two weeks had passed and Kennedy finally agreed to have the DNA test performed. She knew that she was doing the right thing but was still scared. She was afraid the test would reveal she was wrong about the paternity of her child. Either way she knew that she couldn't lose with Jared or Michael. Both were very good men who would take care of their child. At least she knew that Jared would, his track record had proven that. And Michael was elated about being a father, so her worries were only minor ones.

Not knowing bothered her the most. She had always harshly judged women who didn't know who fathered their children and prided herself for not being like them. But she wasn't one of those women; she had no intentions of playing the lying game. She would find out the truth and raise her child knowing the truth. Kennedy wasn't going to have her child look upon her with contempt later on in life for lying or not caring enough to find out. After all, the child's stability was at stake, not hers.

Kennedy looked at her watch and searched frantically for her house keys. Michael was due to pick her up any moment and she wanted to be ready. She had looked everywhere and couldn't find them. As her pregnancy progressed, Kennedy was always losing things. She wiped the sweat from her forehead with her shirtsleeve and sat down. She was tired from looking, her feet hurt, and she was thirsty.

When Kennedy opened the refrigerator to get some water, she broke out in laughter. She laughed so hard that she almost wet herself, which wasn't a hard task, since the baby was getting bigger by the day. Right next to the gallon of milk was her house keys and the cordless phone. Kennedy shook her head in disbelief at her forgetfulness and walked to the front door. She looked at her watch again and saw Michael pulling up out front. As usual he was on time.

Kennedy unlocked the front door and walked back into her bedroom to get her purse and refreshen her lip gloss. She hated to make Michael wait but she couldn't go out looking dull *and* swollen. The front door slammed. Michael was probably standing there waiting for her.

"Back here in the bedroom," Kennedy yelled.

"Did you know that your front door was wide open? I told you about that," Michael said as he walked into the bedroom and kissed Kennedy on the cheek.

"I didn't know that it was wide open. I just unlocked it and opened it a little when I saw you pull up. It must be really windy outside. Don't worry, I'm crazy but not that crazy. I'll be finished in a sec, okay? I just needed to touch up my lips."

"Yeah, I can tell. So, does Simone know that you're going to buy the nursery set, or is it supposed to be a surprise?" Michael asked as he walked up behind Kennedy and wrapped his arms around her stomach.

"Why? Did she say anything at work about doing the nursery yet? Oh, never mind, she wouldn't tell you anyway, you're not a woman. Ready?" Kennedy grabbed her coat and purse.

"Not yet. Sit here on the bed for a second, I've got something that I need to discuss with you," Michael said as he patted the empty spot beside him.

"Okay. You sound serious. Is everything all right?"

"I don't know. I mean I thought I knew, but I can't be certain. Um, what I'm trying to say is that you've always been forward with me and I trust you, I really do—"

"Just say it, Michael. It can't be that bad."

Michael clasped his hands together and exhaled loudly. "I know that you and Jared had a thing going on before and I know that you two have spent a good amount of time alone. I just need you to reassure me that there is no possible way that he could be the father of the baby. I mean, it is mine, right?"

Simone answered the phone on the first ring and it wasn't Kaisha. She had been waiting all day for Kaisha to call back after Kaisha had left a message saying she would call back at five. It was now a quarter to six. Simone hated waiting, especially for Kaisha, whom she hadn't seen since their argument.

Kaisha had called Simone and apologized for everything

that she had said or done. Under different circumstances, Simone would've hung up in her face. But Kaisha had been very sincere and even cried. Simone guessed that being pregnant had caused her to be more forgiving and sensitive toward others, Kaisha included.

Simone sat next to the phone and went over some office paperwork. She looked at the caller ID and put her paperwork down, she couldn't concentrate. What was so important? Kaisha said that it was urgent that they talk, she didn't say what about. Simone was going through numbers listed on the caller ID when the phone rang.

"Simone, it's me. Sorry it took so long but I had to get away from my baby's daddy. He's crazy. Anyway, can you meet me? I don't want to talk on the phone."

"I hope everything's all right, Kaisha. You sound out of breath. Wait, I thought that Nigel told me that your boyfriend left you?"

"Yeah right, wish he would. Everything is everything, Simone. Anyway, can you meet me?"

"Yeah, where?" Simone asked, hoping that Kaisha didn't say in Brooklyn because she didn't feel like taking the drive.

"Uptown on 145 at Copeland's, the soul food spot. Do you know where that's at?"

"Yes, I've been there before. What time? I know it's going to take you a while on the subway—"

"Come now. I'm already there. Simone, please hurry up, I don't want him to find me." Kaisha sounded scared.

"Okay, I'm on my way. But before I come I want you to know that the only reason that I'm willing to do this is because you're going to be my child's sister."

"Yeah, I know. See you when you get here. I'ma be sitting toward the back, away from the front window."

Kaisha wanted her to leave right away but she decided to call a few important clients first. She needed to tell them that she was going on maternity leave and let them know who would handle them while she was away. After she made her calls she thought about Kaisha and hoped that Kaisha wouldn't ask her to borrow money or to stay with her to get away from her crazy boyfriend. Kaisha was going to be her child's sister but even Simone had her limits.

After Simone retrieved her coat and was headed down the stairs a door slammed. She stopped, looked around, and listened but didn't see anything, so she kept going. When she made it down the stairs she saw Nigel standing out of view.

"What are you doing here and how did you get in my house?" Simone snapped.

"What question do you want me to answer first?" Nigel smiled.

"I'm serious, Nigel. What do you want and how did you get in?" Simone approached him and smelled the liquor seeping out of his pores.

"Your door was unlocked and I was coming by to check on you, see how you were. The last time I was here you were in a lot of pain. Did you go to the doctor?"

"You should be asking if I went to the police, not the doctor. And yes, I'm fine. Is that all? Because if so, you can go now," Simone said. She had exaggerated her pain to make Nigel feel sorry for her and leave her alone.

Nigel's voice rose and his bass got deeper. "No, as a matter of fact, that isn't all. Where were you going?"

"None of your business. I'm going out and so are you," Simone said as she reached for the front door.

"I'm not going any damn place."

"Suit yourself. Lock my door when you leave," Simone said and grabbed the doorknob.

Nigel kicked Simone's hand while it was on the knob. Simone pulled back and yelped out in pain as a loud crack sounded throughout the room.

"You're going to meet a man, huh? Not today, bitch. What did I tell you about talking to me like I'm some kind of child. Telling me to lock your door behind me when I leave.

So what do you have to say now? You got any more instructions for me?" Nigel yelled as spit shot from his mouth.

"What is wrong with you?" Simone screamed as she looked at her limp, bleeding hand. "What have I done to you?"

"What have you done? What have you done? I'll tell you what you did, you . . . you trifling bitch. You disrespected me, that's what!" Nigel yelled in Simone's face and grabbed her by her throat.

"Nigel, I can't breathe—"

"If you couldn't breathe, you wouldn't be talking, now would you? No! I am so sick of your lies. You lied about loving me. You lied about being faithful. You lied about the baby." Nigel slapped her.

Simone stood there defenseless. "I didn't lie to you, Nigel, the baby *is* yours. This is *our* baby, Nigel, mine and yours," Simone said as she rubbed her stomach with her left hand.

"Damn if it is." Nigel grabbed Simone by her hair as she tried to fight back and dragged her through the house into the kitchen.

"Nigel, please. Stop it! Stop it! Just leave, Nigel. You've been drinking. Just get out of my house—"

Nigel pulled Simone from the floor by her hair and punched her and knocked her down. He looked her in the eyes as she screamed out in horror and stepped on her neck as she struggled to breathe.

He ran up to her and kicked her in the side. Simone fell over and screamed out in pain. "Shut up," Nigel shouted and kicked Simone in the face as hard as he could. Everything went black.

———

Derrick sat outside on the cold cement porch, the snow melting under the sun's rays. It was exceptionally warm for

February and perfect for proposing. It was the day he had been waiting for, Valentine's Day.

Derrick pulled the velvet box from his pocket and turned it over and over before opening it. The ring was perfect for Courtney. He only hoped that it was the right size. Derrick had saved the ring for the right time—the time when Courtney was serious enough to commit.

Derrick rose and shook the cold from his pants and walked into the condo. He looked at his red leather chairs sitting opposite each other. He made a mental note to make his home more comfortable because his life felt more comfortable. He decided to call Kennedy later on in the week and ask her to help him because that was more of her area than his.

Feeling family-like, Derrick grabbed his box of photo albums and searched for a picture. When he found the picture of him, Kennedy, Kharri, and Simone at Kharri's last birthday party, he put it into a frame and placed it on top of the entertainment center. Derrick traced his finger along the top of the frame, picked it up, and kissed Kharri's little image. "I miss you, Khar-Khar," Derrick said, grabbed his coat from the sofa, and left.

Derrick placed the balloons on Kharri's headstone and bent on one knee and said a prayer. Kharri had always been such a treasure, as if she had been one of his own. Because of Jericha, he had seen more of Kharri than he had of little Derrick and Anjelica.

Derrick got up and kissed Kharri's picture on the headstone and whispered, "I know you hear me and I know that you're still around. Just look out for your uncle and check on me from time to time. Will you do that for me? I know you will. I love you always, and I'll be back soon. Oh yeah, and don't forget to tell God I said hi and remember to play nice with the angels. Okay, sweetie."

Derrick got back into his car and waited. He didn't know

what he was waiting for but something inside of him told him to. He started his engine and put his car into gear when suddenly two yellow butterflies landed on his windshield. "I know I must be crazy now. Butterflies in February?"

Derrick smiled almost all the way home and his face hurt. He had really enjoyed his visit to the cemetery, but wished it had been a visit to Chuck E. Cheese with his niece instead. Derrick searched through his CDs, looking for Kharri's favorite adult songs that she wasn't supposed to listen to, when he felt his pager vibrate. Whomever would have to wait because he had purposely left his cell phone at home.

When Derrick walked into the house he was greeted by the sound of the telephone ringing. He waited for the answering machine to pick up but remembered that he forgot to turn it on.

"Hello."

"Derrick, where have you been? I've been calling you and paging you. I tried your cell phone—"

"What's the matter, Ken? I was at the cemetery visiting Kharri when the most amazing thing—"

"Later, Derrick, tell me later. Right now you have to get over to the hospital," Kennedy said as she started to cry.

"What happened and which hospital?"

"Simone lost the baby and she's been unconscious for hours. They don't know if she's going to pull through. Please hurry, I don't think I can handle this, not again, Derrick. Not again."

~ *16* ~

*K*ennedy watched as the movers carried the last box into the house. She wasn't looking forward to unpacking and didn't want Michael helping her. Some things would always be private, and she didn't want Michael going through her belongings, even if she didn't have anything to hide.

Michael had insisted that Kennedy move in with him until the baby was born. He didn't want her to be home alone when she went into labor, so he and his mother took turns staying home with her. Kennedy assured him that she could handle it but Michael wasn't having it.

At first Kennedy didn't think she was going to be able to take having Mrs. Montgomery around all the time. Mrs. Montgomery was a sweetheart, and Kennedy genuinely liked her, but when two women shared a kitchen there was bound to be trouble. But Mrs. Montgomery was different; she respected Kennedy's space.

After the movers left, Kennedy went upstairs to change into her unpacking clothes and got to work. Even though she dreaded unpacking she was glad that her things had finally been moved. She had been at Michael's for almost two weeks and didn't have enough clothes to wear, so she had been forced to either go shopping for new things or walk around in Michael's T-shirts.

Kennedy was bending over, grabbing something out of a box, when Mrs. Montgomery walked in.

"Chile, I know I ain't seeing what I think I'm seeing. Why you all bent over that box?" Mrs. Montgomery said as she placed her hands on her ample hips.

"Sorry, Ma, I forgot," Kennedy said and squatted.

"That's better. Squat, don't bend, or else you'll be in more pain than necessary. And don't let me catch you reaching above your head either, cause you can strangle the baby like that. Just call me and I'll do it for you," Mrs. Montgomery instructed.

Kennedy stopped and sat on the floor, and laughed at Mrs. Montgomery's old wives' tale beliefs.

"What's so funny, girl? You young people, I swear," Mrs. Montgomery said and turned to walk back into the kitchen.

"Ma, wait. Do you think that you can come with me to the hospital—"

"Oh Lord, you ready, ain't ya? I told Michael that you was looking a little peakish."

"No Ma, not yet anyway. I need to go see Simone and find out when they're going to release her." Kennedy got up from the floor.

"How is she?"

Kennedy raised her eyebrows.

"That bad, huh? Well I'll call a couple of my church friends—you know the women in my prayer group, and we can pray for her. Do y'all know who did it to her?"

"She hasn't said yet," Kennedy lied, not wanting to spread Simone's business. "I guess she doesn't feel like talking. And I can't say that I blame her, I wouldn't be talking either. Been there, done that." Kennedy tilted her head and poked out her lips. "I just hope she says something soon so the police can get whoever it is before I do. Because if I get to him first, then it's all over."

Mrs. Montgomery nodded and adjusted her bra strap. "Yeah, I guess I can understand your anger but what y'all gotta do is pray about it and let God handle it. You gon' have to pray for the strength to forgive that lost soul. Cause we're all his children and he loves us all and forgives us all if we repent. You hear me?"

"Yes Ma, I hear you. But I don't think you understand, you've never lost a child—"

"Yes, I have. I lost Jimmy."

"Ma, you didn't lose Jimmy. Jimmy's not dead, he's gay. There's a big difference," Kennedy said, shocked by Mrs. Montgomery's narrow-mindedness.

"Same thing. While Jimmy's gay, Jimmy's dead in my eyes. There is no room for him in the house of the Lord."

"You can't be serious, Ma."

"Sure. Jimmy die today, Jimmy's going to burn in hell, that's all to it. It's right in the Bible," Mrs. Montgomery said as if she'd written it herself.

"Okay, Ma, whatever you say. But the only way you're going to convince me is if you show me. And I mean it has to say that word for word. No turning the scriptures around to make them mean what you're saying," Kennedy said, knowing that Mrs. Montgomery couldn't.

Mrs. Montgomery glared. "Chile, I know you're not doubting the word of God."

"No, I'm not doubting anything. I just want you to show me in the Bible that that is the word of God and not just yours, that's all. Didn't you just say that we're all God's children, and he loves every last one of us?" Kennedy said and smiled on the inside because she knew that she had just beat Mrs. Montgomery.

"You ain't funny, is you, Kennedy?" Mrs. Montgomery said, looking at Kennedy from head to toe.

"If you mean as in hilarious, then yes. But if you're asking if I'm gay, no. I just believe that people are who they are, and we can't help who we love or how we're made."

"Well then, get your coat and bring your hilarious tail on then. You still want to go see your sister, right? Well hurry up, I ain't got all day," Mrs. Montgomery said, flinging a kitchen towel in the air and walking out.

Kennedy finished showering and started getting dressed. Mrs. Montgomery had looked wounded, and Kennedy guessed that no one had ever challenged her beliefs before. She could imagine her downstairs on the phone with her prayer group, praying for Kennedy and her lost soul.

Slipping on her shoes, she heard Mrs. Montgomery call out for her to hurry up. Kennedy took her time. She wasn't worried about being left because she was the one who was driving, not Mrs. Montgomery. Kennedy stood in front of the mirror and primped just to delay when her cell phone rang.

"Hello."

"Michael Montgomery, please," a very familiar male voice said.

Kennedy took a good look at the cell phone. Michael had taken the wrong phone with him.

"He's unavailable. May I take a message?" Kennedy asked, thinking that this man sounded like Derrick.

"Can you tell him that Mr. Jacobs—"

"Derrick?" Kennedy asked in disbelief. How did Derrick know where to find her?

"Kennedy? What are you doing answering Mr. Montgomery's phone?"

"I picked it up by mistake, mine looks just like it. Oh, here mine is, right in my purse. I'm at his office picking up something for Simone and he stepped out for a second. What are you doing calling him?" Kennedy asked.

"He's going to do my taxes for me. I guess I can just fax my paperwork over to his secretary," Derrick said.

"Oh, okay. Listen, I'll tell him that you called. I feel like such a fool answering his phone. I hope he doesn't get upset," Kennedy said and reminded herself to go to Simone's office in Manhattan to get something, anything, just in case Derrick asked her about it.

"Don't worry about it, sis, anyone could've made that mistake. I'll talk to you soon, take care," Derrick said and hung up.

———————

Kennedy walked into Simone's room and grew weary. The room was dark and smelled like antiseptic. Simone's hair was a mess, flakes of dandruff lay on top. Her right eye was bandaged, her arm in a cast, and her skin was dull. Kennedy had never seen her look so bad. Cards, flowers, balloons, and teddy bears filled the room and would've made some unknowing person think that all was fine and dandy, but it wasn't. Simone lay in the bed with her light brown eyes open, but when Kennedy looked in them she saw nothing. Not a morsel of life. Yes, she was alive, she was living and breathing, but she was like Kennedy had once been, dead on the inside.

Simone had been devastated when she woke up and all she said that she remembered was Nigel's boot coming at her face. Simone didn't miscarry, but had to give birth unconscious. In the end, the doctors said that the baby just wasn't strong enough to make it and Simone almost didn't either. The doctors had difficulty stopping her from hemorrhaging and later discovered that she had internal bleeding as well.

"Hey, sis, how're you doing? You feel any better today?" Kennedy asked and rubbed Simone's hand.

"I'm trying, Ken, I'm really trying. But you don't know how hard it was for me to wake up and not know where I was. It was terrible to wake up to find out that I lost the baby and almost my life. It tore me apart when the doctor told me that I'll probably never have children. It felt like I lost a part of myself. Now I understand what you felt, but I think mine is a little different. With Kharri, at least you knew what you would be missing. But I don't and I'll never have that. I'll never know what he would've been like, or what he would've looked like alive. I'll never get to see his eyes, Kennedy, or hear him call me Mommy. And I wanted that, Ken, I really did. He wasn't a mistake, you know, I don't think I ever told anyone that, but he wasn't. I knew what I was doing." Simone cried.

"Shh, it'll be alright. It may not seem like it, but it'll get better, trust me. You just concentrate on getting yourself out of here, okay? We need you, I need you, *you* need you. Don't give up, Simone," Kennedy said as she joined her sister in tears.

Simone tried to sit up but couldn't. She squeezed Kennedy's hand. "I believe you, it's just hard. I know that I have to go on, just like I told you to do. But just like you'll never forget Kharri, I'll never forget him."

"I know . . . I know, and it's okay. Now come on and help me get you up. I'm going to give you a shower before these nurses come in and tell me it's against hospital policy," Kennedy said as she took Simone by the arm and gently pulled her.

"I don't know, Kennedy. You know I got an incision on my stomach—"

"Girl, please. I know you don't want to go home smelling like that. Just come on, I'll just wash around it. You know, the important parts," Kennedy teased and was happy that she put a smile on Simone's face.

Kennedy bathed Simone, dressed her, then did her hair and makeup. She stepped back and admired her work and smiled. Simone's coffee-colored skin glowed again, bringing out her light baby browns. She looked just like her old self with the exception of the scar on the side of her head and a faint trace of a black eye. Kennedy beamed and admired her sister's strength.

The doctors said that Simone was a fighter and had fought for her life every second that she was on that operating table. They were surprised that she had pulled through, but Kennedy wasn't. Simone had always been strong; she was the one who held the three of them together after their parents died.

"What are you smiling at?" Simone asked.

"You."

"Why?" Simone tilted her head and pushed her hair out of her face.

"Because I'm admiring you, and I love you." Kennedy smiled.

"No tears, Kennedy. We Jacobs women have cried too much these last few months."

"Amen, sister. Amen."

Courtney had beaten Derrick at four straight games of pool. Derrick was surprised because he considered himself to be a good shot. All night he had watched Courtney intensely, and couldn't wait to get home. Derrick twirled the ice cubes in his glass in an effort to mix his drink.

"Seems like all the liquor's on the bottom. Mine's the same way," Courtney said.

"Yeah, all the Coke seems to be on top, or maybe the Bacardi's hiding," Derrick joked.

"It's definitely hiding. Let's order a double," Courtney said and beckoned the waitress.

"Order some buffalo wings when she gets over here. This liquor is making me hungry again," Derrick said and rubbed his stomach.

"It's not the liquor. You know Chinese food doesn't stick. You want to go over there and sit down?" Courtney pointed to an empty table.

"Yeah, you lead."

As Derrick followed, a much older man walked past and winked at Courtney. He couldn't see Courtney's reaction but whatever it was made the man smile from ear to ear. Derrick guessed that the man assumed he and Courtney were just friends because they hadn't shared any public displays of affection.

"You know him?" Derrick sneered.

"No, why?"

"I was just wondering what would make him react like that."

"Like what? The way he winked at me?"

"No, the way he reacted *after* the wink. What did you do?"

"I winked back. I didn't mean any harm though. I hope that doesn't bother you."

"Well, actually it does. It's disrespectful, don't you think? But I guess since we didn't share any PDA's he didn't know."

"PDA's?"

"Public displays of affection."

Courtney hesitated. "Oh, I'm sorry, Derrick, it'll never happen again. I just thought that I'd repay him the compliment, that's all. I'm not interested in him. I was just trying to make him feel good, he looks old enough to be my father."

Derrick nodded.

Courtney leaned across the table and kissed Derrick passionately. "You don't have anything to worry about. I'm all yours."

On the ride home Derrick felt embarrassed for showing his insecurity. He hadn't planned on the conversation going the way it had. Derrick grabbed Courtney's hand and kissed it. He smiled about the man in the pool hall and the look on his face when he and Courtney shared their first PDA.

"Courtney, I forgot to ask you if you want to come by tomorrow to celebrate with me."

"Celebrate what?"

"My acceptance to law school." Derrick grinned.

"For real? Congrats! Why didn't you tell me earlier?"

"Because I don't think I'm going to go to the one I just got into. I have somewhere else in mind."

"Where?"

"All I'm saying is Ivy League."

"No? You'll get in, baby. Just mark my words, you'll get in."

Derrick loved Courtney's confidence in him. He looked out at the city lights and felt Courtney grab his hand. Damn, he was in love. He couldn't believe that he finally had what he wanted—someone he could really love. "So, will you join me tomorrow?"

"I'm there, sweetie. What time?"

"That depends on the family. Kennedy and Simone are supposed to be coming around six, but I wouldn't set my clock by it, if you know what I mean."

Courtney adjusted the rearview mirror. "Sure, sweetie."

~ *17* ~

*K*ennedy stopped and looked Simone in the face. Simone had been home from the hospital for more than a month but Kennedy was still worried about her and refused to let her stay home alone. If she wasn't there, then Derrick was. Overall Simone had been pretty good about it except for when she kicked one of them out from time to time. Kennedy didn't worry though because that was a sign Simone was getting back to being herself.

"Could you please stop looking at me? I'm fine, Kennedy, really." Simone stopped cooking and put her good hand on her hip and smirked.

"Okay, okay. I was just trying to help. Damn." Kennedy held up her hands in surrender.

Derrick left the room in search of a hiding spot in

Simone's office. He hadn't been in the best of moods since Courtney had stood him up again. Derrick found a corner chair and sat down. He caught on to Simone's mood quick and no one had to tell him twice that she didn't want to be mothered by Kennedy or anyone else. Derrick decided to search Simone's bookcase for a book to borrow when Kennedy came in.

"She kicked you out, huh?" Derrick laughed.

"Yes, of course. So what are you doing? I hope you're not looking for a book to borrow because you know Simone isn't having it."

"Maybe she won't lend you a book but she'll lend me one. *I* return things that I borrow," Derrick said as he pulled *The Prophet* by Kahlil Gibran off one of the shelves.

"Forget it, D. She's definitely not letting that one go. Besides you should know that one by heart. How many times have you read it?"

"Not enough. You should read it sometime, you can learn a lot. Besides, it's mine. I told you that I'm the only one who returns things." Derrick sat down and flipped through the pages.

"Derrick, remember last month when you invited us over to celebrate, and you said that you wanted to tell us something? Well, what was it? I thought about it when I got home and remembered that you never told us." Kennedy walked over to where Derrick sat and leaned against him.

"Get your pregnant butt off me," Derrick teased. "It was nothing really, I had forgotten about it. It was probably something about Jericha," Derrick said. Jericha was the last person Kennedy wanted to hear about.

"Oh, okay. Well I'm going back before Simone burns the house down. You know she calls herself trying to cook again. You coming?"

"Soon. Please go and help that girl but don't be too obvious. You know she's still sensitive. I can't believe Nigel did that to her. When I see him, it's on."

"I know, D, I can't blame you and I wouldn't stop you. But don't worry about Simone, I'll just tiptoe around her. And I don't care how sensitive she is, I'm still not eating her food." Kennedy lightened the mood.

Downstairs she found Simone standing by the sink staring at the running water from the faucet. She stood by the door and watched her for a moment. Kennedy put her arm around Simone and they both just stood there for a few minutes.

"Thanks, Ken."

"No problem, sis. You were there for me too." Kennedy kissed Simone on her cheek.

"How did you know what I was going to say?"

"I know you, girl. Now turn that water off before you drown us all." Kennedy laughed to lighten the mood.

Derrick came into the kitchen and sat down at the table with his book. Simone looked over his shoulder and saw that it wasn't hers and made a face at Kennedy who busted out laughing because she knew that Simone had been trying to keep it. Simone was always trying to keep something of theirs. She had always teased that she was entitled to anything that they had because she helped raise them.

"Forget it, Simone," Derrick said without looking up.

"What?" Simone asked and stuck her tongue out behind his back.

"You're not getting the book, that's what," Derrick glanced up and said.

"You're not getting it, that's what," Kennedy mimicked.

"Oh, y'all got jokes." Derrick nodded. "I'm going to the store. Do you two comedians want anything?"

"No." Simone winked at Kennedy.

Kennedy just shook her head.

Derrick paused in the doorway. "Kennedy, I forgot to tell you that I stopped by your apartment. I didn't know you moved."

"When? Where?" Simone asked.

Kennedy bit her lip. "I just recently moved. I thought I

told you," Kennedy lied. "I'll have you two over when I'm finished decorating."

After Derrick left, Simone and Kennedy sat on the sofa, shared a container of ice cream, and gossiped. Kennedy confessed to sleeping with Jared and not knowing who the baby's father was.

"It could happen to anybody," Simone offered.

"Yeah, right anybody, but not me." Kennedy sighed.

"So how does Michael feel about it, and when were you going to tell me?"

Startled, Kennedy asked, "What?"

"You heard me. When were you planning on telling me that you and Michael were involved? That's where you live, huh? Do I look that stupid to you? Now you know that I was going to find out eventually. And how on earth did you think that you were going to have his baby and cover it up? I work with him, remember?"

Kennedy searched Simone's cold face before she answered, "Listen, I didn't plan on hiding it from you forever. I just figured that you couldn't do anything else but accept it once the baby was born. I would've told you about him and me, I just didn't want to hear your mouth, Simone. Sometimes you can get a little too carried away. Does Derrick know, too?"

"No, Derrick doesn't have a clue about you and Michael. As far as me getting upset, I have reason to get carried away. Remember Derrick and his fiasco that cost me my job? You'd be the same way if you were me," Simone said and passed Kennedy the ice cream.

"But Derrick's situation was completely different from mine. I love Michael and I've been seeing him more than a year now," Kennedy said and passed the ice cream back.

"Well, what about Jared?"

"I love him too." Kennedy smiled.

"Okay, I can accept that. *But* who are you *in* love with?"

Think about that for a moment, I'm going to get the mail." Simone passed the ice cream back to Kennedy and got up.

Kennedy didn't have to think long to make a choice between Michael and Jared. She was in love with Jared. He would always be the love of her life. But she had to be honest with herself—the days of her and Jared were over a long time ago.

A few minutes later, Simone plopped down on the sofa next to Kennedy, cleared her throat, but didn't say anything. She cleared her throat again.

"Well, what is it? Are you going to say anything or do you need a drink of water?" Kennedy asked.

"I asked you a question first. Don't you think it's common courtesy for you to answer mine?" Simone said and opened an envelope without looking at it.

"Jared. I'll always be in love with Jared. Happy now?"

"The question is, are *you* happy? I'm not the one in a relationship with one man and in love with another," Simone said as she tore open another piece of mail.

Kennedy eyed the mail in Simone's freshly manicured hands. "Well, what am I supposed to do, break Michael's heart and go to Jared when I don't even want to be with Jared?"

"I don't know, you tell me." Simone opened another envelope while looking at Kennedy.

"I don't know if I would've done that if I were you." Kennedy looked down at the mail in Simone's hands.

"What?"

"You just opened Derrick's mail." Kennedy peeked over Simone's shoulder at the envelope.

"Damn, he's going to have a fit. But *you* know I wasn't paying attention. He shouldn't of had it sent here. Do you see who this is from, Kennedy? It's from Harvard Law School." Simone held up the envelope to the light.

"What are you holding it up to the light for, silly? It's already opened, just read it. And why did he have it sent here?"

Derrick had been accepted into Harvard. He'd be thrilled to say the least. He'd also be pissed that they opened his mail, even if it was by accident. Simone said if he had it sent to her house, that meant he was too scared to open it himself.

They contemplated when would be the best time to give him the news. They had both noticed that Derrick had been in a sullen mood lately and disagreed as to when they should give it to him. Derrick walked into the house while they were debating and Simone stuffed the letter behind the sofa pillow before he had a chance to see.

"So, what's in the bag?" Simone asked as she went to peek.

"I got you just what you asked for, nothing," Derrick joked as he pulled the bag away from Simone.

"What are you doing later on, Derrick?" Kennedy asked.

Derrick shrugged. "I don't know. I'm supposed to be meeting Courtney for dinner. Why, you plan on going into labor?"

"Funny, very funny. No, I was just asking. Simone and I were thinking about doing something later. But you go ahead and have a good time with Ms. Courtney." Kennedy nudged Simone and laughed.

"What's so funny? Don't tell me that you two are trying to be comedians again." Derrick looked at Simone.

"So when do we get to meet her?" Simone asked.

"Soon. As a matter of fact, I have to call her right now," Derrick said and went into the kitchen.

Kennedy and Simone sat on the sofa and whispered. Why had Derrick been hiding Courtney from them? He had never been as secretive as they were about his love life and never hid any of his women from them before.

Simone went to the kitchen door and listened. Kennedy shook her head no but Simone just waved her off.

"It's my house. I can listen if I want to," Simone whispered.

"Don't let him catch you," Kennedy whispered back.

Simone came back to the sofa and told Kennedy that she

knew when and where Derrick was meeting Courtney for dinner. She told Kennedy to go home and get dressed. They were going to surprise Derrick with a cake and his acceptance letter and find out who Courtney was.

———

Kennedy walked into the house and was thankful that Mrs. Montgomery wasn't there. She didn't want to be asked a million and one questions about how she was feeling. She was pregnant, not dying. Michael was nowhere to be found, so she paged him. Kennedy wanted him to come with her and Simone to surprise Derrick.

Before stepping into the shower she called the florist to have flowers and balloons sent to Simone's house for Derrick. Then she paged Michael again, leaving a message asking him to meet her at the restaurant, and stepped into the shower.

Kennedy arrived at Simone's at six, and Simone wasn't finished dressing yet. Michael hadn't answered her page, so she was already pissed. Why was Simone so slow when Kennedy was the one who was fat? Kennedy went upstairs and into the bathroom. "What's taking you so long? You told me to be ready and you're not even ready."

In the mirror Simone was applying mascara. "I had to wait on the cake. Can you pass me that brush?"

"Could you *please* hurry up. We're going to surprise Derrick, not find you a man."

"You never know." Simone winked.

Kennedy and Simone arrived at the restaurant at seven on the dot. Simone saw Michael's car and tapped Kennedy on the shoulder and pointed to it. Kennedy smiled.

"So I guess everybody's here tonight. So are you going to invite him over to our table or are you two still going to act like you barely know each other?" Simone smiled and bumped into Kennedy.

Kennedy walked over to Michael's car, looked inside, and then checked the license plate. It was definitely his.

"Oh, I'm going to act like I know him all right. Do you know I left two messages on his pager, and he didn't call back."

Simone waved her hands in the air. "Don't worry about it. I heard that we're trying to land a couple of major corporations. He's probably entertaining them and trying to convince them that they should let us crunch their numbers."

They entered the restaurant and Simone asked for the manager on duty. She had contacted the restaurant earlier, pulled a couple of strings, and got a reservation. The place was packed and they didn't see Derrick anywhere.

Kennedy just knew that Simone hadn't heard correctly and went over to the hostess. "I'm looking for a Derrick Jacobs. We're supposed to be meeting him, it's a surprise . . . the manager knows," Kennedy explained to the tight-lipped hostess.

"I'm sorry, we don't have anyone on the reservation list by that name."

"Okay, how about Michael Montgomery from Montgomery and Klein?" They might as well crash Michael's dinner party since Derrick wasn't there.

Kennedy told Simone that Derrick wasn't on the list. Simone sucked her teeth.

"Are you sure Derrick isn't here? Did you ask her to double-check? You should've looked at the list," Simone said and followed Kennedy.

"I did look at the list. He wasn't on it. So are you ready to see Michael's face? He's going to be so surprised that you know about us, Simone. Come on. The hostess said that he's all the way in the back by the corner behind some divider sort of thing."

When they reached the back, Kennedy froze. Simone

nudged her from behind and Kennedy let out a loud whew, as she dropped the cake. Simone went and stood next to Kennedy to see what the problem was.

"Oh my God. This has got to be wrong," Simone said to no one in particular.

Derrick and Michael were sitting about ten feet away from them, laughing and whispering in each other's ears, oblivious to their surroundings. Their dining together would've seemed innocent if they hadn't have kissed and held hands like two people in love. Kennedy looked over at Simone. Simone's jaw was on the floor. Kennedy stormed over to the table, Michael's face froze as he snatched his hand from Derrick's, and Derrick's eyes bulged.

Kennedy stuttered, "S-so this . . ."

"Kennedy, Simone . . . I didn't want you two to find out this way . . . this is Courtney—I mean Michael is Courtney," Derrick said.

Michael just sat there looking straight ahead while Simone joined him in his silence.

"So this is why you wouldn't return my pages? I don't even know what to say! What the *fuck* is someone supposed to say?" Kennedy screamed and the restaurant got quiet.

Derrick said, "Kennedy, please. This is embarrassing enough for me as it is—"

"I'm not talking to you, Derrick," Kennedy said through clenched teeth.

"Well, who are you talking to? Simone, who is she talking to?" Derrick turned to Simone.

Kennedy pointed her finger across the table without taking her eyes off Michael. "I'm talking to him, the motherfucker sitting across the table from you, that's who. Ask him, Derrick, ask him who *I* am."

"Michael, what's going on here? Wait a minute, let me guess, you've been seeing my sister too. I knew it, I knew something wasn't right!" Derrick slapped his hand on the table, jumped up, and grabbed Michael by his collar.

"Derrick, Kennedy, look, let's not do this, not here," Michael said and pulled Derrick's hands off him.

Kennedy growled. "Don't say a word, Michael, not a damn word because I don't want to hear it. Truth be told, I don't ever want to hear your voice again. And Derrick, we need to talk because *your* man is the father of my baby . . . your niece or nephew. Now doesn't that just ice your cake." Kennedy laughed angrily.

Derrick just sat with his head in his hands. "Kennedy, I am so sorry—"

"Shut the hell up, Derrick, I'm not in the mood. And you . . . you should've told us. We love you no matter what and you know that," Kennedy snapped and held her glare at Michael.

"Ken, let's just go." Simone grabbed Kennedy's arm.

"I'm not finished yet, Simone."

"I know, Ken, but don't embarrass yourself over him. He's not worth it," Simone continued and pulled Kennedy by the arm.

"Oh yeah, Michael, one more thing. Don't even think about coming home," Kennedy said and spit across the table into Michael's face.

Kennedy and Derrick walked out of the restaurant in silence. She looked at him with tears in her eyes. She thought Michael was the man for her, she was wrong. How could he do this to her after she had bragged about how much he loved her, how good he was? Derrick tried to hug her but she shrugged him off.

"Derrick, here. This is the reason that we came. We opened it by accident and we wanted to surprise you and meet Courtney . . . never mind," Simone said and handed him the letter from Harvard.

Derrick opened the letter, read it, and a hint of a smile spread across his face.

Kennedy invited Simone to stay the night with her at Michael's house. Embarrassed as she was, she didn't want to be alone and didn't want to stay at Simone's. Simone tried to convince her to invite Derrick over but Kennedy couldn't handle it, not right then anyway. Michael had hurt them both.

"Okay, the locksmith is gone and the locks are working," Simone said and handed Kennedy the keys.

"Thanks. You know what, Simone?" Kennedy lay on the bed.

"What?"

"I didn't see it coming, did you?" She turned away, not wanting Simone to see the hurt in her face.

"See what coming, Kennedy?"

"You know, about Michael. He didn't seem bi to me. I never would've guessed." Kennedy faced Simone.

"No, I can't say that I did. But I heard that you can't always tell. All bisexual and gay men aren't feminine, you know," Simone said and lay down next to Kennedy.

"I know now," Kennedy said and closed her eyes.

When Kennedy woke up Simone was standing over her, staring in her face.

"Kennedy, you up?"

"You see me looking at you?"

Simone put her hands on her hips. "Let me ask you a question. Did you pee in the bed last night or did you dream that you were peeing?"

"Simone, are you completely out of your mind?"

"Well, then we better go. I think your water broke," Simone said and smiled.

The bed was wet. Kennedy rubbed the sheets and brought her damp hand to her nose and smelled it.

"Kennedy, that's nasty. What are you doing?" Simone wrinkled her nose up.

"You're right, my water did break, it smells sweet. Amniotic fluid smells sweet, piss doesn't."

~ 18 ~

Kennedy had been in active labor for almost an hour when Jared walked in, carrying a picture of Kharri. He took down the generic hospital reproduction print from the wall and replaced it with Kharri's eight-by-ten. Kennedy smiled at him between pains because he had remembered her focus point. Simone looked at him as though he had two heads.

"What are you doing, Jared. Do you think *that's* good idea?" Simone pointed to the wall.

"Yes, it's a good idea. Kennedy needs something else to focus on besides her contractions. It's a Lamaze trick. We learned it a long time ago when we were expecting Kharri."

Kennedy moaned loud. She had forgotten how painful labor was but had been constantly reminded every few minutes. Focus. Breathe through the pain. She was having a hard time. Jared leaned over her and dabbed the sweat from her face. "Just breathe, Kennedy, don't hold your breath. That's it, in through the nose and out through the mouth. Try to exhale with the pain," Jared instructed with a calmness that only a health professional could master.

"That was a big one, Jared. I know the baby's going to be here any second—"

"Take your time, Ken. Look at Kharri's picture and remember how much of a joy she was to have around and just think that now you get to do it all over again. Simone, how long has she been contracting like this?" Jared held Kennedy's hand and read the graph to check Kennedy's progression.

"I don't know, Jared, I haven't been timing them. I just know that they've been pretty close together," Simone said.

"Jared, I feel like I have to go to the bathroom, and I know what that means." Kennedy gripped the bars on the side of the bed and held her breath.

"Get a nurse!" Jared yelled at Simone.

Kennedy lay on her left side and stared over at her son lying in the bassinet. He had made his appearance to the world at 10:37 on the morning of April fourth. Kennedy reached over, touched his face, and cried tears of joy.

With the tears still flowing down her face, Kennedy sat up and lifted the baby out of the bassinet and held him. He was so handsome, perfect, and small. Kennedy studied his face and saw so much of Kharri. Just as Kharri had, he would look like Kennedy.

"Open your eyes, little man, Mommy needs to see what you look like. I have to see your eyes in order to know what to name you." Kennedy grabbed the baby's little fist and shook it gently. She looked up and saw Jared standing in the doorway. "So are you just going to stand there all day and watch us, or are you going to come in and introduce yourself?" Kennedy smiled at Jared.

"I didn't want to interrupt. You two seemed to be having

a pretty deep conversation." Jared walked over and held out his hands. "Do you mind if I hold him?"

"Be careful. Doesn't he remind you of Kharri? Take a close look at him." Kennedy held out the baby to Jared.

"Now that you mention it, he does. He looks just like Kharri. What's his name?" Jared looked Kennedy in her eyes.

"He looks like a Niles to me. I'm naming him Niles, Niles James . . . after my father. And as far as him and Kharri looking exactly alike, it doesn't mean anything, Jared. Kharri looked just like me, remember. Anyway, when are they going to do the test?"

"Now, if you're ready."

"We're ready." Kennedy smiled at the thought of being a "we" again.

After the DNA test Jared left so Kennedy and the baby could get some rest. She had been so excited with the birth that she didn't realize how exhausted she really was. She lay the baby next to her and carefully cuddled him. She wasn't letting him sleep in the bassinet. He was exactly where he was meant to be—right next to her.

Kennedy felt herself drifting off in a deep sleep when Mrs. Montgomery's voice woke her up. Kennedy opened her eyes and saw Mrs. Montgomery standing by her bed, smiling. She looked so happy, and Kennedy hated to crush her spirits but she had to tell her the truth. Mrs. Montgomery would want to know why Michael wasn't there with her and the baby.

"Hey, Ma. How did you know I was here?"

"One of the sisters from the church was in the Emergency Room and saw you come in. She called me, bless her heart. You all right, sweetie?" Mrs. Montgomery bent down and kissed Kennedy's forehead.

"Yeah, Ma, I'm fine. Look at you all dolled up. Where are you going?"

"I ain't goin' nowhere but here, child. When Sister

Moreland called me, I just knew you were gonna have that baby. So I rushed to the church to pray and I asked God to minimize your pain. That's why I'm all dressed up—you know I ain't goin' in nobody's church in my street clothes. Although, it is all right. God says to come as you are, but I like to give Him my best because that's what he gives me, Hallelujah!" Mrs. Montgomery raised her hand in worship and held her own private prayer service.

Kennedy closed her eyes and waited for Mrs. Montgomery to finish asking God to bless the baby when the hospital room door clicked close. Kennedy opened her eyes and saw Michael standing there.

"Get out!" Kennedy yelled.

"What's goin' on, Kennedy? You all right?" Mrs. Montgomery held her chest.

"Get him out of here," Kennedy said, and Mrs. Montgomery turned to see Michael standing at the door.

"Kennedy, I know you're mad at me and you have a right to be, but please let me see the baby," Michael pleaded.

Kennedy ignored Michael and turned to Mrs. Montgomery. "Ma, do you know what your son did to me?" Kennedy watched Michael put his head down.

"Kennedy, don't—"

"Don't what, boy? Whatcha done did now, Michael?" Mrs. Montgomery turned to Michael and waited.

Michael put his hand out in defense. "Ma, it's between me and Kennedy."

"You heard your mother, Michael, now answer her question. Either you be a man and tell her, or I'll be a snitch and tell her for you. It's time to pay the piper, baby, now pay up." Kennedy laughed.

"Michael, you got two seconds to come clean with me, boy. Now what did you do to this girl to make her so mad? You know betta than to get her all worked up and she in here. Don'tcha know she could have died during labor? You mens don't think about that, but it's possible, you know. You got

Kennedy all upset and that precious baby is laying right next to her. Don't you know by now that a child can feel its momma's pain? I know I raised you betta than what you actin'."

The door creaked open, temporarily saving Michael from his mother's wrath. Simone walked in Kennedy's room, turned around, and walked back out.

———

As Simone stood in front of the door Derrick sauntered down the hall. She had called and told him to come to the hospital and was now sorry that she did. Simone waved and watched as he and Jared, who had shown up as soon as she stepped out of the room, shared a brotherly hug and then talked as they walked toward the waiting room. With Jared and Derrick gone, Simone peeked into Kennedy's room and asked if she was okay.

After Kennedy assured her that she was fine, she went to the waiting room and sat next to Derrick and whispered in his ear. She hated to be rude but had to let him know who was in Kennedy's room. Derrick scooted forward in his seat as though preparing to get up and leave.

Simone grabbed his sleeve. "Don't leave, Derrick. You don't have to go."

Jared sat looking through a magazine.

"I wasn't leaving. I'm going to Kennedy's room. I think I should be in there just in case my name comes up."

Jared put his magazine down. "Is everything okay? Is there something I need to know about that you guys aren't telling me?"

"Oh, it's nothing," Simone lied.

"Nothing?" Derrick turned and crinkled his face. "I'll tell you what happened, man, and it's not nothing. Maybe

Simone won't tell you, but I will. Our code of ethics, that's what you doctors go by, right? Well our code of ethics, mine and Simone's, are different."

Simone cleared her throat. "Jared, I don't mean to be rude, but I think that it's up to Kennedy to tell you. It's her business to tell, not ours."

"Well, if you say so," Jared said, shrugging.

"Simone, don't make me come over there and shake some sense into you. You went through all of that schooling and lost your common sense. It may not be your business to tell, but it's mine. I went through it too."

Simone listened as Derrick told Jared about his year-long relationship with Michael. Jared offered no expression at Derrick's admittance to being bisexual. Simone cringed as she heard the hurt in her brother's voice. Damn, she had only been feeling sorry for Kennedy, when she should've sympathized with them both. Derrick had lost more than Kennedy did. Even though Kennedy might have given Michael a child, it couldn't compare, because Derrick had given him his heart. Derrick was in love with Michael and Kennedy wasn't. Kennedy was in love with Jared.

Mrs. Montgomery was stunned. Her once flawless makeup was ruined by tears. Kennedy couldn't believe that Michael had stepped up and faced his mother like the man she knew he could be. No one had a dry eye in the room when Michael finished confessing his love for both men and women. Kennedy didn't know if she cried because she felt sorry for him or because she felt sorry for her child. All she knew was that she didn't hate Michael. As much as she wanted to, she couldn't.

Kennedy's heart went out to Michael. How unfair for a person to have to hide who he was. Life was hard enough without having to try to find a way to incorporate a hidden life. But as sorry as Kennedy felt for Michael, she felt even sorrier for Mrs. Montgomery.

Mrs. Montgomery was from the old school, the school that had been updated and revised, but one couldn't convince Mrs. Montgomery of that. Mrs. Montgomery thought she was right and the rest of the world was wrong and condemned to hell. But Kennedy knew the truth was, Mrs. Montgomery was afraid. She judged harshly because she was scared that someone would look down on her and her parenting skills because her sons weren't "all man."

Kennedy wiped her eyes. "Ma, let me ask you a question. How come you can't accept your sons for who they are?"

"Because I didn't raise no sissies, that's why. I didn't birth no boys in dresses." Mrs. Montgomery crossed her heavy arms over her massive chest.

"I understand that. But you know what, I just had a son and he's perfect—"

"Ain't nobody perfect in this world. Only Adam and Jesus, and Adam lost it. A perfect man ruined it for us and a perfect one saved us." Mrs. Montgomery pursed her lips.

"Ma, let me speak for a moment, okay? No one is here to judge you or your beliefs. All I was saying is, my son *is* perfect, whether you believe it or not. He's perfect just the way he is. You understand? We are all perfect being us, no one can be us better than we can. You got me? I can't be you better than you can and you can't be me. Just like I can't change you. I think you're just scared, Ma, I do."

"Kennedy, you talking a whole lotta jibber-jabber. And I ain't scared of nothing. I beg your pardon."

Kennedy, nodded hard. "Yes you are, Ma. You're scared that it's your fault that your sons are gay, but it's not. It's nobody's fault. You're scared that one of your church friends is going to look down on you. And I'll be honest with you,

I'm a little scared myself. I'm scared to have my son around you." Kennedy pointed out.

Mrs. Montgomery's jaw dropped. "What'cha mean. You know I wouldn't do nothing to that baby. Michael, you hear this, now you got this girl's mind polluted too."

"No, I'm afraid he doesn't. Nobody controls my mind. And the reason that I'm not too sure about having my child around you is because you would hurt him. You would love him with your all one day, and if he came up to you on another day and told you that he was gay, you would shun him and act as if he never lived or mattered. I'm right, aren't I, Ma?" Kennedy sat up and waited.

Michael stepped up. "Kennedy, you don't have to do this. I'll be okay."

"I'm not doing this for you, Michael, believe me I'm not. I'm doing this for my brother and your mother. I'm doing this because my brother must've thought that we'd treat him like your mom's treating you. And I'm trying to let your mom know that life is just life. It may not always be good, it may not always give us what we want, but it *is*. Take it or leave it, life is . . . life, and it's too short to waste with judgments and insecurities. Tantrums don't get us what we want. Are you listening, Ma?"

Mrs. Montgomery closed her eyes and shook her head. "Uh-huh, but don't mean I gotta agree."

Michael smiled for the first time since he had been in the room.

"You're right, you don't. But remember when that young woman who really loved you told you that life is hard enough as it is without trying to please everyone else by becoming two people. The person you really are and the someone else for everybody else?"

"Uh-uh, what young woman?" Mrs. Montgomery stopped shaking her head and stared at Kennedy.

"Me, Ma. I'm telling you this because I love you and you're just as much at fault as Michael is for hurting me. If you opened up your mind and your heart, he would've been able to be himself and he wouldn't have used me—without my permission or knowledge, I might add—to fool you."

Mrs. Montgomery held her Bible in the air. "That's nice that you're trying to take up for him, but it won't work. It says right here in Leviticus 20:13, that being gay is a sin—"

"Ma, stop it. Did you hear anything I just said? Answer me this, doesn't the Bible also say that one sin isn't greater than another?"

"Yes." Mrs. Montgomery flipped through her Bible.

Kennedy crossed her arms. "Well, what did you cook for dinner last Sunday?"

Mrs. Montgomery paused. "Last Sunday? Let me see . . . pork chops . . . I think. Why?"

Kennedy laughed. "In Leviticus eleven, verses one through seven, it says eating pork is a sin."

Simone twiddled her thumbs and Jared sat in silence. Derrick paced so many times that Simone thought that he was going to wear out a path in the carpet. Simone would've given anything to be a fly on the wall in Kennedy's room. She couldn't wait to find out what happened.

"Simone, did all that really happen? I believe Derrick but it's a little much to digest, you know," Jared said.

"Yeah, except he left out the part about Kennedy spitting in Michael's face. Other than that, that was everything. So how do you feel about what Derrick told you?"

"About him being attracted to men?"

Simone nodded.

"Nothing. I already knew—"

"What do you mean you already knew? He told you? Why didn't you say anything?"

Jared shook his head. "No, he didn't have to. I overheard

him on the phone one day. It wasn't my place to say anything. I felt when he was ready to tell us, he would. Besides I'm comfortable with who I am and who he is. It doesn't bother me. But what about Kennedy, how is she taking it?"

Simone sighed. "Honestly, I don't know. He went to hug her yesterday and she shrugged him off."

"That doesn't mean anything, that's just Kennedy being Kennedy. When we were together, when she was upset with someone else or something else she'd shrug my hugs away too. I don't think it was personal. But I'll tell you what's personal, that guy hurting her. I know we're not together but I don't want anybody hurting her. I hope I don't have to knock that fool out up in here, because I will," Jared said and flexed his right arm.

"Check you out, Jared. You got skills, huh." Simone bumped him.

Jared nodded seriously and tightened his jaw muscles.

Derrick went to the water fountain and saw an older woman come out of Kennedy's room. She had to be Michael's mother. Derrick stared at her as she came his way and she returned his stare with cold, glaring eyes. Derrick stood with his head held high. He refused to allow her to intimidate him as he had heard she had the power to do.

Derrick put his hands in his pockets as she got closer and then stopped about two feet in front of him. He held his ground and didn't say a word. He waited for her to speak because he wasn't going to explain himself to anybody, especially a woman he didn't know. And he was damned certain that he wasn't going to apologize. He was proud of who he was, and now that his family knew and loved and accepted him, he wasn't going to apologize to a stranger.

"You must be Derrick, Kennedy's brother. I can tell by your eyes. You have honest eyes like your sister. Will you be honest with me and answer a question for me?" Mrs. Montgomery wore a faint smile.

"Sure, what is it?" Derrick asked in a safe businesslike tone.

"Did my son approach you, or did you approach him?"

"Are you asking me if I turned your son gay?" Derrick asked bluntly.

Mrs. Montgomery looked at the floor and then into Derrick's eyes. "I guess, I don't understand gayness, so you'll have to excuse me."

"Well, I'll tell you this much. One, no one can turn someone gay, and two, it's not something you can catch. But I'm sure you already know it's not contagious. And no, I didn't approach your son first and he didn't approach me first either. It kind of just happened," Derrick explained and covered his mouth as he let out a laugh.

"Well, did you love him?"

"Yes, and as a matter of fact, I still do. It's unfortunate for me, but it's true." Derrick cleared his throat as he rocked back and forth on his heels.

Mrs. Montgomery surprised Derrick and hugged him. She stood on her tiptoes and whispered in his ear, "You know I may not agree. No, I don't agree. But you know love is all I ever wanted for my children, all of them. That's what any mother wants for her children—someone to love them. You take care, and I'll see you around. You know we got blood between us now. He's such a sweet baby." Mrs. Montgomery stepped back and continued, "Well, you are handsome, if I may say so myself. I can see why you turned my child's head."

Derrick stood in disbelief as Mrs. Montgomery sashayed down the hospital corridor in her matching purple skirt, blouse, and hat. He could tell she had really been something to reckon with in her day. She was feisty and quite a character with her beliefs. He turned and saw Simone and Jared staring at him. He held up his hands in the air.

Michael came out of Kennedy's room and tried to walk past but Derrick stopped him. "Michael, I need to talk to you. Now."

"I don't think now is such a good time, maybe later."

"I don't believe you're in the position to be declining or putting me off. You owe me an explanation."

"Okay, you're right. Meet me in the cafeteria in five minutes. I don't want to talk in front of them," he said, looking at Simone and Jared.

~ *19* ~

*S*imone unlocked the front door and eased it halfway open. Leery about walking into the house, she hesitated. A chill ran through her body. She was almost certain that she had only left one light on, but now almost all of them were on.

Simone stuck her head inside and peeked in. Everything seemed fine and in its place. *Dang, something smells good, the neighbors must be cooking up a storm,* she thought as she walked in and locked the door behind her. As she was about to put her keys on the table, she stopped. The garlicky smell was coming from inside the house. The farther she walked in, the more she smelled it.

Simone turned toward the front door and froze.

Someone was behind her. She was being watched; she felt it in the pit of her empty stomach.

"Nice of you to come home. Are you hungry?" Nigel asked in a pleasant tone.

Simone stood still and didn't say a word. She was afraid to turn around and afraid not to turn around. Nigel had a definite mental problem, and she didn't want to light his fuse. It wouldn't be hard to make him blow up. Simone decided to play along with Nigel's game and chose her words carefully.

"Hey, Nigel, I didn't know you were here. I must've left my door open again." Simone turned around and tried to read his face.

"No, you didn't leave the door open, you left a window open. I let myself in, I hope you don't mind. It's just that I was trying to get in touch with you . . . and I was worried about you. Where were you?"

"How long have you been waiting?" Simone plastered a fake smile on her face.

"A few hours. Just long enough to cook and dust."

"Oh, I've been gone a couple of days. I had my cast removed, then Kennedy had her baby and I stayed at her place getting it all ready for when the baby goes home. You know, as much shopping as that girl does, she hadn't even furnished the nursery yet," Simone rambled out of nervousness.

"That's great. What did she have?" Nigel asked, wiping his large hands on his stained apron.

"A boy. My, something smells good, I'm starving."

Nigel smiled. "Come on into the kitchen, I'll fix you a plate."

At the kitchen table Simone played with her food. She was waiting for Nigel to take a bite of his first. She didn't trust him and she didn't use the plates that he had laid out on the table. She even insisted that she fix the plates since he had been nice enough to cook.

Simone watched Nigel as he ate and hated that he had turned out bad. The truth was, Nigel had been a good man in the beginning, a man with whom she would've loved to have settled down. But the sad part was, that he was no longer that man. She had no idea who he was now, except for someone who put fear in her heart.

Nigel cleared the table and took Simone by the hand and led her to the living room. He gently grabbed her by the shoulders and sat her down. Nigel squatted down in front of her and swept her hair out of her eyes and kissed her on the cheek.

"I need to talk to you. I'm sorry about breaking in your house like I did, but I was worried."

"Don't worry about it. I'm just glad you took care of the house for me," Simone lied again. She prayed someone would call or come over.

"Simone, you don't have to lie to me. I know you're upset about it. It's okay, I'm not going to do anything to you. I've changed. I started seeing a therapist and I've even been going to anger-management classes. I didn't realize that I had so many issues and insecurities." Nigel laughed.

"That's good, Nigel. I'm proud of you. It takes a big person to make a move like that. None of us likes to admit to needing help. I could use some therapy myself."

"You? Please, you're the sanest person that I know. You don't need therapy. If anything, you should be the one counseling somebody." Nigel smiled.

The longer Simone and Nigel talked, the more at ease Simone became. He seemed like the same laid-back man he used to be. She was still careful, reminding herself of what he had done. She knew if she didn't act right, he could harm her again.

Nigel suggested that they go out for drinks, and for some reason unbeknownst to Simone she agreed. Nigel had been a perfect gentleman and even suggested that for Simone's comfort, they drive separate cars. He let Simone decide on the place and how long they should stay.

Simone sat across the booth from Nigel, falling into his

trap again. She had to keep reminding herself that he was half-man and half-monster. But the more she drank, the more her memory faded.

Simone woke up with a hangover. Her head was killing her and her mouth was drier than hot cotton. Afraid to sit up, she didn't even want to think about what she had done the night before.

Nigel walked in the room and opened the curtains. Simone grabbed the pillow next to her and covered her face. She didn't know how he could be up and walking around after the previous night. He drank more than she did.

"Good morning, sleepy head, how're you feeling?"

"Terrible, what time is it?"

"Two in the afternoon. Here, drink this and you'll feel better." Nigel handed Simone a tall glass of fizzing water.

"Alka Seltzer? That's Kennedy's remedy." Simone laughed and downed the drink.

"Come downstairs and eat. I'll warm up the leftovers."

"In a minute. I have to take a shower first."

Simone walked in the kitchen and smiled. Nigel was at the sink washing dishes. In all their time together she had never seen him lift a finger to clean up anything related to the kitchen. The table was spread with chicken and waffles.

"You like it?" Nigel asked as Simone gobbled down the last bite of food on her plate.

"Mmm-hmm," Simone mumbled with a mouth full of food.

"Simone, I need to talk to you."

"I don't know if that's such a good idea."

"Don't worry, it's not about what you think."

Nigel shocked Simone. He said that they moved too fast. Simone had agreed and suggested that they remain friends. But she purposely left out that she didn't want to be close friends and she didn't want him coming around her house.

The night before had been a mistake, and she vowed not to let it happen twice. Nigel had gotten his and she had gotten hers a couple of times, so all was fair.

"Simone, do you mind if my granddaughter comes over? Kaisha paged me while you were still asleep and asked if I'd watch her."

"Sure, it's no problem. Bring her over, I'd like to see her," Simone said, hoping that Kaisha would pick her up so Simone could find out what Kaisha wanted to tell her so badly.

"Great, I'll call Kaisha right away and tell her. You sure you don't mind? Because if so, it's no problem."

Simone merely waved at him.

Simone instantly fell in love with Kaisha's daughter and refused to put her down. Everywhere Simone went, the baby went. She was such a little doll, and Simone started calling her Kiss because she reminded Simone of the candy—little, sweet, with skin a smooth, flawless brown.

Simone laid Kiss down for a nap in the crib that was meant for the baby she lost. She had planned to clear out the nursery for months, but didn't have the courage to go in. Kiss changed all of that.

"Nigel, does Kiss have a nursery set?"

"Who? Oh, you mean Uniqua? No, I don't think so. Besides the things that I bought, I think she just has some little cheap crib that Kaisha bought her, why?"

"Because I was thinking that she could have the furniture in the nursery. It's still brand-new, I even have plenty of extra wallpaper and borders to match."

"I think that would be a good idea. I'll ask Kaisha. I'm sure she won't mind. She'll know it's good quality stuff. She knows your style."

Simone woke up on the sofa to the sound of the telephone ringing. She reached to get it too late. She looked at the caller ID. Simone scratched her head and glanced at her watch. She hadn't planned on falling asleep. Simone smiled as she heard Kiss breathing over the baby monitor.

Simone propped her feet up on the coffee table and Nigel walked in the front door carrying bags. She hadn't even known that he was gone.

"Oh, you're up. I was sure you were going to be asleep for a while, the way you were going at it." Nigel set the bags on the dining room table in the adjoining room.

"I just got up. What you got there? Anything sweet?"

"Nope, just Pampers and formula. She up yet?"

"Not yet." Simone stretched. "Oh, Kaisha called while I was asleep. I didn't make it to the phone in time. Her number's on the caller ID."

"She's probably just calling to check on Uniqua. I'll call her in a minute." Nigel walked into the kitchen.

Simone lay back down on the sofa to do something she rarely did, watch television. She could overhear Nigel in the kitchen talking to himself as he sterilized Kiss's bottles.

Simone was flipping through the channels on the television when Nigel walked past her with a bottle. He picked up the cordless phone from the coffee table and went upstairs. What was he going to do with a bottle? Kiss was still asleep. She hoped that Kaisha wasn't listening to the hospital and waking Kiss up to be fed. Babies needed to learn how to sleep through the night, and if continually awakened they'd never get used to sleeping for long periods.

Fed up with the junk on television, Simone decided to go over some paperwork. She reached in her purse, found her reading glasses, and got to work.

A deep raspy mumble came over the baby monitor. Simone guessed that Kiss was still asleep because Nigel was whispering, but she could hear him loud and clear talking to Kaisha. Simone got out of her seat to turn down the volume on the monitor, but changed her mind.

Simone dropped her pen to the floor. She almost couldn't believe her ears but knew that they wouldn't lie to her as

Nigel did. Simone took off her glasses and chewed on one of the tips while she pondered on what to do. Should she go upstairs and risk her life again, or sit and be stupid? Simone jumped up from the sofa, reached for her cell phone, and decided to go upstairs.

Kennedy held Niles as she looked at the envelope in her hands. She was scared to death to open it. Since Jared would be there any minute, she'd wait for him. He wouldn't be scared.

Kennedy checked the water in the baby bathtub. Niles's umbilical cord had finally fallen off and Kennedy couldn't wait to bathe him. It had taken his so much longer than Kharri's, but she had to remember—he wasn't Kharri. He was Niles. And she knew she couldn't bathe him before it fell off, but she felt so sorry for him. The poor thing had to wait almost a month before having a bath.

Niles was just getting settled into the bath when Jared rang the bell. Kennedy shook her head in disbelief. She didn't want to make Jared wait outside. Even though spring had warmed the weather a bit, it was still flu season. Kennedy picked up Niles and wrapped him in a heavy, over-sized Egyptian cotton bath towel and went to answer the door.

Kennedy cracked the door and yelled for Jared to wait thirty seconds before coming in. She didn't want Niles to get a chill from the draft, so she made sure that she took him back in the bathroom first.

Jared walked into the bathroom and closed the door tight behind him.

"How did you know we were in here? I didn't say any-thing about the bathroom."

"You're kidding, right? Please, you used to pull the same

thirty-second thing when Kharri was a baby, remember? So how's my little man doing? He's getting big. Ain't that right, little man?" Jared shook Niles's little hand.

"Big and heavy. So I see it didn't take you any time to get here. What did you do, get a police escort or something?" Kennedy teased.

"Almost." Jared smiled. "Do you have his clothes out already?"

"No, I usually dress him in his room. His underclothes and PJ's are in the top two drawers of the chest."

"I'll get them together. I'll go warm his bottle up too. Looks like it's sleepy time for somebody." Jared walked out.

Kennedy sat in front of the fireplace with her legs crossed Indian style. Waiting for Jared to finish putting Niles to sleep, she traced her fingers between the bricks on the fireplace. She thought about the letter. If Jared were Niles's father, it'd be easier.

The last thing Kennedy wanted was to have her child doing the split custody thing again. If Jared was the father, maybe they could get back together. Kennedy wanted him back anyway, but didn't think it fair to ask him to take her back if Niles wasn't his.

Jared walked in and plopped down on the sofa. Kennedy stepped over to sit on his lap. Her mind told her that she was supposed to wait six weeks, but her body was screaming "feed me." Kennedy ignored the mind-over-matter logic and started to rock back and forth. Jared's penis became hard and pressed against her bottom, so she slowed her rock and added pressure.

"You sure you want to do this?" Jared whispered.

"Do what? I'm not doing anything." Kennedy bit her bottom lip seductively.

"Stop playing. You know what you're doing. Did you go to the doctor yet?"

Kennedy turned toward him, kissed him, and nodded. She

was playing dirty, but she didn't care. She wanted to feel Jared. And once that envelope was opened, she knew that she might never get the chance again.

Jared lifted Kennedy off him and kissed her. "Where at?"

Kennedy pointed upstairs toward her bedroom. Jared took her by the hand and led her there.

Jared turned up the volume on the baby monitor and Kennedy went to the bathroom to get a condom. She held the condom up in the air and waved it toward Jared, wanting him to know that she was prepared this time. She pushed him back on the bed and climbed on top of him. She planned on giving him the ride of his life.

Jared ran his hands up and down her legs, then finally made it up under her dress. Kennedy moaned as he touched where her panties were supposed to be. She smiled. Today was one of her "free," no-panty days. Kennedy bent to kiss Jared as he caressed, teased, and played hide-and-seek with his fingers. He tasted so good. Kennedy slid off him and undid his pants and pulled them and his boxers off at the same time. She licked her lips at the sight of his penis and tingled all over. Jared was a package deal, his manhood was big and pretty, curving up just so. He had the most perfect piece of chocolate she had ever seen and she couldn't wait to taste it. She reached between her legs and stuck her finger inside while Jared watched. She took her finger out and stuck it in his mouth.

She grabbed Jared's penis and traced the top with her finger. She looked at it and then at Jared.

"Did you bathe today?" she asked bluntly.

"Of course." Jared grinned slyly.

"Good," Kennedy said as she bit her bottom lip and then licked her friend in her right hand. It was her turn to play hide-and-seek with Jared in her mouth. Jared moaned and sat partially up and grabbed Kennedy by her shoulders—his signal that the volcano could erupt any moment. Kennedy slowed and worked her way up Jared's body, kissing and licking here and there. When she got to his nipples she stopped and began nibbling them.

Jared grabbed Kennedy and flipped her under him. He pulled the switch so fast that Kennedy didn't know he was on top of her until she felt him working his way down her stomach. Jared stopped at her navel and put his tongue in it. Kennedy loved to watch him work his tongue, he was the best.

Jared's tongue lapped Kennedy's navel and traveled to her breasts. First her left one and then her right. Kennedy arched her back each time he licked, sucked, and nibbled. Jared grabbed both of her breasts at the same time and gave them equal treatment. He lifted his head and kissed her deeply as he pulled her short hair. He stopped and looked into her eyes. Kennedy was crying and he licked away her tears.

Kennedy couldn't take anymore of the foreplay. She wanted Jared, and she wanted him that very second. But he wasn't having it. Jared slid to the floor, at the bottom of the bed, and positioned himself on his knees. He grabbed Kennedy by her thighs and pulled her down until her butt was hanging off the bed. Jared put his arms under her thighs and lifted her until her entrance met his face.

Jared licked her thighs deeply. The closer he got to her entrance the deeper he licked. He played lick, kiss, suck, in rotation, switching from one thigh to the other. Finally he licked between her lips and above them. She shivered as he sucked her clit, and cried when she reached the point of no return.

Kennedy grabbed Jared and led him into her. She moaned as she felt him separate her. How she could take all of him, she never knew. He was definitely blessed. She closed her eyes and let him take her to heaven over and over. While there she planned to ask God to please let the DNA results say that Jared was the father.

~ 20 ~

*D*errick never met Michael in the cafeteria. He planned to, but sneaking made him feel like old times when he was still hiding himself from the world. Michael called him a few times but Derrick refused to answer or return his calls. What was done was done. The person he really needed to speak to was Kennedy. He hadn't called her and she hadn't called him.

Derrick waited for the light to turn green on Central Park West, so he could make a right into the park. He hated not being able to make a right on red in New York. He sat, waited, thought about Kennedy, and decided to stop by Simone's house. She would want to help. Maybe she would play mediator again. But that would never work. He had to face Kennedy on his own.

Finally he called Kennedy.

"Hello."

"Hey, sis, it's me, Derrick. Did I catch you at a bad time?"

"Well sort of, Jared's over. But it's okay. What's up?"

"I was just wondering if I could talk to you for a second." Derrick mentally crossed his fingers.

"Come on over. You know where I'm at, right?" Kennedy laughed.

"Actually, I do. Give me about ten," Derrick said and hung up.

Derrick knocked on Kennedy's door a few minutes later, and Jared let him in. Derrick didn't know what he had just walked into, but he could take a good guess. Kennedy and Jared both had permanent smiles plastered on their faces. They all spoke and Jared went upstairs.

"So what's up, D? You want to know if I'm mad at you, right?"

"Yeah. I haven't heard from you, so I-I thought that maybe you were." Derrick sat down.

"Did it ever occur to you to call me? I wasn't sure how you felt about me. I did sort of push you away that night. But I was upset, so no hard feelings? I'm not mad at you, D. You're my brother and I know you would never hurt me. I know that you didn't know about me either." Kennedy stood with her arms open.

Derrick hugged her.

"So do you still love him?" Kennedy asked.

"Unfortunately, but it'll fade. It always does, right?"

"Not always. Look at me and Jared. So what are you going to do about it?"

"What do you mean, what am I going to do? He was sleeping with you, my sister. Niles may be his son—"

"And he might not. Let's pray it's not. But seriously, I think that you should talk to him. I don't think he really cared about me, he was just using me. You were who he really wanted."

"But he slept with you. That's nasty . . . I don't mean it like it sounds. But it's sort of incestuous, don't you think?"

"I guess so. But you know what, we never had sex unless we were drinking . . . usually a lot, now that I think about it. See, I didn't catch on. I assume he needed alcohol to be with a woman." Kennedy shrugged. "I don't know. He was smooth, played the I respect-you-too-much, I-love-you-for-more-than-that card on me. I lost the game, D. He was a card shark for real." Kennedy grinned.

"I don't know, Ken . . . I can't. I won't talk to him."

Kennedy and Derrick talked a while more before he left. He didn't want to disturb what was going on with her and Jared. She wasn't rude about it, but he knew that she wanted him to go. If he had someone in his life that could plaster a permanent smile on his face, he wouldn't want company either.

Derrick decided to go home. Against his better judgment he was going to call Michael. Although he had no intentions of getting back with him, he did feel that he was owed a formal apology and explanation.

Derrick turned on his street. Michael's black car sat parked in front of his brick condo like old times. "Careful what you ask for," he said and pulled into his driveway.

Simone called 911 from her cell phone and reported that Nigel had broken into her house and was beating her up. She knew that the cops would take at least thirty minutes to get there. Nigel hadn't touched her yet, but once she confronted him, he would.

When Simone was eavesdropping courtesy of the baby monitor she learned that she had been lied to, cheated on, and tricked. Nigel and Kaisha had pulled the ultimate betrayal.

Kaisha wasn't Nigel's daughter, she was his teenage girlfriend. And the baby was his child, not his grandchild. Simone had heard Nigel threaten to blacken Kaisha's other eye and kill her if she didn't do what he wanted. He never said what it was, but Simone could tell that Kaisha wasn't too keen on doing it.

Simone cracked open the front door and went into the kitchen and turned the fire on under a pan of chicken grease. Then she went upstairs to Kiss's room and pulled Nigel by his arm. He looked up at her and smiled. Simone quietly beckoned him to come downstairs.

Simone was in the kitchen packing the baby's things in the diaper bag when Nigel walked in.

"What are you doing? You're ready for us to go?" Nigel came up behind Simone and tried to hug her.

Simone pushed Nigel off her. "You can get your shit and get out. I can't believe you or Kaisha. I guess you didn't know that I could hear your whole conversation, did you?"

Nigel stood stuck-on-stupid still.

"Well, I could hear everything over the baby monitor, stupid. I can't believe you! How could you? Tell me that. How long, Nigel? How long?" Simone said and pushed him.

"Simone, look man, don't. I don't want to have to hurt you—"

"Yes, you do. The only reason you're not is because you're wrong and you're scared. You see I'm not afraid this time and I've got something for you. You got one minute to get out of my house." Simone leaned against the counter.

Nigel snapped just as Simone knew that he would. He grabbed her by her throat. Simone dug her fingernails into his eyes and he let her go. "Is that all you got?" Simone said and slapped him. Nigel punched Simone in the side of her face and then in her stomach. He tried to knock her down but the counter kept her up.

Simone grabbed her stomach as she caught her breath and reached for the pan on the stove. Nigel took one step toward Simone and she threw the hot chicken grease on him.

Simone slid down the cabinet and onto the floor. The police yelled from the front door. She hollered back. They came in and took one look at her face and read Nigel his rights while the paramedics took care of him.

Simone told the police that Nigel had killed her baby. Nigel didn't know that she had reported his name to the hospital, and to the officers on duty who questioned her. She could only give them a name, because she didn't know his new address or place of employment.

After the cops left, Simone cleaned up the kitchen and sat down in the chair with a cup of coffee. She was just starting to settle herself when the baby cried. Simone picked up the phone and pressed redial. Kaisha answered on the first ring.

————

Kennedy stared at the floor while Jared opened the envelope. She tightened her hold on Niles and hugged him hard. She gathered her nerve and looked up at Jared. His deep brown eyes were misty and he took a slow loud swallow of nothing.

"I knew it, Jared. I knew it was going to be you. I prayed and prayed. I see you over there getting all emotional." Kennedy went to hug him with Niles in her arms.

"I'm not the father, Kennedy. It says there is no possible way that I can be the biological father." Jared hung his head.

"No, Jared, don't tell me that. Please don't tell me that." Kennedy started to cry and rocked Niles, who was also crying.

Dear God. She didn't want her child to be passed back and forth as though he were some borrowed item. She didn't want to have to explain to him that his father didn't prefer women. She didn't want him to have Michael's blood. She didn't want him to be anyone's other than Jared's.

Jared reached out for Niles. Reluctantly she let Jared hold him.

"Do you mind if Niles and I have a few minutes alone?" Jared hugged Niles and kissed him on the cheek.

"Okay. I think it'll do me some good to be alone for a few anyway. I'll be in the shower if he needs anything." Kennedy walked out of the room.

———

Derrick sat at the kitchen table and sipped his coffee, waiting for Michael to speak. Michael had drank two cups of coffee and hadn't said a word.

"So why did you come here again, to talk to me?" Derrick said.

"Yes. I wanted to tell you that I am truly sorry. I didn't mean to hurt you—"

"Or Kennedy."

Michael set down his cup. "Yes, or Kennedy. I want you to know that I didn't plan on seeing both of you—"

Derrick tapped his foot on the kitchen floor. "Who did you start seeing first?"

"It's kind of hard to say. I became friends with both of you around the same time. Kennedy and I started out the same way you and I did . . . just friends. I didn't mean to, I really didn't. Did Kennedy tell you that she and I talked?"

"Yes, but I already knew. I was at the hospital, remember? Did your mom tell you that she talked to me?"

Michael's eyebrows shot up. "No. She wasn't rude, was she?"

"Actually, she wasn't. Michael, I want you to know that I don't forgive you. Maybe one day, but not today." Derrick set his cup down.

"That's understandable. Do you mind if I get my things that I left here?"

"No, I would prefer it if you did, but you're not getting the car back." Derrick smirked.

Kaisha sat down on Simone's sofa while Simone went upstairs to get the baby. Simone swallowed hard—she would never see Kiss again. Simone carefully got her dressed and then kissed her on the cheek.

"I'm going to miss you, Kiss. You're so beautiful and I hope you have a wonderful life." Simone hugged and kissed her some more.

Simone walked slowly down the stairs, trying to compose herself. Even though Kiss was just a baby, she didn't want to argue in front of her. The nerve of Kaisha, comfortably sitting on her sofa.

"Here's your baby. I packed all of her stuff in those diaper bags. The one Nigel brought with her and one that I gave to her." Simone handed the baby to Kaisha.

"No, you hold her. I still have something that I need to tell you. When is Dad—Nigel getting back?" Kaisha watched the door.

"Oh, I'm afraid that you won't be seeing your man for a long time. He's locked up *under* the jail." Simone smiled her sweetest smile.

"Oh my God—"

"Don't be too upset, God didn't do it, Nigel did, and he deserved it. And if it was up to me, you'd be with him."

"I'm not upset, I'm happy." Tears started to roll down Kaisha's beaming face.

"What?"

"That's what I wanted to talk to you about, and that's why I was so scared."

Simone sat and listened to Kaisha's horror story. Nigel had done Kaisha worse than he had done Simone. He had met Kaisha when she was sixteen years old and living in a group home. He took her out, bought her clothes and jewelry, made her call him Daddy, and convinced her to run away and be with him. He promised to take care of her. But all he did was beat her and then turn around and screw her. He wouldn't let her have any friends or go anywhere. For two years he didn't allow her out of the house without him.

"Well, why didn't you just say something while you were here?" Simone asked.

Kaisha stared at her feet. "Because he'd beat me. He brought me here so I'd learn to be like you. That's what he told me. He said I had to pretend to be his daughter and you'd never know the difference because me and him look alike. That's what everybody says. He also told me if I said anything that he'd pistol whip me again." Kaisha cried uncontrollably.

Simone's jaw dropped. "He pistol whipped you?"

"Yes. He pistol whipped me when I didn't feel like going down on him. I was only sixteen, I was scared."

"Kaisha, I am so sorry for you. Honey, you should've reported him. You should've done something, but I guess you didn't know. So that's why you were so scared that day on the phone. You were hiding from him, huh?" Simone rubbed Kaisha's back as she cried.

"Simone, I need to ask you something. I heard you talking on the monitor to Uniqua—"

Simone laughed. "That's how I found out about you and Nigel. He was in the nursery talking to you. What is it you want to ask? Take your time, try to stop crying."

Kaisha wiped her eyes and looked at Simone. "I was just wondering if me and my baby could spend the night. I can't move into my new place until tomorrow and we don't have anywhere to go tonight."

Simone hesitated. She really wanted to be alone. "Sure, Kaisha, that'll be just fine."

Simone made up the guest bedroom for Kaisha. As mad as she was earlier, she didn't have the heart to send her out into the street. Besides, Kaisha was just as banged up as she was. They had twin scars on the sides of their heads and fresh black eyes.

Simone patted the baby's back and put her to sleep. She decided to let Kiss sleep with her while Kaisha slept on the sofa. Deadly thoughts of Nigel clouded her mind. Simone had become a statistic. *Never again,* she thought as she turned off the light.

Simone woke up bright and early the next morning. She didn't know how she had so much energy after Kiss had kept her up most of the night. As soon as the clock struck eight, Simone called in sick. She couldn't go to work bruised up. She checked on Kiss, who was sound asleep, and went to get a bottle.

Simone called Kaisha's name from the stairs and received no answer. "She must have beat me to the punch," Simone said. *I guess I'll just make coffee instead of formula,* she thought, as she walked into the kitchen. Kaisha wasn't there either. Simone tilted her head in deep thought. Something wasn't right. She proceeded to check every room in the house. Kaisha wasn't to be found anywhere. Simone plopped down on the sofa where Kaisha had slept. On the coffee table she saw a note.

Please take care of Uniqua because I can't. She deserves a good home and mother, things I can't give her and you can. I'm sorry, but I'm too young to be a mother, so I want you to have her.
Kaisha

Kennedy lay on the bed and stared at the ceiling. She clutched Kharri's journal tightly. She had forgotten about it. When she had tried to go back to the living room, Jared had kicked her out. He and Niles were still having their talk, as Jared referred to it. She went upstairs to clean out her closet, and tucked in the back was the journal. She sat up and opened the cover.

> *For my sweet daughter, Kharri,*
> *By the time you read this you will no longer be a little girl, but you will forever be my baby. I have always loved you—even before you were born. You are my everything and I promise to do my best, give my all, and if need be, sacrifice my life for your happiness. This journal is my gift to you. I start this today, the day of your birth and will continue to write in it until you're a woman. I will record all the important things in life—good and bad, to help you in your journey through womanhood. These thoughts are only my own . . . take them and do with them your will. I am sure that by the time you receive this, you will have more to add, for you will be a woman yourself. Pay close attention to the words because behind them is my love.*
> *Love,*
> *Mommy*

Kennedy ran her finger across the page. Kharri would never receive the journal. A lump formed in her throat. "Why baby, why? Why did you have to leave so soon? I had so many plans for you. And I know you had millions of smiles left," she said to herself.

Kennedy put the journal on the dresser and picked up Kharri's picture. She thought of Simone losing her baby. At least God had blessed her with her Kharri for a little while. At least He had given her that happiness. She smiled at Niles's picture. What was taking Jared and Niles so long? Didn't they realize what she was going through? No, they couldn't.

Kennedy's smile faded. She had gambled with sex, and

Niles lost. No matter how hard she prayed, Jared wouldn't be his father. She dreaded the phone call that she had to make, but eventually she'd have to. There was no way around it.

Jared knocked on the open door. "Can we come in?"

"Don't be silly, of course you can. Isn't that right, Niles?" Kennedy sat up and reached for her son.

"Not just yet. We have something to tell you." Jared pulled Niles back, smiled, and sat next to Kennedy.

"I'm listening."

"Well, we decided . . . that I can still be Niles's father. Maybe not his biological, but still, his father. Niles gave me his permission, he loves me. Can't you tell, just look at his face." Jared smiled and held Niles in the air.

"What, you're serious, aren't you? You mean you still want to be in his life even though he's not yours—"

"Oh, but he *is* mine. And he has something he wants to ask you, here, you take him." Jared handed Niles to Kennedy.

Niles started to fuss. "What is it, little man, you hungry?"

"I think he wants his pacifier, it's tucked in his shirt," Jared offered.

"Why is it tucked in his shirt?" Kennedy asked as she pulled Niles's pacifier ribbon out of his shirt. She screamed.

On the same ribbon as Niles's pacifier was an engagement ring. At a loss for words, all she could do was give the biggest smile that she had.

Kennedy put Niles's empty bottle in the sink and had just begun to run the dishwater when the doorbell rang. She thought about Jared's proposal. She loved him, but she needed to get herself together first. She hated crushing his heart but she couldn't give him an answer. Kennedy picked up a drying towel and smiled. She must look like Mrs. Montgomery, walking to the front door with a towel in her hands.

Kennedy opened the door and Michael nodded. Ever since the incident in the restaurant and the hospital, he had not been his usual charming self. He talked less, smiled even less, and didn't look like himself. But then again, he wasn't. He was a man free of his secrets.

Kennedy stepped back and held open the door. Michael walked in and looked around. She had changed the place completely since throwing him out. She had gotten rid of everything that reminded her of him and his deception.

"You don't have to just stand there. You can sit down, you know. The house is still in your name," Kennedy teased uncomfortably.

"Oh, okay. I was just admiring your handiwork. The house looks good, but I really couldn't expect less from you. You did a really good job," Michael said as he pulled up his pants leg and sat down.

"Thanks for coming." Kennedy sat opposite him.

"No, thank you for asking. I never would've thought that you'd want to see me again. Where's Niles?"

"I just finished putting him to sleep less than twenty minutes ago."

"And Jared?" Michael rubbed his hands together.

"Oh, he left a couple of hours ago. But I didn't ask you here so we could talk about Jared. We need to talk about Niles. Niles's not . . ." Kennedy hesitated.

"Kennedy, really, we could've done this over the phone. I know that I hurt you and I've said it I don't know how many times, but I am truly sorry. I know you hate me, and you have every right. But did you really have to call me over here to break my heart? Must you see the look on my face when you tell me that he isn't mine?" Michael frowned and clasped his hands together.

Kennedy cleared her throat before she spoke. "As I was saying, Niles isn't Jared's son, he's yours—"

"Are you serious?" Michael jumped up and laughed. "I don't know what to say. It's like everything is going . . . I'm finally happy. Thank you. Thank you for my beautiful son. Thank you for telling me. I just knew that you were going to tell me that he wasn't mine. I promise to be the best father to him, better than anyone has ever had. Do you mind if I go in and take a look at him? I just want to watch him breathe. I want to watch my son breathe."

"Sure, but we have to finish talking first." Kennedy began to cry.

"Kennedy, what's wrong? I promise that I won't hurt him. And I promise that I won't do anything to confuse him when he gets older. I know that you didn't want to have a baby by a man who's . . . a man of my sexual preferences. But I won't do anything wrong." Michael knelt down and grabbed Kennedy's hand.

"No, it's not that. I don't care about your sexuality. Apart from you hurting me, I know that you'd never do anything to hurt Niles. It's just that I didn't want to go through this. It's not supposed to be like this." Kennedy sobbed.

"Like what, Ken?"

"Like this, just look around. I didn't want to raise a child alone again. I know that you're going to be there. I don't question that. But we're not together and we never can be. I was supposed to have children by someone that I'd spend my life with . . . that's how I always planned it. I didn't want to go through the back and forth. I get him on certain days and you get him on certain days. It's bullshit and it's not fair to him. What kind of life is he supposed to have like that, being split in two?" Kennedy pulled her hand from Michael's grasp and got up and started to pace, wiping tears from her face.

"Are you trying to tell me that you want full custody? Please don't say that—"

"Michael, don't. I'm not that kind of woman. Do I look

that horrible to you? Do you think that I would just pull my child's father from under his feet? I would never deny my child his father, never! I just didn't want to go through the same thing as I went through with Kharri."

"Ken, it's going to be okay, I promise." Michael went and held Kennedy as Jared walked through the door.

~ *21* ~

*D*errick grabbed his black linen pants from the closet and put them on. He turned around in front of the mirror and winked. In his own way, he had always been vain, but only when he knew that he looked good. He straightened the collar on his cream-colored linen shirt and adjusted his gold cross. He was ready to go.

The sun's vibrant rays mingled with the blue sky. At seventy-seven degrees the weather was perfect. It wasn't too hot or too sticky. It was definitely a day for a party. The breeze just barely tickled the green leaves on the trees, while the birds seemed to sing their own rendition of "Happy Birthday" to him.

Derrick opened the glass doors and paused. Contagious

laughter drifted in the air, forcing him to smile. Summer engulfed him, greeting him when he stepped out. Gripping the redwood deck, Derrick rocked his body to the familiar song blasting from his neighbor's open windows. Evelyn Champagne-King. Bobbing his head to the melodic voice, he began dancing and thanking the heavenly Father for shining his light on him. Derrick finally felt at ease in his life. He'd reached his point of honesty, and Michael no longer permeated his thoughts—not too often.

After watching the neighborhood kids play kickball, he went back inside. He locked everything up and adjusted the temperature on his A/C. He loved coming home to the icebox-cool air. On his way out he grabbed Kennedy's gift. A smile spread across his face. He knew she would love it; she always loved his gifts.

Derrick turned on his car ignition and Maxwell filled the air. He turned the volume up. Nothing like a Maxwell song to help him get out and on his way. Derrick cruised while tapping his fingers to the beat on the steering wheel. He looked in the rearview mirror and put on his shades.

Jericha had the kids ready when he got to her house. He was surprised to see her smiling at him. Usually she just frowned and put her hand out for money. But today she was different, she was nice.

Derrick kissed little Derrick and Angelica and strapped them into the backseat. Lately Jericha had been letting him see them a lot, and nothing could've pleased him more. He loved his kids but wasn't able to be the kind of father he wanted to be. Jericha had seen to that.

"You're looking nice, Jericha. How've you been?" Derrick gave Jericha a slight peck on the cheek.

Jericha drew back. "Fine, just great. I guess you heard, 'cause you're being awfully nice."

"No, heard what?"

"Oh, I'm expecting another baby. And we're moving out of town—"

"What do you mean *we're* moving out of town? Don't you think you should've discussed it with me first?" Derrick's temples started to throb.

"Not all of us. The kids don't want to go, they don't like my boyfriend. They're going to stay behind and live with my sister. I thought you knew."

"No, I didn't. But do you think they should stay with your sister? I mean she has five kids of her own and a small apartment. I think they should stay with me. I am their father. When are you leaving?" Derrick asked.

"Well, I'm leaving in three days. I thought they told you. Are you sure that you want them with you?"

Derrick softened his tone because he could see that Jericha wasn't trying to be disagreeable. "Of course, they're my children."

"Okay, fine. I'll get their stuff together. I think they'll be more happier with you anyway." Jericha smiled and hugged Derrick.

———

Simone finished tidying her house. She double-checked to make sure that everything was just so. Satisfied with her work indoors, she headed out to the backyard. The food was almost finished on the grill, thanks to Jared. He had been a great help.

Simone straightened the patio furniture and finished putting out the plastic plates and plastic-ware. She went into the kitchen and took the lasagna from the oven and finished frying the chicken. The baked macaroni was done and she put it back in the stove to keep warm. Now the only thing left to do was to take the potato salad out of the refrigerator.

Miranda had drove in for the party and brought some food

and drinks. Simone had all of the juices, soda, and water, but she didn't know what to get as far as alcohol, so she left it up to Miranda.

Jared carried out extra chairs, but not before he started peeking in the food dishes.

"Jared, you better get out of that food. But it smells good, doesn't it?" Simone asked, scratching her arm where the cast had been.

"Yep. Do you think we could sneak a taste without everybody knowing?" Jared picked up a fork.

"No, and you better not. Everyone will be here soon. Are you sure that you're okay with Michael coming over? It's going to be a little intense." Simone leaned against the kitchen counter.

Jared raised his thick eyebrows. "Why should it bother me? I have his woman and I'm raising his child, it doesn't bother me at all. If anything, he's going to be the one uncomfortable."

"Be nice now, Jared, okay. It's Kennedy's and Derrick's birthday and I don't want anyone to ruin it." Simone crossed her arms.

"Simone, now you know better than that. That's not my M.O., and I see him all the time. He does come over to visit his son, you know. I don't have a problem with Michael, and we just had a man-to-man last week. I walked in and he was holding Kennedy, or at least I thought he was. He was just comforting her. I guess she really broke down when she told him that he was Niles's biological father. He seemed pretty cool after I spoke to him for a few. Besides, I don't have anything to worry about. My life is together. I have a beautiful woman I plan to knock up as soon as possible and a wonderful son I plan to raise as my own." Jared kissed Simone on the cheek and walked out as she laughed.

Kennedy stopped by Michael's house to pick up Niles. She hated to go in his house but he never had Niles ready on time. He knew when she had said she'd be there, but that didn't make him move any faster.

In Niles's room she was surprised to see a ceiling full of balloons. She smiled and found her way to the other side of the nursery to get Niles's diaper bag.

"Do you like them?" Michael asked from the doorway.

"Yeah, they're cute. I know Niles was amused to see all the colors."

"They're for you from Niles. Pop the red one."

Kennedy popped the biggest red one and out dropped a key. She cocked her head up at him. "What's this?"

"It's a key—"

"Oh, really? I wasn't sure," Kennedy said sarcastically.

Michael smiled. "It goes to that briefcase sitting next to the dresser. Open it."

Kennedy opened the briefcase and found a bunch of papers. At first she didn't know what they were but as she held them up to the light she could see the word "deed" written across the top of one of them. She looked up at Michael and held it up in the air.

"What's this?" Kennedy asked, making sure she wasn't mistaken.

"It's the deed to the house in the Hamptons. It's yours and Niles's. I have no use for it anymore."

"So what, you want me to move out of the town house? I don't know, I'd rather have the house in the city. It's more convenient."

"Well, we can talk about it. You know I have the other place across the park too. Don't worry, we'll figure something out. Happy birthday, Kennedy." Michael kissed her on the cheek.

Derrick arrived at Simone's first. He smiled as little Derrick and Angelica oohed and ahhed at the decorations. Simone and Miranda had really done a good job. He was glad that they were his family. Derrick hugged Miranda and thanked her. He was impressed that anyone would drive in to see him, although Miranda wasn't just anybody. She was like a sister to all of them. And she had played a big part in the whole planning of the party and had even driven in from Connecticut.

Jared gave Derrick a brotherly hug. The two of them walked into the house while the children played, and Simone and Miranda ran around as though they were on fire.

Jared told Derrick of his plan to relocate to the area permanently. He had even bought a house in New Jersey. He planned on surprising Kennedy with it and hoped that she'd move in with him, since she didn't give a definite answer to his marriage proposal. This didn't surprise Derrick a bit, Jared was a good man for his sister.

Derrick told Jared about Jericha's plan to move, and that he was really exited about having his kids all to himself. Derrick planned to go to court as soon as she left, to petition for full custody. The children were better off with him because Jericha had always been unstable. So if Derrick had to play a little dirty, so what. Jericha was abandoning the kids anyway. Just because a woman could give birth didn't necessarily make her a mother.

———————

Kennedy finally arrived with Niles. Jared and Derrick ran up to get him at the same time but stopped when they saw Michael walk through the door.

Jared stared at Michael and kissed Kennedy. Derrick shook his head, gently took his nephew in his arms and turned away. Michael bid his cool hellos and excused himself.

"All-righty then." Kennedy rubbed her palms together. "It's gonna be a long day. Or is it just me?"

Simone stood behind her. "It's just you, baby girl." Simone pinched her cheek and hugged her. "Jared and Derrick, could you meet us outside?"

Jared kissed Kennedy on the cheek and ran his fingers through her hair. "I'll be right outside."

"Me, too." Derrick playfully imitated Jared, running his fingers through Kennedy's hair and kissing her on the cheek.

Kennedy laughed. "You know you two are nuts."

Simone shook her head, holding her stomach in laughter. "Get out. I swear this has got to be the craziest family . . . but it's good to see everyone laughing again."

Kennedy plopped down on the sofa. "So, what's up, sis?"

"Nothing. I was just on my way to get Kiss out of bed before making my announcement—"

"What announcement?"

"You'll see. Anyway, are you sure you're okay with Michael being here? I know you guys came together—"

Kennedy shook her head. "No, we didn't come together, we drove separate cars. And it's a fine time to ask, don'tcha think? I guess I'll be okay . . . I've survived so far."

Simone hesitated. "I just thought I'd ask. I mean . . . I know it's soon . . . but . . . I don't know. If you don't want him here—"

"Don't worry about it. I can deal with it . . . I have to deal with it. He's Niles's father, you know." Kennedy bit her lip. "Besides, I still care about him. As much as I don't want to, I do—"

Simone raised her eyebrows.

"Not like that, Simone. I care about him as a person, as my son's father . . . as a friend. We've all been through a lot. I just wish that everyone, you included, could be as happy as I am with Jared."

Simone kissed Kennedy on the cheek and stared at her with

misting eyes. "Me too, sis. Me too." She exhaled loudly. "Now get your butt outside before you make me cry."

"Good tears, sis?"

"Yes, Ken. Good, happy tears."

Kennedy spotted Miranda as soon as she stepped outside. She ran over to her and hugged her. As they squealed like two schoolgirls, it was clear how much they missed each other. Miranda informed Kennedy that she was doing well and heard that Rich had gotten five years. Kennedy smiled and nodded, glad that Miranda wouldn't have to watch her back for a while.

Tears streamed down Kennedy's face. "You look so good, Miranda."

"You too, Ken. Don't cry."

"No, I'm okay. It's just that it never seemed like we'd get to the good part. It was rough for a while, huh?"

"Yes, girl. Yes. But you know what, Ken? We made it through."

Kennedy nodded as Simone walked toward the front of the crowd.

"Okay, I want everyone to listen up for a moment. I don't want to hear a word until I say it's okay to speak. Kennedy and Derrick, I realize that it's your birthdays, but that means you too. Go ahead, Michael." Simone signaled for Michael to come to the front while everyone wore looks of disgust.

Michael came to the front of the crowd and stood next to Simone. He fidgeted around for a moment or two and then cleared his throat. He whispered into Simone's ear and Simone directed the children to go inside the house for a few minutes.

Finally he began, "I know that none of you want me here. Actually, I didn't want to come. But you all know how persuasive Simone can be. I just want to start off by telling everyone how sorry I am. I'm sorry for causing a lot of unnecessary hurt to all of you. Because although all of you weren't directly involved, you were still involved because I hurt your loved ones. And believe it or not, I hurt myself. I won't go all into it because most of us know what happened. Besides, I can bet money that the kids are listening, wouldn't you?" Michael laughed nervously. "Anyway, I just want to tell Kennedy and Derrick happy birthday, and I mean it from the bottom of my heart. And, Derrick, I want to thank you for being so mature about this and for showing me that it's okay to be me. You taught me a lesson about being who I am and you warned me that eventually it would all come out. I didn't know how right you were. Kennedy, I want to thank you for such a beautiful son and for allowing me to be your friend. Lord knows that you should hate me, but you don't . . . at least I hope not. Thank you for your honesty and double thank you for standing up to the one person I feared—my mother. Thanks to you, she's coming around a bit." Michael stopped and grabbed his head.

"Take your time Michael, I know this is hard." Simone patted him on the back.

"As I was saying, Kennedy, I thank you, my brother thanks you. You just don't know how much you've led my family to accomplish. I promise that I'll always be honest with you and that I'll die trying for Niles. Jared, I know you of all people don't want hear from me. So I'll just say this and finish. I want you to know that I respect you. There are not too many men who'll step up and do what you're doing. You're there for my son, and I'll admit it bothers me, but I'd rather him grow up with a stepfather who loves him as his own. How can he lose as long as we both love and take care of him? He can't. Thanks, brother. I'm going to end this now but first I have to tell you all how difficult this has been for me. I'm not trying to make anyone feel sorry for me. But it's hard enough being a successful black man in this society. As every man here knows, it's hard enough just being a black man. But when you have broken that glass ceiling, it's still hard not to get cut. Derrick, for me and you it's worse because of our lifestyle. Because of my lifestyle, or rather because I wasn't upfront about it, I almost lost my family, and you all. And you may not believe me, but one day, we'll all get along. I'm not going anywhere. My son's a part of this family, and you're not going anywhere. So I guess we'll all have to get used to one another. Maybe one day, we can all care about one another. Happy birthday." Michael held his champagne glass up in the air and everyone else joined him.

After Michael's long speech Kennedy was surprised to see everyone talking. Even Jared and Michael were conversing. She criticized herself for not wanting Michael there, but she knew Michael wouldn't have been heard any other way. If not for the party, no one would've given him the time of day to apologize. But since everyone wanted to save face, no one exploded. The Jacobs family had never been one to put on public shows.

Kennedy and Derrick laughed as they exchanged gifts, something that they weren't supposed to do. Everyone had agreed that all of the money that they would've spent on birthday gifts was to go to the kids' college fund. Kennedy and Derrick, on the other hand, never listened.

Derrick gave Kennedy an eighteen-carat engraved bookmark that read: *For my sister, the one I love, talk to, live for and will breathe for. Family starts with love and love starts with honesty. No more secrets and never a lie, I'm your friend and brother. With you all the way, even after I die.*

Kennedy cried and Simone complained. Derrick had given her the same gift, but hers was silver. Kennedy nudged Simone with her elbow. "We never cease to amaze you, huh?"

Simone rolled her eyes and smiled.

Kennedy gave Derrick an expensive luggage set and inside one of the pieces were airline tickets, so that he'd be home from Harvard for Thanksgiving and Christmas. Derrick smiled and hugged her. But he told her that he'd need more. Then he turned to everyone and told them that he would have sole custody of the kids from now on. Everyone applauded.

"Hey, wait up," Simone said. "I forgot to tell you all that Kiss's adoption will be finalized in a couple of months. We go to court September third. And her name is now officially Alissa Taylor Jacobs. Now everyone eat up, I didn't cook all day for nothing." Simone bowed.

Michael patted Jared on his back and pushed him toward Kennedy. Jared walked up to Kennedy and got down on one knee. Simone jumped up and down and Miranda shouted, "Hell yeah!" while Michael nodded and bounced Niles.

"Kennedy, the last time I did this, you said you needed time. Well, I plan on giving you all the time in the world, all happy times. It won't always be easy, and some days you may wake up and wish I'd disappear. But as long as we love each other as we always have, we'll have that happiness. Would you do me the honor of being my wife?" Jared held Kennedy's hand while a tear streamed down his face.

Kennedy looked up defiantly with a sly smile on her face. "I don't know, I do have another man in my life now. I think you're going to have to ask him. How about it Niles, does Mommy have your permission?" Kennedy turned toward Niles.

Michael nodded Niles's head. Everyone screamed, whistled, and clapped. The birthday party officially began while Kennedy silently prayed they'd always be this happy.

COMING IN 2005

A Novel by

Jamise L. Dames

Pushing Up Daisies

Sneak Preview . . .

*D*aisy Parker's blood boiled as she balled up her boyfriend Jasper Stevens's favorite brown suede Armani jacket and threw it out of the second-story window. She stuck her head out into the warm breeze and surveyed her work and smiled wickedly. Clothes and shoes decorated her front lawn. The red roses that climbed the white lattice were flanked by silk shirts in every color imaginable. Boxer shorts scattered on the flagstone walkway resembled freckles, while an isolated pair hung from the limb of an oak tree. A beige loafer lay in the neighbor's yard across the street.

Neighbors shamelessly stood outside and watched in amazement. "Mind your own business," Daisy hissed and yanked the navy sheers closed.

She placed her hands on her hips. Now for his grandmother's good china, she thought, running down the stairs. A stabbing pain shot through her right foot. She winced as she watched blood trickle from her big toe. She shook her head in disgust, pulling the half-inch masonry nail out. "Goddamn . . . ooh." She cringed, grinding her teeth as she grabbed her foot. "I hate these stairs. I hate this house." Daisy's adrenaline rushed, and her heart raced. "Lord, don't let him walk through that door right now"— she ran her tongue across her teeth—"'cause I swear I'm gonna kill him." Daisy wiped a tear from her eye. The pain from her wound, which was beginning to swell, deepened her anger. She held her breath, wiped her bloody foot across Jasper's earth-tone Persian wool rug, and went to treat her injury.

Limping into the first-floor bathroom, Daisy scowled. Tiny spots of blood left burgundy stains on the sandstone tile. *If it's not one thing, then it's something worse,* she thought, yanking open the medicine cabinet while watching all of its contents tumble into the sink. "Jesus!" she yelled, closing her eyes. Her heart felt as if it were jack hammering its way out of her chest. She had to calm herself before she had another nervous breakdown like she'd experienced almost eight years before. She didn't want to go through that again—Jasper wasn't worth it, she reminded herself while taking a cleansing breath. Inhaling slowly, Daisy held her breath until the count of ten and exhaled. Repeating the process several times, she began to relax. Seven years of yoga classes taught her how to alleviate stress. When her pulse slowed, she rummaged through the toiletries and located the small first aid kit. After wiping her toe with an alcohol pad she applied antibiotic ointment, then gently bandaged it. Resting her hands on the sides of the sink, she balanced herself and stared into the basin. Something wasn't right. The medicine cabinet was usually full but the sink only contained a few items. Daisy chewed her bottom lip and snapped her fingers. *All of Jasper's toiletries are missing . . . even his extra toothbrush,* she thought, shaking her head. "Now I'm really going to throw the china out of the window!"

Stacking the china on the floor in separate piles, plates and bowls respectively, Daisy wiped sweat from her brow with the back of her white shirtsleeve. Her *Jungle Fever* reenactment of throwing clothes out of the window would have to wait until later. Her mouth felt like cotton.

She headed to the kitchen and froze. Slowly she eyed the layout and the decor. It was nice, but too dark. The cold that emanated from the black marble-tiled floor soothed her injured foot. She yanked open the mahogany cabinet to retrieve a glass, then changed her mind and slammed it shut. Snatching a bottle of water from the black refrigerator, Daisy wrestled with the cap. The ridges reddened her palms. Didn't the manufacturers know that women's hands were too soft for the lines sharply carved in the tops?

Standing by the large black acrylic sink, she grabbed a damp dishtowel and opened the water. She threw her head back and let the coolness of the needed liquid pass over her tongue and caress her dry throat. Leaning on the charcoal-colored countertop, she stared out of the bay window. The pool's aqua water shimmered under the sun's rays. It would be a welcome relief when she was finished throwing Jasper's belongings out.

Daisy sat on the sofa Indian-style, waiting for Jasper to come through the front door. She reminded herself of the awaiting china. She was fuming. Jasper should've had enough decency to call. Daisy sucked her teeth and picked up Jasper's photo from the end table. *One would think you'd want to spend every available minute with me, considering your job has you out of town four days a week. But no, not you, Jasper. That would be asking too much,* Daisy thought, glaring at the picture before tossing it across the room. Daisy played with her medium-length, cinnamon-colored hair, which she had disheveled—when aggravated, she couldn't keep her hands out of it. She stared at the glass-paned door, willing the brass knob to turn and give her what she wanted—Jasper's head.

The loud chime from the grandfather clock startled her out of her stone-faced gaze and onto her feet. Opening the drapes, she peered out one window and then another. Where the hell was Jasper?

Tears streamed out of Daisy's deep-brown eyes. Pounding her fist into her palm, she frantically paced back and forth. As much as she loved him, she couldn't take Jasper's disrespecting her anymore. Wouldn't take it anymore. She picked up her Iyanla Vanzant book, which Jasper had bought her, from the coffee table. She reread the pages although she already knew them by heart. Jasper didn't know how much of a disservice he had done for himself by buying the book. He thought he had given her something to occupy her time, but in reality he had given her something to think about. She sneered and tossed the book back onto the table.

"A reason. A season. A lifetime. Well, Iyanla, you were right. I don't know the reason but Jasper is definitely a season kind of man—here yesterday, gone today. I guess I missed this time. Every time. Jasper definitely isn't here for a lifetime," she said and began to pick at the loose acrylic that was starting to lift at the base of her fingernails, a result of her biting while upset. She'd have to call her friend Ming Li; she needed a fill badly.

She plopped down on the overpriced, overstuffed sofa. She'd give Jasper one more hour. If he didn't come home or call, she would change the locks. She'd show him.

She engulfed her body in the hard cushions and questioned herself. Why did she sit and drown herself in thoughts of Jasper? Evidently he wasn't thinking about her. The longer she sat, the madder she got at not only him, but herself. Why should she allow him to drain her of her happiness? He wasn't God; he didn't deserve her undivided attention. Although she had to admit that she treated him like a god. She placed him on a pedestal from which he refused to come down, and she had been punished for being the type of woman who loved completely. There wasn't anything on the green earth that she hadn't done for him. So why hadn't he come home?

Daisy took up residence on the sofa she had adorned in too many fringed throw pillows, trying to give it a *Better Homes* look, and repeatedly asked herself the same question for three hours. Why? She came to the realization that she could question all she wanted, but no one could tell her what she already knew. She had been cheated on before and her gut told her that Jasper was out doing something that he had no business doing. That was why he didn't answer his cell phone or call her back after her numerous attempts to page him.

The more upset she got, the more she raked her eyes around the room. The room wasn't even her. The house wasn't her; it was Jasper. It was all Jasper. He had been the one who wanted rooms too pretty to sit in. "Posh" was what he had called them. Daisy grimaced. She'd throw out the sofa too. She just didn't see the point of having furniture that couldn't be sat on. *As a matter of fact, I'm getting rid of all his stuff. I'll have a moving sale, that's what I'll do. But it won't be one of those* Waiting to Exhale *sales. Uh-uh, I'm not selling anything for a dollar. I want all that I can get,* she thought.

The furniture had cost a lot of money. More than what she would've paid for it if she could've afforded it. But Jasper had wanted it and paid for it. Too busy with work to get out and get it himself, Daisy had to purchase it. She smiled. The receipts, all of them, were in her name.

There was one thing that she refused to get rid of—the grandfather clock. It had accompanied her through the night and hadn't missed a beat. She would keep it to remind herself about the wake-up call that she had finally answered. The same call that told her to put Jasper where he belonged—out with yesterday's trash.

The clock chimed again. One hour had turned into four.

Time to make the doughnuts, Daisy thought as she reached for the phone. She called the locksmith and then forwarded her calls to a local psychic hotline. Jasper had really taken it too far.

Daisy imagined the look on Jasper's face when he found his things scattered across the lawn. He would be beyond pissed. Hell, the locksmith had better hurry. She couldn't have some deranged man running up in the house trying to kill her. Not that Jasper had ever laid a hand on her, but she knew if he had thrown her stuff out, she'd take it back to junior high school, complete with Vaseline on her face and a ponytail tight enough to make her eyes look Asian. Please, she might do that anyway. Just jump on him at first sight. And he didn't want that.

It had been almost an hour since she called the locksmith. How many people needed locks changed on a Sunday afternoon? Didn't people go to church anymore? She looked out her window and saw all the neighborhood kids and decided that church attendance had definitely declined. Where was he? Now she was waiting on two men, Jasper and the locksmith. She shook her head. Now wasn't that a trip? It was bad enough that she was going to have to pay a surcharge because it wasn't normal business hours. In the phone book the ad claimed to have the speediest service in town. Please, she had seen turtles move faster. But she was patient, she could wait. She'd been waiting almost seven years for Jasper to act right, so waiting a few more minutes for the locksmith would be a breeze, unless Jasper made it home first.

"I'm getting my Mace," Daisy said and turned toward the stairs. There was no way she was going to try to fight a man fairly. She was twenty-nine, too old to be fighting, but never too old to defend herself. She knew Jasper would flip, and she was going to be ready for whatever came next.

Her weight sank into the thickness of the tightly woven rug and her brown-sugar-complected feet blended in with the harmonious colors of sage, tan, and earthy reds. She scrunched her burgundy-painted toes deep into the intricate patterns, wishing she could just dive and disappear in the inviting colors. She hated having to face the loss of seven years of her life. She'd given him so much, too much.

The doorbell rang. Her heart raced. Jasper? No, he had a key. She calmed herself, tried to fix her wild hair in the in the large cherry-wood framed mirror which hung next to the front door, and let the locksmith in.

Three hundred dollars and five changed locks later, Daisy was even more pissed. There went the new outfit she wanted.

Slowly she walked up the stairs, counting every pewter-framed picture of her and Jasper that hung on the wall in stair-step succession. There were seven in all, one for every year they had been together.

Daisy removed the picture that was hanging at the top of the stairs and traced her finger over it. They were the ideal couple when they had posed for it. She remembered being young and newly in love. Jasper had been her days and nights. Now the bastard didn't even know how to come home, or he just didn't want to. A tear rolled down her tired face. I *should've known better. You didn't deserve me. Huh, and just think, I thought you were the world,* she thought. "I can't believe I played myself for this long," she said aloud. "Seven years. Seven whole years and not once did you pro-pose. And you thought that I was going to give you a child? You must've been crazy. What kind of fool did you take me for, telling me to have your baby first and then you'd marry me? Hell, I could've had just about any man I wanted, and I settled for your tired behind." Daisy smashed the photo against the others, shattering them to pieces. She stared down at the pictures scattered on the stairs. She had been so happy then; they both had.

She paused at the top of the staircase. Every door in the hallway was closed. After all the time and effort she had put into decorating the rooms, he insisted the doors stay closed.

"Too much dust," Jasper had said. But he wasn't the one who cleaned the house, she was.

Daisy threw open the first door. The citrus scent from the guestroom greeted her. She inhaled the tropical-mango freshness that she'd carefully chosen to match the colors of the room. The queen-size bamboo canopy bed covered with a salmon-colored duvet and matching sheers draping the posts looked inviting. Daisy was tired; her soul had become heavy. Her feet sank in the plush lavender pile as she strode across the room to the closet. She knew not to open the door, but was tempted. Just the sight of what it contained would irritate her, and the last thing she needed was to be face to face with hurt. She grabbed the gold knob and hesitated. She had cried enough. She walked out of the room and closed the door.

"This is one door that needs to stay closed," she said. "But the rest will stay open, and I mean it!" Daisy yelled, walking down the hall, thrusting doors open. Tripping over one of Jasper's ill-placed shoes, she fell, crushing her face into the carpet. She sobbed, "I can't. I just can't . . . take this." She pounded her fist and pushed herself up. Daisy rolled her eyes. Day-old makeup left faint traces of color on the blanket of white carpet underfoot. "Who puts white carpet in a hallway, anyway?" she mumbled and snatched up Jasper's shoe.

Daisy started rummaging through her top drawer looking for the red lace panties that matched the bra she planned to wear. Her phone rang. She picked up the receiver and no one was there. *My cell phone,* she thought.

"Hel-llo," Daisy snapped.

"Day-um, what's wrong with you? You okay?" her best friend, Gigi Mitchell, asked.

"Yes. I mean, no. Jasper didn't come home last night." Daisy clasped her panties in her hand, slammed her drawer shut and walked into the bathroom.

"No? Are you serious? Girl, you are having all kind of trouble today—men problems and phone issues. Did you

know something was wrong with your phone? 'Cause I just
tried to call twice and some lady who claimed to be psychic
kept answering . . . had the nerve to ask me which credit card
I'd be using. I told her since she was psychic she should be
telling me." Gigi rambled.

Daisy laughed. "I forwarded my calls there just in case
Jasper decides to call. Since they're psychic maybe they'll
tell him that he doesn't have a home," Daisy said, spreading
Noxzema on her face. "So what's up? You feel like going to
see Ming Li?"

"Sure. I'm not doing anything else, and Marcus won't be
over until later. So I'll meet you there in about an hour?"

"Yeah, I should be there by then. Make it an hour and a
half. I have to stop by the ATM first. Oh, and Gigi?"

"Yeah?"

"When was the last time you talked to Marcus? Did he
come over last night?" Daisy quizzed.

"We had lunch yesterday, and he stopped by last night
around nine and left around midnight. Why?"

"Just asking. Listen, if Marcus calls you, don't say anything, okay? I'll see you at Ming Li's."

Daisy couldn't believe her ears. Jasper was slowly dig-
ging his own grave. The night before, around ten o'clock,
Jasper strolled into the den looking scrumptious. His Gucci
cream-colored silk blazer and matching cream silk twill
pants highlighted the twinkle in his slanted bedroom brown
eyes. His chalk-white teeth brightened up the room when he
smiled and announced that he was going out with Marcus.
He looked Gucci good and smelled Gucci fine. Daisy shook
her head. It was terrible when a woman had a man who
looked and dressed better than she did. She should've never
let him go out without her. But she had always prided herself on her security. This had been the only time that it had
betrayed her.

Daisy stood naked in front of the mirror and studied her
body. She still had it together thanks to years of working out.

She refused to give in to gravity. She cupped her full breasts and gently squeezed them. Still firm and upright. She turned her backside to the mirror, checking her behind. She ran her hands over the roundness and shook it. It jiggled just a little. Not as tight as it should be, with a dimple here and there, but it was tight enough. I'll show you, Jasper. You wanna play games, huh? Okay, I still got everything that attracted you to me, plus more, she thought.

Drawing back the shower curtain, she stepped into the oversized Roman tub. She turned the lever, opening the bibcock, enjoying the warmness of the water as it gushed out, kissing her feet. Lifting the shower gauge, the water rushed from the showerhead, baptizing her and relinquishing her of all her deadly thoughts.

———————

Daisy sat patiently next to Gigi as she waited for her nails to dry in Ming Li Nails of New York and smiled as she absorbed her surroundings. Gold-framed authentic African art adorned the celery-green walls and custom carpet of a similar green and pale pink inscribed with Ming Li's name covered the floor. New York's Hot 97 filled the air while the televisions broadcasted BET. *So much for stereotypes,* Daisy thought as she admired the afrocentric decor in what would've been mistaken as a typical Asian nail salon by its name.

"Gigi, can you do me a favor? Would you look in my purse and hand me a fifty?" Daisy blew her nails.

Gigi raised her eyebrows. "For what? Don't tell me Ming Li's gonna start charging us now. I mean, business is business, but fifty dollars—"

Daisy covered Gigi's mouth. "Girl, hush and stop worrying. It's for a bet. And it's not like you can't afford to get your nails done."

Gigi fanned her face. "Oh, okay. What did you two bet on

this time? Not the Lenox Lewis fight? Don't tell me that you lost your money betting on—"

"Please. I won. This is Ming Li's change," Daisy said, carefully holding the fifty up that Gigi had retrieved for her. "She already put the salon's money in the drop box. If she had bet on Lenox she could've dropped this cash in the bank too," Daisy whispered and walked away laughing.

Ming Li confidently strutted toward Daisy, grinning. Her light-mocha complexion complemented her slanted hazel eyes, which lit up a room when she smiled. She ran her hands through her waist-length blue-black hair and pointed her long finger at Daisy. "I know your nails aren't dry yet. Don't mess them up again."

Daisy frowned, then smiled. "Now you know better than that. Do I look like Gigi to you? You know I'm careful with my nails."

"I don't know. Do you?" Ming Li laughed and patted her pockets. "Damn."

"Need a smoke, huh?" Daisy tried to suppress her smile.

Ming Li pulled her pearl-pink cigar case from her back pocket and waved it in Daisy's face. "A drink too. Care to join me?" She bared her top and bottom teeth, forcing a smile. "Just give me my damn change and leave me alone. I don't bother you about your bad habits, so don't bother me about mine." Ming Li winked.

"Leave Jasper out of this, girl."

Ming Li licked the tip of her unlit cigar. "I never said Jasper's name, you did, sweetie. Remember that!"

Daisy playfully pushed Ming Li, and they both laughed then swapped money as Gigi approached.

Gigi placed her hands on her hips. "I know you two heifers aren't talking about me. I don't purposely try to mess up my nails," Gigi said, snatching the fifty from Ming Li.

Ming Li flung her hair, bit her top lip, and gave Gigi a quizzical look.

"Uh-uh," Daisy muttered.

Gigi smacked her lips, straightened the fifty-dollar bill, and jerked her head back. "Ming Li, don't even try it. You know you bet me too."

Ming Li dramatically rolled her eyes at Gigi and turned to Daisy. "So, Daisy, what do you think now that the renovation's finished? You like it?"

"Yes, it's nice . . . real nice." Daisy raised her eyebrows and nodded, admiring Ming Li's taste.

Gigi's jaw dropped. "Nice? As much time as Ming Li and I put into this place, all you can say is nice? Come on, Daisy, you know it's more than nice. You love it, admit it. You're going to have to excuse Daisy, Ming Li. She's having man problems."

Daisy shot Gigi a dirty look, then smiled at Ming Li. Ming Li and Daisy glanced at Gigi and laughed.

Gigi exhaled loudly. "What? What's so funny? I helped pick out the colors."

Ming Li patted Gigi on the back. "Daisy, you tell her." Ming Li retrieved a golden flask from her pocket and took a swig. "I'm going to find my lighter."

Gigi crossed her arms. "Well?"

"Okay, I'll tell you. But you have to sit down and promise you won't be loud. I don't want everybody in my business."

Gigi sat and crossed her legs. "Alright, alright."

"You may have helped with the colors, but Ming Li and I decorated this place. Well, actually she did most of the work but I paid for it—"

"Daisy, you paid for it? Why? Don't tell me that Ming Li needed money. I would've helped her . . . she should've asked me."

"Gigi, Ming Li didn't need the money. It was an investment. She offered me the opportunity, and I jumped on it. The money that she was going to use to renovate, she used to purchase a foreclosure in Los Angeles."

"And where—"

"Don't even ask," Daisy said, feeling her anger return. "I got the money from Jasper . . . sort of. Let's just say I wrote myself a check." Daisy rolled her eyes.

"Oh, let me guess. He was gone, right? Well, good for you. Someone needs to put that money to good use."

Daisy stared straight ahead.

Ming Li waved from across the almost empty salon. "I'm closing up, ladies. Y'all want to grab a bite to eat?"

Daisy took a bite of her Caesar salad and dabbed her mouth with her napkin. Gigi sat across from her with tears streaming down her face. Ming Li held her stomach. They were laughing loud and uncontrollably. Daisy, embarrassed, smiled politely at the people who walked by staring. The outdoor restaurant was bustling, and Greenwich Village was in full-swing mode, crowded as usual on a hot Sunday evening.

"Girl, no you didn't." Gigi threw her napkin across the wrought-iron bistro table.

Ming Li swept hair from her face. "Did you?" She eyed Daisy and nodded. "Oh hell, you did. Didn't you? Hmm." She crossed her arms. "'Bout time."

"Yes, I did. He didn't come home, so I did what I had to do." Daisy nodded to a man across the street who kept shouting: "Hey. Hey, baby girl. Psst. Shorty, you got a man?"

Gigi waved her hand at the rude intruder, dismissing him. "Jasper's clothes, Daisy? Girl . . . he's gonna kill you. You of all people know how much that man spends on his clothes."

Ming Li cleared her throat and slapped her hand on the table. "Good for him . . . screw him. Screw them all but don't fuck yourself in the process." Ming Li bit her top lip and reduced her eyes to tiny slits. "You know what I mean."

"Nobody told him to pay that much for clothes. Besides, he should've come home last night." Daisy took another forkful of salad and chased it with a bite of garlic bread.

"Uh-oh," Gigi said. "You sound serious. Don't tell me that you're really gonna put him out this time."

Daisy took a sip of her iced tea and stared across the table. "What do you mean, this time? You know something about Jasper that I don't know?"

Ming Li sat erect, rested her chin in her hands and looked at Gigi.

Gigi glanced at Ming Li, then bit a bread stick. She turned to Daisy. "No. It's just that you always say that you're gonna put him out . . . you know, when you get mad. And I'm sorry, but I just have to say it . . . you need to put those degrees to use—"

"You got that right, Gigi," Ming Li agreed and tapped her spoon on her glass. "What you have to do, Daisy, is think about yourself and think for yourself. Just because Jasper was your knight in shining armor once upon a time doesn't mean you owe him your life. You never asked him to intervene when that guy tried to rob you. He interfered on his own. Maybe Jasper was your human savior then. But who knows . . . maybe that crook just wanted your purse . . . not your life. You're supposed to return an act of kindness by reciprocity, not slavery. I admit it was fairytale sweet the way you two met, but damn. How long do you plan on being a puppet, sweetie? Never mind—"

"Ming Li—"

"No, Daisy, you need to hear this." Ming Li turned toward Gigi. "Doesn't she need to hear this?"

Gigi nodded.

"Thank you." Ming Li nodded. "Daisy, don't say you're gonna put Jasper out. Just do it or he'll never take you serious. You need tactical skills . . . maybe you should read *The Art of War* by Sun Tzu. Personally, I would not give anyone that much control over me . . . telling me I can't work. Please, for what? So I can be dependent? You really need to think about it."

Daisy crossed her arms, sucked her teeth, and was silent for a moment. She wanted to curse Ming Li out and scream at Gigi for agreeing, but she couldn't. "Well, ladies, getting mad is one thing, and not coming home is another. Evidently Jasper had a place to rest his head last night, so he can stay there. And I hear what you're saying, Ming Li, I do. But as far as working . . . I don't know . . . Jasper's never wanted me to. But that doesn't matter now. He's leaving. Point blank—end of story, there's nothing more to be said."

Gigi twisted her lips and tapped her short manicured nails on the table. "You sure? 'Cause you know you can always stay with me."

"Stay with you? Girl, have you lost your mind? I'm not leaving. He is!" Daisy wiped her mouth, placed her napkin across the plate, and pushed her chair back. "But thanks for the offer. I really appreciate it."

"Anytime."

Ming Li reached across the table and put her hand on top of Daisy's. "Daisy, I'm harsh because that's how I'm made, you know that. I have to tell you the truth because I care. And as much as I don't agree with your situation, you know if you need me . . . if you need anything, I'm here. I don't care what it is, or what time it is. Okay?" Ming Li offered as she retrieved a Montecristo mini cigar from her case.

Daisy's eyes moistened with tears. She knew if she couldn't depend on anyone else, she had Gigi and Ming Li. Both possessed something Daisy didn't. Gigi's marketing career was a perfect outlet for her pushiness, and Ming Li's levelheadedness proved the perfect match for her radical business sense. While Daisy and Gigi had been friends since age three, she and Ming Li had been friends for more than six years. Equally, they had always been there for Daisy, and she would always be there for them. Men had come and gone, but their sisterly bond remained.

———————

Daisy lay on the sofa, staring at the ceiling. Not wanting to face her reality alone, which had become a nightmare, she was glad that Ming Li and Gigi were there. Daisy exhaled loudly, covering her face with a throw pillow. Tears streamed uncontrollably down her cheeks. "That bastard!" she muttered, feeling a hand tap her shoulder.

"You okay?" Gigi asked.

"Yes . . . no! I thought you two were gone."

"We just stepped out to get something to eat and a bottle of wine." Gigi clinked wineglasses together. "I think we all need a drink."

Daisy sat up and ran her fingers through her hair. "Gigi, we just ate."

Ming Li walked in and set Chinese carryout on the coffee table. "No, Daisy, we ate more than six hours ago. I don't know about you, but a salad doesn't do it for me. Some of us do eat," she said as she nudged Daisy to scoot over.

I've been asleep that long, Daisy thought as her stomach growled. Ming Li and Gigi laughed. Daisy cried. She hadn't felt so betrayed before. Jasper had hurt her beyond measure.

"You know I hate that motherfucka. I really and truly hate him." Daisy raised her voice, startling her friends.

Ming Li glanced at Gigi and rubbed Daisy's shoulder. "It's gonna be alright. Trust me."

"I know . . . I appreciate what you're trying—" Daisy held her face in her hands. "Can somebody please tell me why. Why is he so lowdown? Not coming home? What type of mess is that? I mean . . . if Jasper's going to cheat, the least he could do is not be so blatant about it. I don't know whether to be mad or cry. If I don't ever see that motherfucka again, it'd be too soon. I swear to God, if I could do it and get away with it . . . I'd kill him."

Gigi cupped Daisy's face in her hands. "Listen to me, Daisy. Look at me. Don't put yourself through this. Jasper's not worth it. I know you may think he is because you love him and you've been with him for years but trust me when I tell you this, and don't ever forget it: No one, and I mean nobody, is worth your happiness. You understand me?"

Daisy nodded and wiped her tears.

"Good, now let's eat. Ming Li, pass me a plate please."

Daisy sat force-feeding herself. Her growling stomach reminded her that she needed to eat, but her emotional pain took over. I have to get it together, she thought as she poured a glass of wine. Together, get it together, Daisy.

After five drinks Daisy sank into the sofa cushions. She, Ming Li and Gigi had reminisced, argued over the upcoming boxing match and cried tears of laughter. For a moment everything in Daisy's life was normal and she relaxed.

The sound of the cell phone ringing startled Daisy from sleep. "Hello," Daisy mumbled.

"Daisy, you gotta get up now!" Gigi demanded.

"What? What time is it, and where are you?" Daisy sat up, rubbing her eyes.

"Daisy, Ming Li and I left in the middle of the night. I'm home now. It's five in the morning, and Marcus just called. Just get up!"

"What?"

"Marcus told me to meet him at your house. If he's on his way there, then you know Jasper has to be on his way too."

"Gigi, I don't understand. How come Jasper couldn't just call me himself? Why didn't he try my cell?"

"I don't know . . . it's five in the morning. Daisy, just go outside and get his clothes now. I'm not going to work today, so I'll be over in a bit. Hurry up. You don't have much time."